Maximum Moxie

Maggie Sullivan mystery #5

M. Ruth Myers

Copyright © 2016 Mary Ruth Myers

All rights reserved. No part of this book may be used or reproduced in any manner whatsoever without written permission from the author, except in the case of brief quotations embodied in critical articles and reviews. Contact www.mruthmyers.com

Cover design by W. Alan Raney

This books is a work of fiction. Names, characters and incidents are products of the author's imagination or are used fictitiously. Any resemblance to actual events or persons, living or dead, is entirely coincidental.

Thanks to the usual culprits:
Henry
Lee, JoAnn and Sandy
Steve Grismer & the Dayton Police History Foundation

ISBN: 1539199088
ISBN-13: 978-1539199083

ALSO BY
M. RUTH MYERS

Maggie Sullivan mysteries

No Game for a Dame
Tough Cookie
Don't Dare a Dame
Shamus in a Skirt

Other Novels

The Whiskey Tide
A Touch of Magic
A Journey to Cuzco
Captain's Pleasure
Friday's Daughter
Costly Pleasures
Insights
Love Unspoken
An Officer and a Lady
A Private Matter

ONE

It wasn't my habit to shoot a new client.

For Loren Collingswood, I made an exception.

"I'm told you're one of the best detectives in Dayton," he said as I unlocked the door to my office and flipped on the lights. It was half-past eight in the morning. He'd been waiting for me when I stepped off the elevator.

"That's always nice to hear, Mr.—"

"Collingswood. Loren Collingswood." He was somewhere past fifty with rounded shoulders and thoughtful eyes.

"Could I hang up your coat?"

"No thank you. I haven't much time."

Draping his folded coat over the arm of the chair in front of my desk, he sat down. My own found its usual peg on a wooden rack, followed by my red hat which was seasonally trimmed with a sprig of fake holly. I was five-foot-two and the coat rack was taller than I was, but I counted the stretching as exercise. As soon as I slid into place across from Collingswood, he launched in.

"My partner and I want to hire you, Miss Sullivan."

"Maggie. Please."

"Yes, very well."

After the determined start, he faltered. His gaze moved to the calendar from my DeSoto dealer hanging drunkenly on its final page. The hole at the top had just about worn through on the nail that held it. Three days into December odds were the calendar would hit the floor before 1941 ended.

"What sort of problem are you having, Mr. Collingswood?" I asked softly.

People came to me scared or distressed, but almost invariably embarrassed at needing my services. Getting started was the hard part. Collingswood sighed.

"A man who works for us has disappeared. A brilliant young engineer." He knitted salt-and-pepper brows that matched the hair retreating from his forehead. "Well, he's in his thirties, but that's young by my standards. A company's coming in next week to talk to us about - about something he's been working on. It's absolutely vital that we find him. Without Gil—"

I held up a hand to halt his flow while I took out a lined tablet.

"What do you mean, 'disappeared'? We need to start with some basics."

"Oh. Yes."

"He's an employee?"

"Yes. My partner and I have a company. C&S Signals."

"You said the missing man's an engineer. I take it that's what you do?"

"Yes. We-we develop technology which we sell to other firms. We specialize in—"

I held up my hand again. I'd done okay at geometry and a year of algebra, and the nuns at Julienne High School could probably hold their own with most college professors, but I was pretty sure whatever C&S Signals specialized in was over my head. There were other aspects of finding someone which were more useful.

"What's the man's name and the last time you saw him?"

"Gilbert Tremain. Gil. He was in early Monday and left the building and that's the last we've heard from him."

Two days ago.

"Was that unusual?"

"Not coming in early. He did that quite often. But certainly going off and not coming back or calling. Gil's extremely responsible. That's what's got us worried."

"You've tried to reach him by phone?"

"Oh yes. And Frank — that's my partner, Frank Scott — Frank went over yesterday and knocked, thinking perhaps he'd been taken ill or had an accident and couldn't get to the phone."

That implied Gilbert Tremain was single.

"We'd worry about him in any case. We're small, C&S. He's quite a resource for us. And the presentation next week... unless we find him, it can't go forward."

I saw him swallow.

"That's why I - we - thought we should hire an investigator."

"What do the police say?"

"We prefer not to involve the police. For business reasons."

I'd heard that tune before. It was never music to my ears, and from what he'd told me, I knew what I had to ask next.

"Has there been a ransom request?"

"No, of course not, or-or—. Well, we would have gone to the police in that case, I suppose."

I breathed easier.

"Do you have any reason to suspect foul play?"

"Good heavens no! Nothing like that. At least it hadn't occurred to me... No, surely they couldn't..."

"Who couldn't what, Mr. Collingswood?"

"I-I-I don't see how they could possibly be related, but..." He swallowed again. "I've had some phone calls."

"What sort of phone calls?"

"Just a little odd, that's all." He gestured vaguely. "Wrong numbers, probably."

"Since Gil Tremain has been missing."

"Oh, no. No. They started about a month ago. Just a fluke, surely."

Six years ago, at age twenty-one, I'd opened my office. Since then I'd learned coincidences seldom existed for people who came through my door seeking help.

"You're probably right, but lots of what I do is hunt connections. What did the phone calls say?"

"Nothing. Mostly." His voice dropped so much I wasn't sure I'd heard the second word.

"How many calls have there been?"

"Half a dozen. Possibly eight."

"And all you hear is silence? No breathing? No noises in the background?"

"Breathing, yes. Just that." He steeled himself. "Until last week. It rang and I answered and someone said, 'Be careful.' Then they hung up."

If possible, he looked more worried than when he'd come in.

"But it's all got to be some ghastly mistake. It can't have anything to do with Gil. It can't have anything to do with *me*. Someone's muddled a phone number."

"You're sure no one has a grievance against you? A reason they'd want to harass you? Maybe an employee you let go?"

If there was a connection, someone who knew the workings of his company was the obvious place to start. My would-be client was shaking his head.

"One of the girls who typed left last year to get married. But as far as firing anyone, it's been three years. At least. And before you ask, I'm not involved with any women or — or anything of that nature."

"Have there been any calls since the one that warned you to be careful?"

"No." He said it too quickly. "Look, the main thing is to find Gil."

The room was getting overly warm, a novelty since the radiator usually gave off only a trickle of heat. Removing the handkerchief from his breast pocket, Collingswood patted his forehead.

"I need to get to the office." He edged forward on his chair. "Can you help us? Can you start today?"

I told him I would, and what I charged.

"I'm due to make a final report to another client in about an hour. I can stop by after I finish there."

Something caught my eye. A movement in the pocket of Collingswood's coat. Oblivious to my wandering gaze, he talked on.

"Here's the address." He slid a business card onto my desk. "I'll have a check for a week's wages waiting for you."

A head emerged, swaying slowly above the narrow body oozing after. Eight inches, maybe less, separated it from Collingswood's arm.

"If you find Gil in only a day or two, I'll consider the rest of it money well spent," he was saying.

It's amazing how many thoughts fit into a split second:

That the snake might be harmless — or not.

That someone had warned the man across from me to be careful.

That this was the wrong time of year for snakes.

"Mr. Collingswood. Before you go, I need you to close your eyes and keep them closed until I tell you otherwise. Sit absolutely still. Try and remember, ah, everything Tremain said the last time you saw him."

"But—"

"Now!"

My fingers already were closing around the Smith & Wesson I kept in a holster-like sling beneath my chair. Collingswood looked anything but happy, but his eyes were closed. I eased to my feet.

The snake emerged another inch. Pinkish belly. Dark splotches. It veered toward Collingswood. It veered away. I squeezed the trigger.

TWO

Collingswood let out a yell and opened his eyes.

"What in the name—?" As he lurched to his feet, he caught sight of the headless form now half out of the coat pocket and writhing violently. With a whimper of terror he thrust out a hand to ward it off.

"It's dead!" I shouted. My volume moderated. "Muscle contractions or something make them keep moving. It's dead. It's harmless. The head is gone."

I thought I saw a splatter of something across the room, but I wasn't sure. I put down my gun. Collingswood was white as buttermilk.

"It was in— it was in my—"

Eyes bulging, he pointed a trembling finger, but drew it back abruptly to claw at his chest.

"Mr. Collingswood!"

He sagged against my desk. *Dear God, was he having a heart attack?* I gave my chair a shove on its casters and lowered him into it.

"Mr. Collingswood, who's your doctor?"

He shook his head.

"Pills." His scrabbling hand succeeded in freeing them from an inside pocket. Thumbing open the lid, he managed to shove one under his tongue without spilling them all.

Nitro. Digitalis. Something like that. He did have a heart problem. This might not be an out-and-out attack though. His breathing steadied. The pinched look was leaving his face. He nodded as if to indicate he was okay.

"I'm not sure what I should do," I said uncertainly. "I doubt it's the right thing, but there's a bottle of gin in my desk."

A faint sideways move of his head signaled No.

"Water." The brief word didn't sound strained.

This year, in a burst of largess, the building management had put a water cooler in the hall. I filled one of the glasses I kept for the gin. They'd had water in them before without showing ill effects.

"Maggie?" A worried face peered out of the domestic staffing agency one office next to mine. "Is everything okay? We heard a bang."

"Oh, I bumped my coatrack and it fell over into the wall. Sorry to scare you."

I hurried back with the water. Collingswood took two gulps and paused, sipped the next two, repeated the sipping until the water was gone. His eyes closed briefly as he let out a breath.

"I'm sorry I scared you. I probably wouldn't have done what I did if I'd known you had heart trouble."

"No. I think you probably saved my life. What kind...?" His eyes slid toward his coat. He couldn't bring himself to look directly.

"I'm no snake expert. I just knew it didn't belong in somebody's coat pocket. And with you carrying those pills you have, I'm pretty sure you shouldn't be sitting here gabbing about it. You need to get home and lie down. I'll call you a cab."

"I can't. I need to get to the office. I ducked in to drop off some papers on my way here. My partner was coming down with one of his headaches. They flatten him. I sent him home. I need to be there."

"Mr. Collingswood..."

I leaned my hip on my desk, keeping a healthy distance between me and the all-too-active remains of the snake.

"I'm in better shape than I appear at the moment." He gave a determined smile. "I would appreciate a cab, though. I'll have someone get my car later. We can talk about — this — when you come to C&S."

***

"What do you know about snakes?" I asked when Rachel Minsky's secretary put me through to her. Rachel owned a commercial building firm and could walk a construction site with the best of them, albeit in high heels and, preferably, furs.

"The two-legged kind or the Pentateuch kind?"

"The kind you find in the woods."

I'd just put Collingswood into a cab. He'd regained some color and still insisted on seeing me later.

"You're not thinking of going somewhere to put up a tent and drink from a canteen and swat flies, are you?" Rachel asked.

"No."

My chair was back in its proper spot behind my desk and I was keeping an eye on what was left of the snake. It didn't seem quite as dead as I'd assured Collingswood, but its movements weren't getting it anywhere either.

"Well, then. Chances are you'll never see one. I seldom do tramping around when they're clearing things for a new project."

"I'm looking at one right now. In my office. I'm optimistic it's dead. At any rate, it's missing a head. It's not a garter snake, which is the extent of my knowledge. I was hoping you might recognize a few other kinds from the tramping you mentioned."

She was silent a second before uttering words quite colorfully profane.

"In your office? You're serious, aren't you?"

"Yes."

"I may be slightly more conversant, but the smartest thing would be for me to bring over one of the men who know what they are when we do come across one. Shall I?"

"Please."

"I may have to check at more than one site. Give me forty-five minutes."

***

Waiting for Rachel gave me time enough to call the client who was expecting me with my final report. She agreed that I could mail it and I'd stop by later if she had any questions. She already knew the gist of it. I'd found her missing husband playing house with someone else two counties away. I hoped my hunt for Gil Tremain had a happier ending.

At the moment, the man who had hired me to find him concerned me more. Loren Collingswood had a bad heart. He'd been getting unsettling phone calls. A snake had turned up in his pocket — enough to scare the bejeezus out of anyone. It had all the hallmarks of someone trying to kill him.

What did it have to do with a missing engineer? Before I got far in thinking about it, my door flew open and Rachel strode in. More accurately, she strode two steps and stopped. Her eyes swept my floor, then rose to give the rest of the room a similar treatment.

"That?" she asked aiming a fingernail gleaming with polish the color of burgundy at the coat hanging over the arm of the chair.

"Yes."

Rachel was my height with a cloud of raven hair and a chest that made men turn to admire it. As usual she was dressed like a million dollars, her cranberry wool suit topped by a black fur shrug.

"This is Mr. Taylor." She indicated a raw-boned man in workman's garb and hobnail boots behind her. "He knows an amazing lot about snakes."

He ducked his sandy head in awkward greeting.

"Saw a-plenty growin' up down in the hills."

The two of them came all the way in. Rachel stood within chatting distance of me and cupped her elbows with her hands. I sat on the edge of my desk. We watched Taylor circle the chair that held the folded coat. Squatting on his haunches, he surveyed the length of slowly moving reptile. After several moments he picked up the coat and carried it to the far side of the room. He dumped its contents, nudging them with the toe of his boot.

"This here's a plain old Kirtland," he said. "Harmless 'cept for scarin' you."

"It's winter. Don't snakes hibernate or something?"

He twisted a finger in his ear and squinted.

"Well, they do tuck up in someplace out of the weather and sleep some. But come a nice sunny day, anyplace there's a nice rock or two to hold heat, you might see a snake."

But not in a coat pocket, I thought grimly.

THREE

Based on what Rachel's expert had told me, the snake had most likely been placed into Collingswood's coat pocket while still in a deep-sleep, motionless state from being outside in winter. A warm room, particularly one as warm as my office that morning, had revived it. When and where that would happen would have been impossible to predict. That didn't matter. Regardless of where it happened, Collingswood would have been scared within an inch of his life.

I got to C&S Signals ten minutes late. The red brick building was simple and modern. A strip of gravel in front and along one side provided parking. I pulled my DeSoto in and killed the engine.

"Mr. Collingswood's expecting me. I'm Maggie Sullivan," I told a white haired woman at the front desk. With her dash of bright pink lipstick and wavy hair she would have looked warm and motherly save for a pair of eyes worthy of a Doberman pincer assessing a threat.

"Oh, yes. The detective."

A potted plant brightened one corner of her desk. Either she'd terrified it into being lush and green or she watered it.

"Don't drag your toes finding Mr. Tremain, and don't take too much of Mr. Collingswood's time. He has a bad heart and he's looking very peaked this morning."

Rising magisterially, she marched through an archway in the wall behind her, leaving me to follow.

On the other side of the wall, four girls pounded typewriters. Two young men worked away at some sort of drawing tables next to metal boxes with knobs on the front and glass screens. We threaded our way around them and went down a hall with doors left and right. Collingswood had the last room on the end.

"How are you feeling?" I asked as soon as the two of us were alone. He had a good deal more color than when I'd last seen him.

"Much better, thanks." He nodded toward a couch behind him. "I stretched out with my feet up for a while. Silly, but it's what the doctor says I must do. Sit down."

"It was harmless," I said. "The snake. I had someone look at it."

"But—"

"You said you stopped here before you came to see me. Where did you put your coat?"

"Where I always do."

He pointed to a coat rack next to his door. One step in, drop it in, one step out. The snake could have been tucked into it here, or at his house. He was starting to frown.

"You think someone put it into my pocket?"

"Either that, or your roof has a very odd leak."

"But that would mean..."

"That someone wanted to scare you. Yes. Let's start with the premise Gil Tremain's disappearance has nothing to do with that, though, or with the phone calls you got. I don't think that's true, but it makes sense to start there and see where it leads. Meanwhile, you need to take some precautions. Don't go anywhere by yourself. Keep people around you. Take a taxi back and forth to work."

"Yes, all right."

"Tell me more about the project Tremain was working on."

His desk was neat as a pin. Slide-rule, cup of sharpened pencils, everything aligned perfectly. He took time selecting his words.

"C&S Signals develops what you could think of as technological bits that are used as part of larger units," he said at last. "We come up with improvements to existing technology in some cases, solutions to problems that are holding up advances in a particular industry, primarily radio signals and sound transmission."

"You're telling me you don't actually make anything — invent some gadget. You make, so to speak, a piece. And what? Sell it to somebody else?"

"In a nutshell." He smiled faintly. "The project we've been working on offers a significant improvement. In and of itself, it's the most valuable thing we've ever developed. But if America joins the fight against Hitler—" He sighed deeply. "*When* we do, it-it might be of some use to our military defenses."

"Are you suggesting the Bund might be behind Tremain's disappearance?"

"No. I can't—. It would be too farfetched. How would they even know about us?"

I had a hard enough time absorbing the reality of the war going on in Europe. The thought of cloak and dagger hijinks by America's pro-Nazi group right here on my doorstep unsettled me enough to search for other explanations.

"What about competitors? Would another company try to hire him away from you?"

"No! Absolutely not! Gil isn't the sort to be bought. He's absolutely loyal."

"But would anyone try?" And get rid of a man if he turned them down, I added silently.

"I suppose it's in the realm of possibility. Gil presented a paper about the problem we were working on at a symposium four months back. Several men from the company we're to meet with next week were there also, and his presentation made them suspect we were nearing a breakthrough. I suppose others might have done likewise."

"How much of the project — the knowledge or calculations or whatever it is — could Tremain take with him if he did, to put it bluntly, take a bribe?"

"All of it. Frank and two other engineers worked on it with him, but it was Gil who had the breakthrough."

"You must have copies. He's not carrying the whole thing around in his head."

"Even Gil wouldn't be up to memorizing the entire thing. Yes, we have copies. In the safe. But... yesterday, when we took a close look because we were starting to worry about our meeting.... We think they may not be our latest calculations. There was a knot, you see. When we were almost there. It had us tearing our hair out for two weeks or better."

"And Gil Tremain was the one who cut the knot," I guessed.

He nodded.

"I thought — I *know* — he'd put in the change and the girls had typed a finished copy to take to Photostat. We'd passed it around to make sure nothing had gotten miscopied. We'd followed the calculations on it to make sure they worked." He swallowed. "The ones in the safe don't."

To me, it looked more and more like Collingswood's fair-haired boy had scampered off into the arms of a higher bidder. More than a few smart, efficient men had thrown away a prosperous future in their hunger for more money faster. Their shortcuts usually led to a jail cell.

"Did Gil know how to get into the safe?"

"No, but he most likely kept his worksheets. Gil was very orderly."

"I'll talk to your employees, and have a look around Gil's office, if you don't object."

"I thought as much. It's why I was so keen to have you come today. So you could get started. I'm sorry Frank isn't here, but the headaches he gets are ghastly. Nausea. Can't stand light. I don't suppose worry over Gil helped it any."

"I can stop back tomorrow to talk to your partner."

"Yes, but you see, he knew Gil better than anyone else around here. They saw each other outside the office occasionally. Went to lunch so they could discuss whatever project they were on. I don't want to give the impression Gil's a cold fish. He's cordial enough. But around here at least, he's never been one for idle chatter. He keeps his mind on his work."

Collingswood's tone left no doubt he approved of that attitude. It also left me wondering who in C&S Signals did indulge in idle chatter. If I could tap into it, chatter might yield something useful.

"There's an explanation for this, I know it," he said. "Please. Just find him. It's not merely the monetary loss we'll face if we can't find him. I also like the boy. Although I'm not sure he'd believe that right now," he added softly.

"Had you two had a falling out?"

"I wouldn't call it that."

"Over what?"

"I'd asked him to stop seeing my daughter."

Was that enough to turn a loyal employee into a thief?

"May I ask why?"

"He's divorced." He looked down uncomfortably. "Gil's a fine man, but I didn't want her subjected to that sort of social stigma."

From what I'd seen, it was only the divorced woman who got snubbed. Ex-husbands went free under the 'boys will be boys' clause.

Prudence said it might be smart to look at Tremain's office before my tongue got me in trouble. For once I listened to the old girl.

* * *

Tremain's office didn't accommodate me by offering signs of whether or not he'd disappeared voluntarily. No marks on the wall suggested a scuffle. No travel brochures or phone numbers scribbled on the office blotter hinted of departure for a happier clime. The only decoration on his desk was a picture frame containing the likeness of a girl who looked about eleven. His daughter, maybe?

I talked to the employees next: three other engineers, a technician, two draftsmen, two clerk-typists and three secretaries. Not to mention the guardian of the front desk. All gave the same story I'd heard already. Gil Tremain was pleasant but kept to himself. Finally I went back to my office, where even the stairwell now had a tropical feel, and called the number I had for Tremain's apartment. Since nobody answered, I decided to have a look at the place.

The two-story building had a spare look suggesting it would appeal more to people busy with jobs than to retirees. Tremain's apartment was upstairs at the rear, I'd learned from one of the secretaries who had dropped off papers there once. I carried a folder so I could claim the same mission if anyone stopped me. Nobody did.

Upstairs, the hall had carpet. It wasn't thick, but it felt rugged and did a nice job of soaking up footsteps. There were four apartments, two on each side, before I reached Tremain's. No sounds issued from any of them. No radio playing, no electric sweeper. No dishes rattling even though it was lunchtime by now. The silence supported my theory the place would appeal to people who were elsewhere during the day.

At Tremain's door I raised my hand to tap, preparatory to taking out my Number Three Boye. Just before my knuckles connected with wood, I heard movement inside. The fact I had my ear pressed to the door helped. The sounds were muffled, but unmistakable. Scrape. Thump. Like drawers being opened and closed.

If it was Tremain and he was just now packing to take off somewhere, then he was an idiot.

The man who'd been described to me didn't sound like an idiot.

I took out the crochet hook.

The shiny little shaft had never put its nose to any kind of fancywork, but it unlocked the door in about a minute. I slid through and stood stock still, wishing I'd brought the Smith & Wesson.

The room I'd stepped into had been torn apart by someone unconcerned about tidying up. A little modern kitchenette was to my right. Above the sink, weak November light made its way through an outside window whose sash was halfway up. At first I thought the noises had stopped, that the other intruder had somehow become aware of my presence. Then, from the room to my left, which I judged to be the bedroom, I heard what sounded like coins or pencils being dumped out on a hard surface.

Cautiously I crept forward, hugging the wall. A few feet short of the bedroom door, I nearly stepped on papers that had spilled from a small occasional table which stood in what seemed an odd place. Keeping one eye on the door, I stooped and gave them a fast once over. They were blank pages and sheets advertising music events, not scientific calculations.

Resuming my stealthy movements, I eased through the mostly closed bedroom door and found myself engulfed in thick darkness. Vision obscured by the sudden change in light, I ducked to avoid the blow which, if I'd been heard, would come from the side. Instead, a broad shape flew through the air toward me.

Instinctively I threw up my arm to block it. Even as I deflected whatever it was, a man's shape charged and a fist slammed into my chin.

FOUR

The floor tilted under me and I felt my knees buckle. Out of little more than reflex, I caught my attacker around the waist and brought him down with me.

I managed to hit him pretty hard in the snoot. We rolled, with me trying to get a good grip on the front of his shirt. His knee drove into my breast so hard I flinched. It gave him the opening he needed. I made a grab for him as he started to stand.

Something hard smashed down on my head and everything around me dissolved.

* * *

When I woke up, somebody was holding a cold wash cloth against the side of my head. I heard voices. Ones I recognized.

One of them grated. The stench of cigarettes made my head ache worse than it already did.

"She's coming around," someone said.

I forced my eyes open. A grizzled cop with an inch of burning tobacco hanging out of his mouth was bending over me. His name was Freeze.

"You mind telling me how it happens I bump into you so often at homicide scenes?" he asked, sitting back on his heels.

"Gee, I guess we must move in the same social circles," I said thickly. "And yeah, I'm okay. Thanks for asking, lieutenant."

I wondered why my mouth was shooting itself off when the rest of me couldn't even see straight. Maybe because Freeze and I rubbed each other the wrong way. He headed the homicide unit, the only detectives on Dayton's force that specialized. He was a good cop, but he had trouble listening to any ideas that weren't his own. It galled him that mine had been right a few times when we were getting in each other's way.

"Lie still for a while," said the cop with the washcloth, holding me back as I tried to sit. He was a blocky blond junior detective named Boike.

Like Freeze's other boys, he didn't normally speak unless his boss told him to. He got a frown for his efforts, but I'd seen Freeze give a lot worse.

Accumulating evidence, most notably my pounding head, suggested I wasn't yet dead. That meant Freeze and Boike and the several men I could hear in the front room must have come here over other matters.

"The room was dark when I came in. Did I miss a stiff somewhere?" I asked.

It was full of light now. Uncomfortable as it was to move my eyeballs, I could see the room had served Gil Tremain as both bedroom and work area. I lay next to a desk and could see the end of a bed.

"Not up here, you didn't. Just the one downstairs." The homicide chief got up and rubbed out the end of his cigarette just before it burned his fingers.

"There's a body downstairs?" Maybe the knock on the head had knocked me goofy and I wasn't understanding.

"Boike here started up to knock on doors, see if anyone else was around who might have seen something, heard something. Noticed some drips of blood on the stairs. They led back here."

"I punched the guy. Guess I gave him a nosebleed. Can I sit up, Boike?"

"Stay put til I'm done asking questions."

I started to get the strong impression I'd understood fine.

"Come on. You don't think I had anything to do with whatever you found downstairs."

"I want to find out what you know before you sit up. In case your brain busts or something."

Swell bedside manner. He was watching me closely.

"I thought I heard somebody in here. I came in. He jumped me and we traded some punches. Then he clobbered me."

"Yeah, with that."

Following his gaze, I saw broken chunks of brightly colored plaster. Judging by the remains, it had depicted old King Tut in his casket.

"So let's get back to the first question I asked you. How's it happen we find you at a homicide scene?"

It wasn't exactly what he'd asked, but I didn't feel like quibbling. I gave him a highly edited version: Hired by a company to find an employee who hadn't come in. Said employee was working on an important project. I gave them Gil Tremain's name and my client's name. Collingswood could tell them more if he wanted. The shape I was in just now, the less I said the better.

"Any idea what the guy who jumped you was hunting?"

"Something to do with the project Gilbert Tremain was working on, maybe? Or some hint to Tremain's whereabouts if whoever came here thought he was hiding."

"Why would he hide?"

"How should I know? I'm a simple private detective, remember?"

I thought such modesty would please him. He narrowed his eyes.

"Hey, can I take a couple of aspirin at least? I've got some in my purse."

Freeze jerked his head at Boike.

"Go get her some water. I'll see she doesn't get up."

He came to my side and stood looking down, prepared to put a foot on me if I stirred.

"How come you didn't stick your nose in downstairs?"

"Into what?"

"The door that was standing ajar."

"There wasn't one standing ajar when I came in."

Freeze lighted a cigarette.

"You claim you thought something was off with this place because the door wasn't quite latched. The one downstairs where we found the stiff was open a foot or more and you didn't notice? It standing open's what made the woman dropping off ironing for one of the tenants peek in."

That woman, I gathered, had called the police. Boike returned with a glass of water. Freeze had the decency to let me sit up. I took the aspirin and kept on sitting. As far as I could tell, it didn't feel any worse than lying down. Neither choice was a picnic.

"If the man who attacked me had already killed the woman downstairs, I'd have noticed her door open," I processed. "He'd have had no qualms about killing me too. But if he panicked that someone might have heard the two of us thrashing around in here, and raced down and the woman downstairs opened her door — she was the manager, after all—"

"So?"

He hadn't exactly confirmed my guess, but since the apartment was one I'd passed, and the manager typically had one at the front, it was logical.

"So she opened her door to see what was happening and he knew the game was up since she'd seen him. Maybe he thought he'd killed me. He was worked up, and willing to kill now to cover his tracks, and he did. On the way out."

"Yeah, that's the way we see it too."

"How? Did he kill her?"

The detective's mouth clamped tightly closed.

"You know anyone at this place that hired you?" he answered.

"No."

"Never dated someone who worked there, say?"

It was one of the stranger questions he'd ever asked me.

"No. Why?"

He knocked some ash into a saucer he'd found to use as an ashtray.

"Just seems strange that a place that works on engineering things would hunt for a woman detective."

"You telling me you're more of a whiz at physics than I am, Freeze?" I didn't really know what that was, other than high-powered math, but I was willing to bet he didn't either. "They wouldn't have to hunt very hard, since I'm in the phone book. Can I go now? I want to go home and nurse my head."

An irritated breath escaped Freeze.

"Yeah, go on. We know where to find you."

I got up slowly and made my way toward the door. I was almost there, when he spoke again.

"You got your car here? You'd better let Boike drive you. See if she remembers anything else on the way, Boike. Then go on back to the office and build a fire under the evidence boys. I'll meet you there."

My instinct was to argue, but it wouldn't remove the thought I knew was stuck in Freeze's mind that a male detective wouldn't have let an intruder get the best of him.

"What's he up to?" I asked Boike when the two of us were in the hall outside Tremain's apartment.

"The boss is okay," Boike defended. "When we first walked into that room and saw you stretched out bleeding, he thought you were dead."

"Bleeding?" I touched the sorest part of my head. My fingers came away with the stickiness of mostly dried blood.

At the foot of the stairs, the door to the first apartment on the right stood halfway open. I wanted to get a look. It might not help at all, but again, it might.

"Jeez, I'm wobblier than I realized. Need to rest for a minute." Wavering toward the wall, I sagged against it.

From where I stood, I could see inside the apartment where another detective and some uniforms were working.

The view wasn't great. A chair and one of the cops were in the way.

"Uh..." Boike possibly suspected I was up to something.

I put a hand to my forehead as if to ward off dizziness. It shielded my eyes so Boike couldn't see their direction.

The apartment showed traces of being searched. Sofa cushions tossed on the floor, the drawer of a writing table pulled open. But it didn't begin to compare to how things had been torn apart upstairs.

The cop who was blocking my view stepped away and I saw what I needed to. A woman lay on her back with one leg splayed. The front of her dress was stained. She'd been shot in the chest.

FIVE

"Eggs and ham," I told Izzy as soon as she noticed me sliding onto a stool at McCrory's lunch counter. On the rare occasions when I wanted something other than my usual oatmeal, I had to speak before my fanny was completely on the stool. "And coffee," I called.

My head ached, which was several notches better than yesterday's pounding. My jaw hurt where the guy had punched me. It was somehow managing to share its displeasure with my eyes. I sipped my coffee gratefully.

When I'd had sufficient coffee, my mind began to groan into gear. Gil Tremain wouldn't have torn his own apartment apart. Everyone who worked with him had mentioned how precise he was. Going to lunch at the same time. Always putting papers for others to look at in the same place. A man like that didn't displace things. Especially not something important. Especially not in his own apartment.

Somebody wanted something in that apartment, though. They wanted it enough to kill for it.

That suggested Tremain hadn't gone off voluntarily, and that he wasn't a traitor.

All at once every one of my senses registered a male presence settling beside me. A particular male presence smelling of soap and shaving cream. A russet haired cop named Mick Connelly. Whenever he came within a foot of me, I felt the same prickle I experienced plunging earthward in a Ferris wheel.

"You didn't show up for our date last night."

What was he talking about? When had we ever had a date? Sometimes when we bumped into each other at Finn's we ended up grabbing a bite to eat together, but we weren't sweethearts, no matter how much he'd like to be.

"I went home with a headache and slept til my alarm went off. Aren't you supposed to be on duty?"

"Not for half an hour. Long enough to have porridge and coffee."

Izzy flashed him one of her shy smiles and scurried away. What was it about him that had an effect on so many women? He was perfectly ordinary looking if you didn't count his fine mouth.

"I'm guessing the fight you were in is what gave you the headache. Or are you going to tell me your yellow jaw is some new beauty fad for brown-haired girls."

I pushed away the fingertips that had come to rest ever so gently beneath my chin as he tilted it up to squint at the bruise.

"Yeah, I got slugged, but I gave worse than I got. And I'll thank you not to paw me in public."

"Does that mean I'm allowed to run my fingers over your still lovely face in private?"

I shoved his hand, which was still close enough for me to feel the warmth of it, further away.

"What date are you talking about?"

"The prizefight?"

I wasn't keen on watching men knock each other silly, but Connelly and most of the other men I knew seemed to enjoy them. Somebody had given him tickets. Now I vaguely recalled that he'd invited me and I'd said yes.

"Sorry I forgot to call you," I said tersely.

"Ah, well. You're okay, and that's the important thing. But Maggie, you've got to start steering clear of situations where you could get punched around. Too many blows to your head and your brains get scrambled like those poor old devils who've lost too many rounds in the ring."

"I know what's what, Connelly. I don't need a lecture, and you wouldn't be sitting here giving me one if I were a man."

Tossing down money to cover my bill and a tip, I stalked off with my heels clicking loudly on the wooden floor. At a spot where it warped a little they gave a particularly satisfying smack. I hated to retreat, but it was the only way I knew to escape an urge to rest my achy head against the solidness of his shoulder and let him comfort me.

* * *

The white-haired Doberman had the phone cradled to her ear when I entered C&S Signals. She was writing something down and listening intently.

"He's expecting you," she said, nodding me back as she covered the mouthpiece. "I'm sorry. Could you repeat that last item?"

I made my way through the same group of typists and draftsmen and headed toward Collingswood's office. As I neared it, I heard two men arguing.

"But you agreed we ought to get a private detective."

"That *we* would!"

"You weren't here, Frank. How could I sit around another day doing nothing? The meeting with Acoff's too important."

"Of course it's important! Which is exactly why I can't believe you hired a — some woman. She's clearly not equipped to deal with a matter like this."

I tapped on the door. The voices ceased. A moment later, Collingswood opened the door a few inches, looking put out.

"Oh, it's you, Miss Sullivan. I, er, didn't expect you so early. Come in. This is my partner, Frank Scott. I was just filling him in...." Embarrassment tinged his cheeks.

"Mr. Scott. Glad to meet you." I offered my hand and a dazzling smile. "I do hope your headache's gone. And yes, you're right in thinking Pythagoras and his hypotenuse is just about as complex as I can manage when it comes to math, but I hold my own when it comes to detecting."

Scott was taller than his partner. Younger, too. He was probably just nudging forty with sandy hair. He had the grace to look embarrassed.

"Miss Sullivan, I apologize for what you must have overheard. I only meant that you work alone, according to Loren. Having more people involved would yield faster results."

"Is that an engineering formula?"

"You're not exactly a giantess, either. And Loren says you've already been attacked?"

"The police were here not much more than half an hour after you called me yesterday," Collingswood put in.

I nodded. The one thing I'd done before downing more aspirin and crawling into bed the previous day was use the hall phone at the rooming house where I lived. I'd given Collingswood a quick rundown of events at Tremain's apartment and told him to expect the police.

"They didn't seem to care much about finding Gil," he said, frowning. "Only how the break-in at his apartment might be related to a woman who was - who was killed."

"What do you think the man who tore up Gil's apartment was hunting?" his partner asked. "It was a man, I take it?"

"Yes. I'd say he was hunting the same thing you're worrying over."

"The project summary? With the right calculations?"

"Which means that Gil didn't take them," said Collingswood eagerly.

"Not necessarily." An hour ago I'd reached the same conclusion. Now I discarded it. "He might have struck a deal with someone, then decided to hold out for more money. Or, if this development of yours is as valuable as you've let on, and people knew about it because of that conference, it's possible someone snatched him thinking he had the whole thing in his head or that he could get it."

Something about that scenario didn't quite match up with the snake in Collingswood's coat pocket, but I wasn't sure what.

"Yesterday when I asked, you said there hadn't been any ransom demands. Is that still true?"

Collingswood bobbed his head once.

"As far as I'm aware," Scott said shortly.

"It's also possible Gil was scared about something and went into hiding," I said. "And though I think this one's extremely remote, it could also be that he took off over something unrelated to your project."

Both men stared at me with equal dismay. While they were still digesting it, the door burst open.

A woman in her late twenties stood there. She had a heart-shaped face and quick gray eyes. They flicked back and forth between the two men, pausing curiously on me before sharpening on Collingswood.

"Dad? Wilma just told me the police were here yesterday. She said Gil's been missing since Monday. Is that true? Why didn't you say anything? What's going on?"

SIX

"Miss Sullivan, this is my daughter, Lucille. Yes, honey, I'm afraid Gil.... No one's seen him since Monday. Miss Sullivan is a detective. We've hired her to find him."

Collingswood looked even more miserable than he had a moment earlier when I'd told him Tremain might have been snatched. His daughter was shaking her head as if it might somehow negate the words.

"Since I wasn't able to talk to you yesterday, I wonder if you could show me some things in your office," I said to Scott.

He took the hint.

"Poor girl," he murmured as we crossed the hall to his office. "They'd been seeing each other. Gil and Lucille."

"Your partner wasn't keen on it, apparently."

"Wasn't he? I didn't know."

Scott's hand swept in an invitation to sit. His office wasn't as tidy, or as sterile, as his partner's. A large seascape hung on the wall facing his desk; another, smaller, where it caught the eye of anyone entering. A copy of Life magazine peeped out from a stack of clipped together pages next to his phone. Next to the desktop baskets marked In and Out sat a pair of dice.

"Do you come from someplace with ocean?" I asked to put him at ease.

"No, I just like to look at the pictures. Daydream occasionally. Look, I do apologize again—"

"Forget it. People shopping for a detective often doubt my ability."

"A mistake on their part, I begin to suspect."

His smile was forced, but that might have to do with the headache that had flattened him the previous day. I had some sympathy at the moment. As if well practiced in the maneuver, he took a capsule from a prescription bottle and swallowed it dry. The shadows under his eyes looked more like bruises.

"'Disaster' might be the best description of what Gil's disappearance is for us. I suppose Loren told you about the meeting? That we might even have an offer to buy out our company? Might have had, anyway."

I nodded.

"What do you think might have happened to him, Mr. Scott?"

He hesitated just a second

"I have no idea."

"If you had to speculate?"

"I couldn't."

"Your partner told me Tremain was closer to you than to anyone else here."

"Loren would consider any type of conversation apart from work closeness," he said drily. "We went to lunch together now and then, but those were mostly spent picking at something that was stumping us in the project of the moment. I'm still heavily involved in actual engineering. Loren mostly oversees now, checks over results as a project progresses, brainstorms with us now and then. Splendid mind, Loren, but he has his hands full with management and keeping abreast of what's going on in the field. We all try to do that, of course."

I waited. He sighed.

"If I had to guess about Gil... Very well. I guess I've begun to wonder exactly what you suggested, if he might have sold out to a higher bidder. Not that I have any reason to think such a thing, and I haven't even hinted as much to Loren. He's fond of Gil."

Not fond enough to want him courting his daughter, I thought.

"He wasn't in debt? Didn't gamble?"

"No. As far as I know. The idea he might have run off and deliberately left us with flawed calculations — it was the only explanation I could come up with. But if someone was tearing his place apart yesterday... Do you really think someone might have nabbed him?"

"As you just said, theories are in short supply. The question is, would it be one of your competitors or someone from the America First crowd? If there's a chance it's the latter, then you need to talk to the police again, or maybe the F.B.I."

"No. Oh, God no!"

Scott flung out his hands as if to fend off my words. His face had gone white. America First was headed by luminaries like the Lindberghs and Kennedys and the Nazi-sympathizing radio priest Father Coughlin, but the group also included thousands, maybe tens of thousands, of ordinary people. Some were volatile. They ranged from wanting to keep America out of the war in Europe to out-and-out supporting Hitler.

"That's simply absurd!" Scott insisted. "It has no military application whatsoever — nothing to attract people like them. The chance one of our competitors is behind it is at least a possibility. After Gil presented that paper, several companies contacted us within days. And we hadn't even achieved our breakthrough yet. Outfits doing work similar to ours would recognize right away it was something to interest the big fish."

"'Big fish' being the companies that you all sell to."

"Yes."

"I'll look at competitors then."

How, I wasn't quite sure. And why did Collingswood think their project might have military uses while Scott didn't?

"What else can you tell me about Tremain? What did he do when he wasn't working?"

"I'm afraid I don't know. I think he said something about a concert once. Mozart or something like that."

"Did he ever mention anyone he might confide in? Or go to in a jam?"

"No. I don't think so. Gil was like Loren. Most of his mind stayed on work."

"Had there been any changes in his behavior lately? Did he seem worried about anything?"

"No, although...." He frowned and picked up the dice, fixing his gaze on them.

"What?"

"He... he might have acted a bit odd of late. Jumpy."

"Any idea why?"

"No."

He said it too hastily.

"Mr. Scott, I need every scrap of information I can get. His life could depend on it."

Scott swallowed. He let the dice slide from his fingers; picked them up; did it again.

"It's just... he told me in confidence. If it turns out to have nothing to do with his disappearing, it could cost him his job."

"Better his job than his life."

He drew a breath.

"Yes, of course. You're right." His lips hovered indecisively over words. "Before he came here, when he was first out of school, Gil used heroin. He became so habituated that he had to spend time in a clinic to kick the habit."

Several moments passed while I absorbed the unexpected bit of input.

"You think he might have started again?" I asked slowly. "Gone off on a jag somewhere?"

"It... crossed my mind. Crescendo — the project — we've all been under considerable stress."

This additional angle was as unexpected as the attack in Tremain's apartment. It was also one I'd never had to factor into a case before.

Across from me, Scott had put the dice down. He massaged the bridge of his nose. I could sense his uneasiness.

"Has he ever said or done anything that suggested he might be?"

"No, no. I'm sure that... problem was well in the past." His conviction sounded on the weak side, though. "Look, I suppose you'll have to look into it, but unless you find a connection, could you please not mention it to Loren? If something has happened to Gil, if he's dead I mean, there's no point smearing him, is there?"

"No."

His concern moved him up a notch in my estimation. He stood. "If there's nothing else, I do need to get back with Loren. We have to plan."

"Of course." I rose too. "I need a photograph of Tremain. And a list of any competitors you think are likely candidates."

He picked up a pad from his desk and wrote quickly.

"I don't think these are candidates, particularly, but they're our main competitors. Feel free to use my office if there are other people you didn't get to talk to yesterday."

He came around and shook my hand again, then hesitated.

"There's something else I should mention, in case someone else does and you get the wrong impression."

I waited.

"Before Lucille and Gil began going out, she was seeing me. We were all but engaged."

My eyebrows raised.

"Did you resent that? The two of them getting together?"

"Of course I did." He gave his lapels a snap. "But I'm a grown man."

SEVEN

If Scott had anything he wanted to hide in his office, he wouldn't have invited me to stay and make use of it. I took out my compact and lipstick as he departed. The pretext would allow me to linger just long enough to have a look at the one thing I wondered about.

As soon as voices across the hall assured me Scott was with his partner and unlikely to duck back in the next thirty seconds, I went to his desk and opened the drawer that held the prescription bottle he'd taken out earlier. I didn't recognize the name of the capsules it held. I assumed they were for his headaches. I jotted the name of the medicine in my notebook and took out one of the pills. The doctor's name and pharmacy I could trust to my memory.

On my previous visit, when I'd questioned all the employees, a draftsman had been out attending a funeral and one of the typists had gone to take something they needed copies of to a Photostat place. A chat with her didn't yield anything interesting, but the one with the draftsman, a young fellow named Roger Lewis, did.

"He's the very devil for having everything perfect," he said when I asked him what Tremain had been like at work. "Not as bad as the old— as Mr. Collingswood, but more of a stickler than Mr. Scott and the others. Hope you find him though."

The last sounded tepid. His curly black hair and good looks probably meant he got enough attention from the ladies to convince him he was something special. Such men often nursed resentment over rebukes others took in stride. Still, it was the first deviation I'd had from the worked-hard-quiet-kept-to-himself recitation.

"Any idea what Mr. Tremain did in his spare time? Did he ever mention anything he enjoyed?"

"Not to me." His mouth gave a smug lift. "Pauline might know. She was always hanging around him."

Flipping back through my notes I tried to place her.

"Pauline. She's the one with the dimples?"

I remembered her now, young and fresh-faced with deep mid-cheek dimples that put Shirley Temple's to shame. When I'd finished with Roger Lewis, I went out to the hive of desks in the open area and asked for a word with her. Eyes widening nervously, she exchanged a look with the women around her. This was the first time I'd asked to talk to someone again.

"Yesterday you told me Mr. Tremain was nice." I'd jotted the word in my notes. No one else had used it. "Nice how?"

"He's-he's patient. When I first started here, I was so scared I'd make a typing mistake and get fired that I made dozens. Well, not dozens really, but I made them. Mr. Collingswood scolds." She winced at the memory. "So much as one letter wrong in five or six pages and he shakes it under your nose and tells you in a really stern voice. In front of everybody.

"Mr. Tremain if he wants something done over just hands it to you and says so quietly. And if it's just one or two letters, he'll say, 'We'll let it go this time.' He even asks for me specifically to type things now, if it's something that has equations. He says I have a better feel for how much space to leave. They have to write those in by hand, you see."

My eyebrows rose a little. I'd just gotten a clearer picture of how things worked at C&S Signals than I had by talking to everyone else.

"Roger Lewis seemed to think Mr. Tremain was too demanding."

"That's because Roger does sloppy work," Pauline said in disgust. "Then he grouses if he has to do something over."

"Were you and Mr. Tremain seeing each other outside of work?"

"Seeing each— No! And if Roger told you that, he's a filthy liar!" Her cheeks flamed with anger. She wasn't as shy as she first appeared.

"What makes you think he did?"

"Because *he* asked me out. Roger did. I turned him down, and I was nice about it, too, but ever since then he's been nasty."

I grinned. "I kind of thought it might be something like that."

Frank Scott was discussing something with one of the junior engineers. He nodded assent when I asked if I could use his office for a few more minutes, so I brought Roger Lewis back for another chat.

"Lying to me is one step short of lying to the police," I said severely. "Authorization to work as a private detective comes from Chief Wurstner himself."

The draftsman squirmed. "I don't know—"

"You tried to make me think Pauline was going out with Gil Tremain because you were mad she wouldn't go out with you."

His manner turned sulky.

"I never lied. Miss Stuck-up wants a bigger fish than me. She was always hanging around him. Ask anyone."

***

"Miss Collingswood asked you to give her a call as soon as you finished." The razor eyed receptionist, whose name I'd learned was Mrs. Hawes, thrust a piece of paper at me as I passed her desk on my way out. "There's her number."

It seemed to me that if Lucille had wanted me to go somewhere more private before I called, she would have left an envelope instead of a message. I asked if I could use the desk phone. Although it produced a small sniff of disapproval, Mrs. Hawes didn't snatch it back. I dialed.

"Just a moment, please. I'll get her," a woman's voice said when I gave my name. A violin was playing in the background. It stopped, and a moment later Lucille came on.

"Miss Sullivan. Thank you so much. I'd - I'd like to talk to you. About Gil. I don't know if I can tell you anything useful, but please. Please, will you stop by? It's almost lunchtime and you'll have to eat somewhere."

Lucille, I thought, might be the most productive source of leads I had at the moment. She'd been dating the missing man. Her father hadn't approved. And she'd jilted her father's partner when she started seeing Gil Tremain.

***

Writing at my own desk was a lot more comfortable than trying to do it on a clipboard wedged against the steering wheel of my DeSoto. I went back to the office to make quick notes on what little I'd learned that morning.

Today the radiator was stone cold. I kept my coat draped over my shoulders as I worked. When I finished, I gave my muscles a pep talk and tilted the heavy Remington typewriter on a stand beside my desk back an inch. I slid the folded sheet of notes beneath the black rubber pad that cushioned the typewriter. Although I didn't expect anyone to search my office because I'd been hired by C&S Signals, the woman killed downstairs at Gil Tremain's apartment building probably hadn't expected that either. Better safe than sorry.

After making a quick call to a man I hoped could tell me about names on the list of C&S competitors, I went upstairs to the ladies room and resettled the tortoiseshell combs holding my hair back. Neat and proper, I went outside and set course for my car which I'd parked half a block up.

"Say, how's the girl with the best set of legs in Dayton doing today?" asked a voice behind me. A fellow in a cheap navy suit and gray fedora trotted up to keep pace with me.

"Better before I saw you." I bit the words off with considerably less antagonism than I felt. His name was Clem Stark and he was an unremarkable waste of skin — medium build, medium height, and enough Brylcreem on his thinning brown hair to smell a mile away.

"Hey, now, doll. Is that any way to talk to a colleague who's come to take you to lunch?"

"Not interested." I picked up my pace.

Clem ran a detective agency with a couple of guys working for him. When I'd first opened my own office, he'd deliberately spoiled an investigation I was halfway through, then poached my client. I'd needed the income, as well as another satisfied customer I could use as a reference. Since then Clem and I had crossed paths often enough for me to know he was lazy, cut corners and was sleazy through and through.

"Not interested?" he said trotting backward now, heedless of a woman and kid who had to duck around him. "You will be when I offer you a job."

"I've got a job, thanks. Right now you're keeping me from doing it."

"I'm talking a nice office, regular paycheck. Nice lunch, too. Work for me and you won't have to settle for a sandwich at the Arcade like ya do now."

I fought an impulse to hit him. We were on a public street. There were witnesses. An assault and battery charge would jeopardize my detective license. We'd reached my DeSoto. I smacked my purse on top of it and came to a stop.

"What is it, Clem? One of the boys who works for you quit?"

A cagey expression flitted across his eyes. He was up to something. Curiosity wasn't enough to make me spend more time in his company, though.

"Let's talk about it," he coaxed.

"Not now, not ever, not if I were starving." Retrieving my purse, I went around to the driver's side and opened the door. "Stand back, Clem. You know how women drivers are. I might get flustered and back over you."

EIGHT

The Collingswoods lived in a very nice area several miles east of Miami Valley Hospital. Their house was dark red brick, two stories, and my cheeks were tingling with cold by the time I made my way up the front walk. A woman in a dark dress and apron let me into a front hall and helped me out of my coat. Polished hardwood floor gleamed at the edges of the pretty Persian rug beneath my feet and holiday greenery wound around the banister of stairs leading up.

"Miss Collingswood said to show you in when you got here," the housekeeper said. She led me toward a room on the right and the sound of a violin like I'd heard on the phone. The piece was something classical with glides and vibratos and an impressive skill to the playing. A long run of notes soared up and quivered. Then Lucille noticed us waiting.

Her bow hovered motionless as her brain made the trip from the sheets of music propped on the walnut stand before her to the here and now.

"Oh, hello," she said. "Do come in. I'm afraid I get rather lost in the music. It...."

She broke off, shaking her head. As if indifferent to fashion, or immune to its whims, she wore her ashy blonde hair in a French twist. With fluid movements she loosened something on her bow and rested it on the edge of the walnut stand, a fine piece of furniture which had probably cost a bundle. Placing the violin in an open case that lay on a table nearby, Lucille Collingswood came toward me with hand extended.

"We didn't exactly meet this morning. Hearing that about Gil — and the fact I didn't even know — it sort of knocked me off my feet, I'm afraid."

Her eyes weren't red from crying, but tension strained the flesh around them. As her father had mentioned, she was a few years older than me. I shook her hand gently, unwilling to risk too much pressure on fingers as talented as hers.

"You're a remarkable musician."

She smiled faintly. "Thanks. I do love it. I don't imagine you've learned anything since I saw you?"

"I've learned quite a lot. I don't know yet whether any of it is important."

"Poor Eve. She must be devastated. Have you talked to them yet?"

Briefly I was at sea. Then I started to put it together. The photograph on Tremain's desk.

"Eve is Tremain's daughter?"

Lucille nodded.

"She's eleven. Smart kid. She adores her father, and he adores her. They're very close." With a shift of focus which I found disconcerting, she gestured toward a console cabinet. "Will you have a glass of sherry before lunch?"

As far as I was concerned, sherry barely passed muster as liquor, so I declined. The violinist led the way to a dining room with cherry furniture. A lacy runner, coupled with place mats of celery green linen, kept the table from feeling overly large as we sat across from each other. By the time we'd been served cups of split pea soup, I'd learned that Lucille's mother had died when she was ten. From that point on, she'd stepped into the role of hostess for her father.

"Not that he entertains in the true sense," she said. "It's mostly just dinner for men who come to town to visit the company, or a couple of local engineers and their wives." She made a face. "I've heard enough equations and theorems tossed about to last me six lifetimes."

I laughed. It seemed like as good an opening as any, so I plunged in.

"Tell me about Gil. When was the last time you saw him?"

In an instant her gray eyes grew grave.

"Sunday evening. We went to a recital. A string trio. We'd originally planned that he'd join us for dinner here first, but..."

"Your father wanted him to stop seeing you," I suggested.

She shrugged. There was something cool and businesslike about her.

"Dad would have come around. He's not unreasonable. But Gil said maybe we shouldn't rub his nose in the fact we were seeing each other."

She paused as the housekeeper set veal birds accompanied by thinly sliced string beans in front of us. It gave me a moment to think.

"Could your father be behind Gil's disappearance?" I asked when we were alone again.

"Good heavens no. He liked Gil, as a matter of fact. It was only when the two of us began to get serious that he started to put up a fuss. The idea, Dad would hire some sort of thug to kill someone or even run him off is quite preposterous!"

There was another possibility she wasn't seeing. Collingswood wouldn't have been the first man to bribe a daughter's suitor to skip town.

"Besides, if Gil's not here, Father stands to lose a fortune on a deal he was making," Lucille said with composure. "And seeing whatever project they've been working on go up in flames would hurt him even more than the money."

Did I detect an edge to her voice?

I gave a bite of veal bird the appreciation it deserved. "So what would you guess has happened to him?"

"I have no idea. None. The possibilities I pried out of Dad — that Gil would sneak off to a rival company with something he'd worked on here, or turn traitor to help someone who sides with Germany, are completely ridiculous. I suppose... it could be a kidnapping that went wrong somehow, couldn't it?"

It could, except for the fact her father and Frank Scott both claimed there had been no ransom demand. I chewed thoughtfully.

"Would the company pay it?"

"Oh yes. If Dad didn't want C&S to take the hit, he'd pay it himself. Even with—" Her wordless gesture, I assumed, referenced her romance with Gil.

Could both partners in C&S Signals be lying to me? Or, as Lucille had suggested, could there have been a kidnapping attempt where something went wrong? If the latter case, Gil Tremain was probably dead.

Taking my silence for agreement with her idea had given the woman across from me her first hint of appetite. She ate, watching me closely.

"How would the snake in your father's pocket fit in with any of this?"

She brought her napkin to her lips and dabbed them as she swallowed the food in her mouth.

"Snake in his pocket? What do you mean?"

I sat back, observing her closely.

"He didn't tell you? It was in his coat pocket yesterday when he came to ask me if I'd look for Gil. It started to slither out."

"What did he do?"

The question struck me as odd. If she was concerned, I couldn't see it. She just seemed curious.

"He didn't have a chance to do anything. I shot it. When he realized what was happening, he began to have chest pains and nearly collapsed. He has a serious heart condition, doesn't he?"

She sipped some water, her only sign of agitation.

"He's had some problems, yes, but he has pills. To answer your question, I don't see how it could possibly be related to Gil's disappearance."

I saw two. For the time being, though, I'd stick with the theory the snake had nothing to do with the fact C&S was missing an engineer and valuable documents.

"The last time you saw Gil was Sunday evening," I said. "Did you hear from him after that? Did he call when he got home?"

"No. He usually called in the evening, but not if we'd seen each other. Neither of us is the moony type."

"So it could be that he never made it back to his apartment. He might have disappeared on the way."

"But what about Daisy seeing him Monday morning? Even if no one else noticed him, he could have been there."

"Who's Daisy? What are you talking about?"

We stared at each other.

"But surely someone told you. Daisy cleans. At the company. She works at night, of course, but she came in Tuesday afternoon to get her pay for the week before and apparently heard the dither over Gil's not showing up for two days. Wilma said Daisy told Mrs. Hawes that she'd seen Gil walking on Fifth Street Monday morning."

No one had mentioned it. Not a peep. And if people at C&S were as eager to find Gil Tremain as they let on, I wondered why.

NINE

I put my napkin down and bid a reluctant adieu to the remnants of my veal bird. I wanted to follow up on what Lucille had just told me. Five minutes later I was headed uptown.

At Third and Main the traffic light turned red ahead of me. To keep my impatience in check, I watched holiday shoppers. FDR's New Deal was working. Their arms held a few more bundles than those of shoppers a few years ago.

Gil Tremain had a daughter. I tried to block the thought that no matter how many gifts she got in her stocking, she was likely to have a lousy Christmas unless I found her father. Apart from when someone went missing voluntarily, the sooner you found them, the higher the odds they'd still be alive. Tremain had been missing going on four days now. The question was, had he vanished because he wanted to?

The light changed.

I moved on.

I wasn't in a holiday mood.

By the time I pulled onto the parking strip outside C&S Signals, I'd planned my order of attack. Mrs. Hawes eyed me without enthusiasm as I entered.

"Have you found him?"

"No. Is Mr. Collingswood in?"

"Where else would he be with everything topsy-turvy here? The office boy went out and got him a sandwich. He's eating it at his desk, poor man."

"I need to see him."

"And *he* needs ten minutes' peace and quiet. Have a seat."

She pointed at four chairs paired on either side of a low table. My impulse was to breeze past her, but she'd been party to the conversation I was interested in. She would probably respond to honey better than horseradish, so I sat. As demurely as when one of the nuns at Holy T. sent me to the principal's office.

The frequency of those visits had given me considerable experience.

Keeping my knees together, I folded my hands in my lap and smiled at Mrs. Hawes. She ignored it. It hadn't worked with the nuns either.

My plan had been to ask Collingswood why he'd neglected to tell me Tremain had been sighted Monday morning. Since Collingswood had hired me, why wouldn't he give me every scrap of information he had? My forced acquaintanceship with the chair in the reception area gave me time to reflect he might not know.

Women in offices talked about things they didn't pass on to the bosses. One got a glimpse of a letter about someone being promoted, or fired, or the target of legal proceedings. That girl passed the information to others. Word spread.

Some might call it gossip. A more accurate term was survival. Women were the disposables, the last to be told officially when jobs or salaries might be cut. They depended on each other for that, and for hearing when one of the men who called the shots was better avoided because he was in a nasty mood.

"Say, I heard somebody caught a glimpse of Mr. Tremain Monday morning," I said innocently. "Did you hear anything about that?"

Mrs. Hawes looked at me over the letter opener poised in her hand.

"Yes."

The opener ripped into the envelope. I gritted my teeth.

"Did you have some sort of grudge against Mr. Tremain that you didn't mention it yesterday when I was asking everyone questions?"

"Of course not! He's a lovely young man."

"Well, then? Why didn't you tell me?"

Another envelope succumbed to the letter opener.

"I'm not one to gossip," she said primly. "I told Mr. Collingswood and left it to him to make what he might of it. It wasn't for me to say how reliable it was. Or how important."

Extricating her latest conquest, she clipped it to its envelope and added them to the pile of opened mail at her elbow. So Collingswood had known, which led me back to the question why he hadn't mentioned it.

"Mr. Collingswood has had a lot on his mind," I said. "The more you can fill in some details on this, the less I'll need to pester him. When you implied Daisy's story might not be reliable, why was that?"

From the way her mouth pursed, I thought she wasn't going to answer.

"I didn't say it *wasn't* reliable; I just don't know that it was. She was on a bus. She can't have had more than a glimpse. And she comes in after everyone else has gone. Mr. Tremain did work late sometimes, but still."

"Still?" At least I'd confirmed it was Daisy who'd claimed to see him. She'd told Mrs. Hawes she was on a bus, the sort of insignificant detail which carried the ring of truth.

"Mr. Tremain would have been in his office. Probably with the door closed. They can't have done more than pass each other and nod a few times. How could Daisy be sure it was him? And at that distance?"

"Mrs. Hawes, you make excellent sense." I was more than willing to stroke her feathers now that I had what I needed. "I think I'll pop in to see Mr. Collingswood now."

Before she could put down the letter opener, I breezed past her.

***

Collingswood was at his desk poring over pages decorated here and there by equations when I rapped on his door. A partly wrapped half-eaten sandwich lay in his wastebasket. He gave a faint frown as I came in.

"Is Mrs. Hawes not at her desk?"

"I'm afraid I didn't give her a chance to tell you I was here. I just need to check something. I won't stay long."

"Yes, of course. Any time."

Standing works when you need to show who's boss, but sitting's better when you want to put them off guard. I sat down.

"I just had a nice lunch with your daughter. She mentioned a woman who works here had seen Tremain down on Fifth Street Monday morning."

"Well, yes. Mrs. Hawes told me Daisy had said that, but I didn't give it much credence."

"Why not?"

His gaze fell to a paperclip on his desk and he pushed it around.

"I hate to say it, but the old dear drinks."

"Why do you keep her on, then?"

"Oh... well... she's a good-hearted soul, and there's nothing wrong with her work. Reliable as can be. Leaves everything ship shape."

"Does she come in tipsy?"

"Oh, no. That is... as far as I know."

Something wasn't adding up.

"How do you know, then? About the drinking?"

Collingswood's expression had begun to grow unhappy.

"Someone must have told me. Wilma? Frank?" He shook his head. "I'm sorry. I can't remember. So much has been going on. By the time I talked to you about helping us, it had slipped—. Frank. I think it was Frank who told me. He'd come by one night to pick up some papers and saw her drinking out of a bottle."

I took my leave and went across the hall to his partner's office. Frank Scott was on the phone. Beckoning me in, he brought the conversation to a quick close.

"Anything to report?" he asked hopefully.

"No, something to ask." This time I stood, leaning a shoulder casually against the wall and crossing one leg over the other. "How do you know that Daisy drinks?"

Scott had been watching my legs. He looked startled.

"Daisy? Oh. You must have heard that rumor she started about seeing Gil somewhere Monday morning."

"Why do you say it's a rumor?"

He spread a hand indulgently.

"The source, the time of day. The woman works nights. Why would she be out and about first thing in the morning? As to your first question, I've come in nights a couple of times and caught her taking a swig from a bottle."

A long time ago my work had taught me one thing about boozers: Sometimes they saw things that weren't there. But sometimes they saw things that were.

TEN

I asked Scott a few more questions, but he didn't have any answers. Unlike his partner, he didn't change his opinion that the charwoman's report was unreliable.

Mrs. Hawes, who had thawed about a degree toward me in spite of my unauthorized trip around her, wrote out Daisy's address when I asked. I didn't broach the question of whether Daisy drank. If she didn't, I didn't want to start rumors.

To my frustration, Daisy Brown wasn't home when I got there. She lived on Robert Drive, a street that was almost at river's edge. What once had been elegant homes to prosperous families now mostly were rooming or boarding houses or, like hers, small apartments. When I knocked on her door, a head of gray curls popped out from a neighboring one.

"Are you here for the cinnamon rolls?"

"I'm here to see Daisy."

"She's not home." The woman frowned. She had on a red apron that went all the way to her neck. It gave her a robin like look. "You're not here for the rolls? She did say she'd told the woman coming for them that they'd be at my place."

"Gee, I didn't even know she baked," I said, recognizing a source of information when it bit my nose.

"Oh my, yes. You wouldn't believe what she makes in a wee little oven no bigger than mine. She takes orders from people, you see, to make a little money on the side."

By now I'd been in the hall long enough that the fragrance of butter and cinnamon permeated my senses. My salivary glands were at high tide.

"A woman she knows sent me to ask her something," I said. "Do you know when she'll be back?"

"Dear me, I'm afraid not. She was going to deliver a cake and stop at the store. After that she looks after some children when they get out of school. Poor tykes lost their dad, so their mother has to work and pays Daisy to stay with them.

"She might be home around six, only sometimes the mother's boss makes her work late. And sometimes Daisy just stops for a sandwich somewhere and goes straight to her regular job."

If Daisy drank, I wondered when she found time.

"Do you happen to know the name of the family? Or where they live?"

She shook her curls.

***

"I'm Mr. Scott's secretary. Mr. Frank Scott, that is." I gave the man behind the pharmacy counter a big smile. "He asked me to check and see if he has a refill left on this prescription."

I slid him the slip of paper with the number I'd copied from the bottle in Scott's desk drawer and held my breath.

"Sure, let me check."

He stepped to one end where he was half-hidden by an enormous glass jar of blue liquid. I was pretty sure it didn't contain anything medicinal, but everyplace I'd ever been to that mixed up potions and powders seemed to keep one out as decoration.

The counter was shoulder height on me, but by standing on tiptoe I could watch the pharmacist walk his fingers through a long box of cards. I wasn't sure what I expected to learn from Scott's bottle of pills. There wasn't any reason to suspect he'd been the one who'd torn up Tremain's apartment and killed a woman on the way out. Still, he hadn't been to the office that day, and his alibi was a bad headache. It would help if I could confirm that's what he'd swallowed pills for this morning.

"Yes, he can refill it," said the pharmacist, returning. "Was there anything else?"

"No, thank you." I peeked over my shoulder, then leaned somberly toward the counter. "Between you and me, though, I don't think those tablets do much good. He's had the most awful headaches this week."

He nodded with professional sympathy.

"Some just have a harder time of it than others. Tell him not to take more of these than he's supposed to, though. They'll knock him cold."

***

For the time being I'd hit a dead end. I'd begun to believe that Daisy the cleaning woman actually might have caught a glimpse of Gil Tremain, but until I talked to her, I was stuck. Fifth Street was long. If Daisy had been on a Main Street bus and crossed it, that would give at least a departure point in trying to pick up his trail. Buses also ran up and down Fifth itself, however. If she'd been riding that line, I'd face endless possibilities.

The sight of Christmas decorations in shop windows did nothing to improve my spirits as I drove back to my office. They reminded me that in addition to making zero progress on my case, I'd made a similar amount on my Christmas shopping. What was I going to get for the two white-haired cops who had been my late father's best friends and part of my life for as long as I could remember? I wanted to find a little something for my landlady, Mrs. Z, too. And for one of the girls in the rooming house who was a pal.

And maybe Mick Connelly?

He'd really gotten my goat this morning, but yeah. Probably Connelly. He always got something for me.

The thought of picking out something for him tied me in knots, though. It had to be something that didn't raise his hopes we had a future together. I'd told him more than once that I wasn't the marrying type. Either his hearing was bad or he wasn't as smart as I thought. The trouble was, he cast some kind of spell when he was around me.

Connelly was too good a man to wind up as hurt and confused as my dad had been by my mother. She cooked, she cleaned, but when my dad paid her a compliment or said something tender, she stared through him. When he asked her a question, her answer was monosyllabic. Her interaction with my brother and me consisted of stony silence or lashing out. How could Connelly possibly think I was a candidate for marriage when the chance of turning into her was in my blood?

Annoyed to find my brain wandering to things besides work, I slowed and waved an old woman with a scarf tied under her chin and shopping bags too heavy for her into a crosswalk. Behind me there was a screech of brakes.

I braced for an impact. It didn't come. Instead, a battered brown sedan swerved around me. Missing the old woman in her fringed kerchief by no more than a couple of feet, it sped into the nearest alley before I gathered my wits enough to catch anything but the final number on the license plate, a six.

The old woman plodded ahead without a glance. On the sidewalk, several people had stopped to crane their necks. Letting the clutch out, I shifted and drove on.

The sedan had been following too closely, surely. Not that it mattered. But since it hadn't hit me, why had it taken off like a frightened rabbit? Was it stolen?

Another possibility crawled into my head. Clem Stark. It stunk of fish the way he'd shown up that morning with his job offer. Or was it just that every time I encountered the man, I found myself wanting to wash myself immediately with lye soap? Maybe he really wanted me to join his firm. Maybe he'd sent one on his boys to follow me, or done it himself so he could come around again and brag how he'd tailed me and I hadn't noticed.

"You'll have to do better than that, Clem," I muttered.

On the off chance I was right, and in penance for my lapse in alertness, I zig-zagged, then looped around a block here and there to make sure no brown sedan turned up behind me sporting a six at the end of its license plate. Finally satisfied, I set course for the address I had for Tremain's ex-wife, doing one more zig-zag halfway there for good measure.

ELEVEN

Nan Hudson Tremain proved to be as inconsiderate of my girlish hopes as Daisy had been. No one answered the door at her nice stone and mortar bungalow. Her daughter, the girl in the photo on Gil Tremain's desk, must still be in school. A look at my watch caused me to revise that assessment. School had been out for at least half an hour. Maybe the kid took piano lessons or went to Girl Scouts or something. After waiting in my car for twenty minutes, I went back to deal with odds and ends at the office.

Since I planned another trip to Daisy's apartment to see if she returned around six the way her neighbor had said she sometimes did, I hunted a parking spot on the street. The gravel lot where I usually parked was only a few blocks away, but maybe because of the roughing up I'd gotten yesterday or the time of month, I wasn't feeling as perky as usual. As I came up Patterson, my grip on the steering wheel tightened. Just ahead of me, across from my building and half a block down, a scruffy brown sedan sat at the curb. The last number on the license plate was a six.

Careful to keep my speed up, I continued past. I was no believer in coincidence. It took discipline not to look to see if anyone was sitting in the car. I waited until I was past, then used my rearview mirror. Yep. He was taller than Clem Stark, though. Broader through the shoulders, too. He wasn't even pretending to read a paper, just sitting behind the wheel. One of Clem's boys?

Adrenalin raised my heart rate. Half was wariness, but the other half was optimism as I thought of another possibility: Could this have something to do with Gil Tremain's disappearance? Had I managed to stir up something I didn't yet recognize?

Circling the block to see if the car would pull out and follow, I tried to decide whether, if it stayed parked, I should mosey up to the driver and say hello or just play dumb. If this was the car that had nearly rear-ended me, there could be an innocent explanation. Maybe the driver had come to apologize. No, because how would he have known where to find me?

By the time I came back around, the brown car was gone. I pulled into the vacated space and sat to see if he'd show up. When there was no sign of him after plenty of time had elapsed for him to go half a dozen blocks and return, I went across the street to my office.

For the next hour I wasted half my time padding across to the window to look down at the street. If the brown car was out there, I didn't see it. I'd kicked off my shoes and was sitting with my feet on the desk trying to figure out what, if anything, the car might have to do with Gil Tremain when I heard the snick of my door latch.

"It's too nice a night to be working late," Connelly said strolling in.

My hand, which had gone beneath my chair to the Smith & Wesson, eased back. Connelly's eyes caught the movement.

"Expecting someone?"

"Just a vigilant gal." I smiled.

He grunted. He knew I was lying.

"What's on your mind?"

"I wondered if you'd settle for a sandwich instead of an olive branch." He made himself at home resting a hip against one corner of my desk as I swung my legs down. His uniform collar was unbuttoned. He'd just gotten off duty.

"An olive branch for what?"

"Giving you grief about the knot on your head this morning. It tears me apart when I see you bruised or hurt, and the worst part is always knowing it could have been worse. But I also know it's not my place to scold. So there. I've said my piece. Seal the truce with a sandwich?"

"A truce implies hostilities can resume."

Crossing his arms, he grinned.

"Ah, Maggie. As long as we're both breathing we'll keep having skirmishes. Don't you know that?"

"I'd like to, Connelly, but I can't. I need to talk to a woman at six. She may be able to help me quit playing Blind Man's Bluff with what I'm working on. And you've got music to play tonight, so we can't go after I finish."

Thursday nights Connelly and half a dozen others played Irish tunes at Finn's pub. Fiddle and concertina and whistle and him on the pipes. It connected him, however briefly, to the life he'd left on the other side of the ocean.

"What about tomorrow?" I wanted to let him know I wasn't sore.

"I can't. You know Brooks? When you didn't show up last night, I sat with him at the prizefight. He won a bet with somebody and got two tickets to the one tomorrow. He invited me. What about Saturday?"

"As long as we go Dutch."

He snagged a strand of my hair and twirled it around his fingertip, a move he knew I hated. He didn't know it also turned me to liquid inside.

"You drive a hard bargain." Eyes twinkling, he straightened and turned toward the door before I could tell him to keep his hands to himself. "Oh, one other thing, *mavourneen*. A wee bell this side of your door would give warning if you're going to sit wool-gathering."

Winking at my indignation, he walked out.

I reconsidered his Christmas present.

***

Even before Connelly made his appearance, daylight had dwindled. Now I couldn't tell the color of cars in the street below except for flashes as they passed under a streetlight.

By the time I set out for Daisy's place, things hadn't improved. I left early since her chatty neighbor's talk about variations in Daisy's child-minding job suggested she could as easily come home half an hour early as not at all. Also it allowed me time to meander a little in case anyone followed me.

Someone did.

A block and a half from my office, a new pair of headlights edged into place behind me, three places back. When I turned right, the first two cars behind me continued straight. The third one didn't. It hung back now, allowing another car to pull in between us. It was too far back for me to make out the color, but our dance through evening traffic made me glad I'd humored my instinct.

Whoever it was, I didn't want to lead them to Daisy. If it turned out to be only Clem Stark or one of his lackeys trying to show me how clever he was or muck up my case, I wanted to rub his nose in it, too. I bobbled over a couple of blocks and looked for a place I'd noticed a few times, a hat shop. I pulled into a spot a customer leaving another small shop vacated. The car that had been playing shadow passed me.

It was brown. With a license plate ending in six.

Time to let the pursuer become the pursued.

***

"Oh, I know it's almost time for you to close, but I've been eyeing a hat in your window for two weeks," I chirped as I entered the hat shop. "I just *had* to have a closer peek. I'll leave when it's time for you to lock up. Scout's honor." I raised my fingers.

The middle-aged clerk who had started around the counter to offer some pleasantry forced a smile.

"Look all you want, dear. I have some items to check off on my inventory. Did you have any questions?"

"Well, I did wonder what the price was." I giggled. "When you can't see the tag, that usually means it costs more than I can afford."

I wanted to see if the brown car came past again. The shop's small display window gave me a dandy view of the street. If I could get the woman running the place to join me, my stop here would look all the more innocent to anyone outside.

"Oh, you mustn't fret about that. We have lay away...."

I kept my ears on the conversation enough to hold up my end and my eyes on the street. Across the way, a car vacated a place at the curb. A moment later, another one left. A moment after that, a shape I was starting to recognize pulled into one of them. I couldn't tell the color, but the last two digits were twenty-six.

"Oh no!" I gasped. "Do you have a back way out?"

"Why?" The woman helping me followed my gaze to the street. "What's wrong?"

"Someone's following me. A - a man who won't take no for an answer. He keeps turning up everywhere. It's starting to scare me."

"We need to call the police." The clerk marched purposely toward the counter and the phone behind it.

"No!" I leaned earnestly over the counter. "I can't." Glancing over my shoulder as if someone might overhear, I lowered my voice to a whisper. "The trouble is, it's – it's my brother-in-law!"

At the cluck of her tongue I knew I was halfway to her back exit.

"Well! Do men get any lower than that?"

"I do want this hat, though. Can I pay now and come back to get it?"

I waved the pretty pink cloche in my hand.

"Oh, of course. And yes, there's a back door. Lights here and there, too, so the alley's not as dark as some."

The merchandise in her shop wasn't up to the quality I generally bought, even though that meant saving up or buying on sale. I'd met a girl who worked in a dime store who was crazy for hats, though. She'd helped me out on a case. I knew she'd be thrilled with the pink hat. Buying it would put me on good terms with the shopkeeper. If anything interesting happened after I left, she'd tell me when I picked up the hat.

She'd already started writing the sale up when she stopped and frowned.

"Didn't I see you get out of a car, though?"

I nodded.

"That DeSoto out there. I'll send my kid brother to get it."

"How will you get home?"

"Oh, I'll take a trolley. I know where the stops are."

Once I'd slipped out her back door, though, I beat it to the nearest pay phone I could find. My fingers were crossed that Calvin, the skinny, bashful eighteen year old who was junior mechanic at Weaver's Garage would still be there working.

TWELVE

"You sure you don't want me to try and get a look at that car, Miss Sullivan? Get the make and the whole license number?"

Calvin had wasted no time in meeting me at a spot three blocks away from the hat shop. His bean pole frame was bent almost double as he looked in through the open passenger window of a jalopy he'd lovingly built from salvaged parts. I sat at the steering wheel of the nondescript vehicle, which under its hood was powerful as a panther. Calvin let me borrow it when I needed a car that wouldn't be recognized.

"Thanks, Calvin, but no. I want you to drive off like you don't even notice it. Leave mine at the garage. I don't want anybody following you home."

Calvin was a good egg. I wasn't about to take even the slightest chance of endangering him.

"Just make it look like my car was acting up and you came to get it," I said.

"I'll pull it in the bay, then. There's room. That'll look like we're going to work on it first thing in the morning."

He unfolded himself and stepped back onto the curb. With a cheerful wave he set off. I reached across the seat and cranked the window up against seeping December cold. Then I found a spot on an intersecting street from which I'd be able to spot Calvin when he drove by. When he had, and I was sure no one had followed him, I tried Daisy's place, but either I'd missed her or she hadn't come home.

I went to a diner and had a hot pork sandwich. The mashed potatoes were first rate, and so were the green beans. When I'd topped it off with a cup of coffee it was time to try catching Daisy at work. I knew the approximate time when she started, so I found the trolley stop closest to

C&S Signals and stood in a sheltered doorway she'd pass when she started walking. Speaking to her on a public street close to a streetlight was likely to frighten her less than pounding on the door of an empty building when she was alone inside.

My fingers were starting to tingle with cold by the time the trolley pulled to a halt and a stocky little woman with nice ankles got off. She started up the side street toward me. She was bundled up in a coat and a muffler and carried a cloth tote in one hand.

As she got closer, I could hear she was singing, half to herself. Something sprightly. Every so often she did a little jig step. Finally she got near enough I could make out her tune. *Sweet Georgia Brown.* Only instead of singing "Georgia", she was singing "Daisy".

Smiling, I stepped out where she could see me.

"Daisy Brown? Lucille Collingswood told me you might be able to tell me something that would help me find Mr. Tremain. I'm a detective. Her dad hired me. They're both worried to death."

I held out one of my business cards as I spoke. She looked from it to me, from it to me again before she took it.

"A detective?"

She was steady on her feet and hadn't swayed a hair when she was doing her little dance steps.

"Like on the radio? Well, I don't know."

She began to walk again, toward C&S Signals. Either the prospect of talking to me made her nervous, or she was thinking about the night of mopping and dusting ahead of her. I fell into step.

"Myrtle Hawes did say he'd brought someone in to ask questions." She was thinking aloud. "I just don't remember her saying it was a woman. Can you show me a badge or something?"

Daisy was sharper than some. I fished the badge out of my purse. It was pinned to a nice leather holder and said

Special Detective. It hadn't been issued by the police, but it saved wear and tear on my paper license, which had been. Daisy stopped to have a good look.

"Well, okay then. But let's get inside, first. Cold gets to me worse now than when I was young."

We walked on.

"He's a nice fellow, Mr. Tremain. Always speaks to me when he's working late, asks how I am. Not many do that. Of course not many of them work late, either." She laughed merrily. "Mr. Collingswood used to, but three or four years ago he began having heart trouble."

"What about Mr. Scott?"

"Oh..." She shrugged. "He pops in and out sometimes. Doesn't sit at his desk for hours figuring and making those funny squiggles like Mr. Tremain does, though to tell the truth, I think he works too much. Mr. Tremain, that is. I was real glad when Myrtle told me he was starting to see Miss Lucille. There ought to be more to life than work, don't you think?"

We'd reached the empty parking strip in front of the building. She gestured to the left where there was a side door.

"Mr. Collingswood says I'm welcome to come in the front where it's lighted, but that doesn't seem right. I use this one."

This side of the building lay in shadow. I followed her, slipping my hand in my reinforced coat pocket where it could rest on my .38. Daisy let us in with a key, then locked up behind us. Flipping on lights here and there, she led the way down to a basement room that housed the furnace and shelves of supplies. One corner held a utility sink and the tidiest assortment of mops and scrub buckets I'd ever seen.

"How long did you stand out there waiting for me?" asked Daisy hanging her coat on a peg. "There's tea in that wrapped up whiskey bottle if you want something hot in you." She nodded at the bag she'd brought in, then turned her attention back to putting soap in a bucket and turning on water. "A man downstairs where I live gives me one now and then when he's emptied it. Put plenty of padding around it and the tea stays warm two or three hours, about as good as one of those Thermos bottles, I bet, and doesn't cost anything. I'd sooner spend my money on a radio. That's what I'm saving for. I do love music."

She did a little dance step.

I didn't need to taste what was in the bottle to know it was just tea. Daisy was a whirlwind. In my experience, that didn't go with being an alkie. I told her I'd smelled her cinnamon rolls when I tried to find her at her apartment. We chatted about her baking as I followed her upstairs.

"Lucille told me you saw Mr. Tremain somewhere Monday morning," I prompted at last.

She'd started her chores in a lunchroom at the back of the building, wiping things down first, emptying trash, then using her rag mop.

"That's right, over on West Fifth. I was riding the Main Street bus, on my way to have a tooth pulled down by the hospital. Dr. Benton. I guess if you've got to go to a dentist he's okay.

"Anyway, we'd stopped to let people off at the intersection, and I was looking out the window, wondering whether the misery before or after I had the tooth out was going to be worse, when I noticed Mr. Tremain walking along."

"How?"

"How?"

"How did you know it was him?"

"The way he walks. That's what caught my eye anyway, and sure enough, it was him."

My silence cued her to my puzzlement. She glanced up from mopping.

"What do you mean, the way he walks? Does he limp?"

Her head shook.

"No, just walks kind of funny. Kind of tipped forward to one side, like he's pushing his shoulder against a door. Then he stopped and I caught a look at his face. Just for a second. The bus started up again right then. But I know it was him. Besides, he had on that muffler his daughter knitted him. Ugliest shade of blue I've ever seen in my life, but he wore it 'cause she made it."

She plopped her mop in the bucket of water for emphasis.

"He's a good man, Mr. Tremain."

It was starting to sound as if Daisy actually had seen him. I let her mop awhile before my next question.

"You said he stopped. Why?"

A frown appeared on her face. She paused to consider.

"I never thought about it. I guess he could have been hunting some place...." All at once her features brightened. "No. I bet he was checking his watch 'cause he had his arm out. Leastwise I think he did." She pantomimed. "He wears one of those on his wrist. These engineer fellows are plumb crazy for newfangled things."

Hunting an address. Checking the time. Both possibilities made me want to dance like Daisy.

"Do you remember how far along Fifth Street he was? Did you notice?" I asked as she gathered her things and started for the next room on her rounds.

She considered.

"It was close to that place with the four bumps in front. The ones that look like they want you to think that they're balconies or towers only they're not."

I had a vague recollection of passing a building like she described. You notice different things at the wheel of an automobile or walking than you do from the vantage point of a passing bus, and I didn't often get to that side of Fifth.

I followed her around for another half hour without learning anything else. She'd already given me more to go on than anyone else. As I was buttoning my coat to leave, the thought of her walking back to the trolley stop alone, in the dark, began to bother me. She did it night after night, and had for a long time, but key employees where she worked didn't disappear every night. Their apartments weren't torn apart every night. Nor did strange cars dog my movements every night.

I went back upstairs.

"Listen, Daisy. I don't like the idea of you walking back to the trolley line in the dark. When are you likely to finish? I'll stop by and give you a lift."

She flapped her hand.

"Oh, you don't need to. I've walked it a million times."

I finally convinced her. We arranged that she'd come out the front door, where she could watch for me through one of the windows that flanked it. I described Calvin's car, and told her I'd blink the headlights on and off two times so she'd know it was me. Then I went back to Mrs. Z's to pick up the key she let me use when my job was likely to keep me out after the time when she locked up.

Thirty minutes or so after midnight I came up the street in front of C&S Signals, checking the few parked cars I passed. I wanted to make sure none were brown, or occupied, before I turned in. None were. The parking lot was deserted, but as I was about to turn in, I thought I saw something by the unlighted side door Daisy and I had gone in earlier. Had there been movement? Some sort of shape?

I circled the block.

This time on my approach, I doused my lights at the last intersection I passed. If anyone up ahead saw them disappear, they would assume I had turned. Traffic was almost nonexistent. There was ambient light enough for me to creep along and pull to a stop just shy of C&S's parking strip.

I waited, with the motor running. Calvin kept it so perfectly tuned that three steps away its sound would be only a whisper. My eyes began to adjust as I watched the area by the side door. Finally... yes. A shape. Its margin stretched and split, becoming recognizable as two men. Their car must be in the shadows behind them. Either they were fixing to break in, or they were lying in wait for someone. And any minute now, Daisy would start wondering why I hadn't shown up, and perhaps step outside.

Would it matter that she came through the front door? No. She could still be in harm's way.

So I did what any red-blooded girl with a car would do. I slid the Smith & Wesson on the seat next to me into my lap. I cranked down my window. Then, letting the clutch out and shifting, with all the speed I could muster, I roared toward the side door. About the time they registered what was happening, I switched on my headlights.

The beams caught two startled figures, blinding them. I heard a shot and one of the headlights in my borrowed car shattered. Sticking my left hand out the window, I got off a few rounds even though my accuracy with that hand wasn't the best. The two fleeing men jumped into a car. One fired again.

"Hey! What's the ruckus?" a voice called.

In my rearview mirror, I saw Daisy run out the front door. She was crouched low, brandishing her empty whiskey bottle like a club.

The car with the thugs tore into the street. I wasn't the only one who'd parked a car with its engine running. If I tried to catch them, Daisy would be left alone. I didn't like that idea. Backing up as fast as I dared, I blinked my lights twice.

"Get in!" I shouted.

THIRTEEN

It took some doing, but Daisy finally agreed to spend the night at my place. She waved off the idea she couldn't look out for herself, but when I suggested someone could be trying to push Collingswood into a heart attack by causing his company trouble, it brought her around. It was mostly a fib, but might be worth considering, nonetheless. Meanwhile, I lent the ebullient little woman a flannel nightie that was too big for me and settled her on a folding cot Mrs. Z let us use for visiting female relatives.

Bright and early Friday morning, I made an appearance at C&S Signals. Mrs. Hawes sprang up to block me as I started around her.

"You can't go in there! He's talking to Mr. Scott, and he doesn't look well. Not well at *all*."

I reached out to plant a persuasive hand on her shoulder. She may have thought I meant to grab her throat, the way she drew back.

"Mrs. Hawes, if you don't let me past, I'll be forced to tell the police that you seem very eager to keep me from finding Mr. Tremain."

"But—"

"They'll find that odd. They'll want to talk to you downtown."

"But—"

"Don't worry, I'm as polite as Emily Post. I'll knock before I go in."

I did, but I didn't wait for an answer. Scott stood with arms crossed in front of his partner's desk. Collingswood did, indeed, look washed out. I didn't waste time on preliminaries.

"Two men were waiting to jump Daisy when she left work last night. When I drove up, they started shooting. I'll put the bill for replacing a headlight on my expense report."

Collingswood sucked in his breath. Frank Scott looked at me in disbelief and swore.

I'd already reclaimed my own car and told Calvin I'd pay for repairs on his. As I launched into details of the would-be attack both partners listened, dumbstruck.

Scott recovered first.

"You mean someone takes her chatter about seeing Gil seriously?"

"Or they're afraid the police might."

His mouth snapped shut as if he had no idea what to say.

"Or," I said, "they know it's true."

"But how would anyone - how would they even know she'd said what she did?" stammered Collingswood. "That would mean - it would mean—"

"That they worked here?" his partner finished. "Poppycock. Maybe it had nothing to do with Daisy. Maybe they were just going to break in."

"Wouldn't that be too coincidental?" objected Collingswood. We've never had a break-in before."

"We've never had an employee vanish before, either!" Scott snapped. "Or one who took off leaving us with the wrong set of data. Maybe whoever it was last night thought they could find it. Maybe Gil made fools of them as well as us."

"Oh, come on! You can't believe—"

"While you two argue, I've got things to do," I interrupted. "Even if something happens to Daisy, she's already given a sworn statement. First thing this morning. That means it can be used in court. I thought you should know, since concern for her safety is clearly topmost in your minds."

I probably left a trail of acid behind me as I walked out.

If one of them or someone else at the company turned out to be a rat, the lie I'd told was Daisy's insurance. I hoped it was a big enough policy.

***

I needed to talk to Lucille again. Privately. Rather than waste time stopping to call, I went to Collingswood's house.

"I'm afraid she's not home. Her group has their first Christmas performance this morning," the housekeeper said. "This is always their busy time of year."

We stood in the front hall. Red bows had been added to the greenery on the bannisters since my last visit.

"Did Miss Collingswood indicate when she'd be back?"

"Not until half-past one or later. There's a luncheon after. Would you like some paper to leave her a message?"

"Just tell her I'll call, or possibly stop by again." I gave her a business card.

I wanted to ask Lucille about Tremain's mannerisms to see if she said anything about how he walked. It would lend support to Daisy's insistence about recognizing him. Maybe this was my comeuppance for getting hot under the collar with Scott and Collingswood. If I hadn't lost my temper, I could have asked them.

***

For the time being I couldn't substantiate Daisy's description of Tremain's walk. I went back to the office and called the man I'd asked to put his ear to the ground about the rival firms Frank Scott had listed. Ed owned a company that made auto parts, and was big-wig enough to sniff around at the Engineers Club where he was a member. The chatter he'd picked up made it extremely unlikely any of the names Scott had given me had the interest or financial situation that would tempt them to dabble in information theft, let alone murder.

My legs needed stretching, so I decided to have a look at the stretch of street where Daisy claimed she'd seen Tremain. If nothing else, I could at least determine whether her account was even feasible. I walked over to Main Street and up a couple of blocks to catch the Main Street trolley.

Daisy had told me the bus had stopped at the intersection with Fifth to let someone off, so as we neared the intersection, I pulled the cord to get out. The big car lumbered over to the curb. I'd been careful to sit on the same side Daisy had been on. I remained in my seat for a moment, looking in the direction she'd indicated. Then, afraid the driver would think I'd changed my mind and would swing back out into traffic, I got off.

I walked back three blocks, waited for the next trolley on the route, and repeated the process. This time I easily spotted the building whose ornate front boasted four projections the shape of oversized bay windows. They ran from floor to ceiling on the two top floors. One final trip on the trolley convinced me it was possible to see gaudy items of apparel, hair color and whether someone wore glasses. Through the bus window I also could make out occasional movements of people on the sidewalk.

Time to poke around and see whether anybody cried "ouch".

Breakfast already seemed like a long time ago, so I had a cup of coffee and a date muffin at a little café down the street from the building Daisy had noticed. Sitting there provided a good vantage point for surveying the area. It also gave me time to think, and nutrition clearly needed by my brain, which hadn't coughed up anything resembling a clue this morning.

"What's that place with the gussied up front?" I asked the waitress when she brought my muffin.

"A lamp shop."

Holding the coffee pot aloft in one hand, she planted the other one on an out-thrust hip, preparing to chat. The breakfast crowd was long gone and there was only one other customer.

"Sells every kind of lamp you've ever seen. Repairs them too. And shades. All kinds of lamp shades. If you're in the market for one, expect to pay a pretty penny if you get it there, though."

"It doesn't look as if he's doing a lot of business. Nobody's gone in or out since I sat down."

She bent and peered across the street.

"I heard he was sick. He's been closed for a couple of days."

I doubted Gil Tremain's destination had been a lamp shop. The building with its ornate facade served as a handy landmark by which Daisy remembered approximately where she'd seen him. Now that small talk had put the waitress in a receptive mood, I got down to real business. Opening my purse, I took out the engineer's photo and lay it before her.

"Say, has this guy ever come in here? He's my sister's old boyfriend and somebody told me they thought they'd seen him coming into an eating place down here not long ago. He's a swell guy, and it didn't take Sis more than two weeks to know she'd made a mistake when she let him go. He'd left town, but if he's back, well, it would sure be worth trying to get them together again."

She picked up the picture and studied it while she refilled my coffee.

"No, don't think so. Nice dresser. Not flashy, but like he's got some quality to him."

We chatted some more. Then she went to check on her other customer and I ate my muffin.

"A place that big and nothing but lamps," I said when I went to pay my bill. "I can't get over it. Has it been around a long time?"

"The man who owns it's been around since before I started working in this place — and that's eight years."

We chuckled together and I went out to see what I could learn at other places along the street.

Daisy had told me Gil Tremain halted as she watched from the bus. She thought he'd consulted his watch. If he had, it meant one of two things. Either he was worried about being late somewhere, or he was supposed to meet somebody and was wondering where they were.

If he hadn't been checking the time... Why else would he stop? To ask for directions? To get a shoeshine? Because he couldn't find an address?

From what I'd heard, Tremain wasn't the sort who'd get a shoeshine on company time. He did, however, sound like a man who would fret at the prospect of being late for work. And if he couldn't find an address, it didn't seem likely he'd continue far beyond where it would logically be.

The probabilities, then, were that he'd been meeting somebody who was late, or hunting a place not far beyond where he'd stopped. It was only a theory, at best. Still, it was something to go on.

Since Daisy had seen Tremain in the vicinity of the lamp shop, I started there. Benning's Lamps and Decor, gold letters across the windows proclaimed. But a sign on the door that I'd expected to say CLOSED, told a different story: FOR RENT.

The lamp shop owner must have taken a turn for the worse. I peeked inside. Four double-wide windows across the front showed off lamps of every description. Some were elegant, their bases brass or crystal or marble. The bottom of one table lamp was a cowboy riding a bronco. Farther back I spotted a floor lamp whose alabaster base was, I was almost certain, a pert nude — though sophisticates probably fancied that up by calling it a nymph.

What I didn't see were any employees. Wouldn't they be struggling along even if the boss had died?

Maybe Gil Tremain had headed here after all, say to pick up a desk lamp he was having repaired or something he'd ordered. He could have been annoyed to find no one there. That still didn't solve what had become of him afterward.

I looked at the FOR RENT sign again, and something hit me:

It had neither the name of a real estate firm nor a number to call.

FOURTEEN

Both curious and alert now, I went into the business next to the lamp shop, a low, square red brick building dwarfed by its larger neighbor. It was an insurance office, and from the look of things, not a very prosperous one. Six desks, each with a chair for a customer, sat at discreet distances from each other. Only two of the desks were occupied. None of the chairs were.

"Gee, that lamp place next door isn't going out of business, is it?" I asked the man nearest the door. "My cousin's getting married and some of us went together thinking we'd get her a really nice lamp."

He sprang up and pumped my hand and told me his name. The half dozen hairs on the top of his head struggled valiantly to hide its shine.

"I hate to be the bearer of bad news," he said heartily, "but I'm afraid they've closed for good."

"When? Why? They'll be having a going-out-of-business sale, won't they?"

"Uh, don't know." He was confused by the onslaught of questions crowned by a zigzag. It was a tactic I'd always found useful.

"The gentleman who owns the business took sick end of last week." The other man in the office left his desk to stroll over and join us. "Lungs." He patted his chest. "He'd had spells before. This time the doc told him it was either move to someplace out West where it's dry or buy himself a nice casket. Just goes to show, nobody knows when their number's going to be up. Right, Don?"

He winked at his co-worker.

"Oh... right. *Right.*" Don–of-the-half-dozen-hairs nodded sudden comprehension. "Even a healthy young lady like you. Do you have insurance?"

"Me? Oh, goodness no." I giggled. "I lead such a humdrum life I don't need it. Didn't the man next door — what was his name?"

"Benning."

"Didn't he have other people who worked there?"

"Uh—"

"Yeah, a clerk and a pimple faced kid that carried things," Don's more adept colleague answered. "Ran the legs off both of 'em. If you're wondering why they're not over there, they probably knew old Walt would like as not stiff them on what he already owed them and they'd be better off hunting new jobs."

"This time of year some stores hire extra help, especially if they've got experience," Don said. "Because of more shoppers. But even somebody in a nice, safe job like selling socks or perfume — or a girl who still lives at home and is just out buying a spool of thread — can still get hit by a car or—"

"How can I find out about the sale?" I interrupted.

The two men looked blank.

"Sale?"

"The going-out-of-business sale." I gestured toward the lamp shop. "The sign that says FOR RENT doesn't have a number to call. Who put it up?"

"Oh, uh, some real estate agent," said Don. "Stopped in to tell us about Walt's health, and that he'd taken off for, was it Arizona?"

The other insurance man nodded.

"Wanted us to know there'd be men coming in to do work. Plastering and that. Nice fellow."

"Did he leave a card? That would have a number, and I really want to find out if there'll be a sale. Oh, I want one of your cards too."

Don nearly fell over himself handing me his business card.

"I don't think the real estate fellow gave me anything. How about you?"

His pal shook his head.

"He had a short name, though. Dixon, I think."

"No, Henson. I'd say it was Henson."

"Well, thanks anyway. Hey, since I'm in here, will you both take a look at this picture?"

I fished out the photograph of Gil Tremain and went through the same story I'd told the waitress. Neither remembered seeing him. I made as if to leave, then turned back.

"When did that real estate man stop in?"

"Yesterday. Yesterday afternoon when he came to switch signs."

"If he comes back, would you get his phone number? I'll stop back and check. And I'll be sure and tell my cousin's husband-to-be that he should buy insurance."

I escaped as Don floundered into another pitch.

***

Chewing on what I'd learned, I walked up the street. The lamp shop owner had taken ill over the weekend, according to the waitress. Monday morning Gil Tremain had been seen in the vicinity, according to Daisy. He might have walked on, or jumped into a cab or onto a trolley, or maybe not even been there at all. And yesterday, according to the insurance gents, a real estate agent had slapped a FOR RENT sign in the window. A sign that had no contact information.

What did all that leave me?

More questions.

It was still too early for Lucille Collingswood to be at home. Since I was already here, it seemed smart to try and find answers. Stopping in businesses along the way to show Tremain's photograph, I retraced my steps. Then I crossed the street and stood admiring the building that housed the lamp shop.

Small wonder Daisy had noticed it. At three stories it was taller than its immediate neighbors. Fancier, too. Bright terra cotta stipes ran the width of the ground floor, one at ankle level and a wider one above the three front doors. Each of the doors was flanked by the generous windows which had given me such a good view of the store's wares.

If that wasn't enough, the two top floors of the building groaned with gingerbread. The octet of curving, three-sided windows Daisy had described wore frills of carving and paint. Above them, stacked one above the other like necklaces, were layers of more carving and paint. The result was gaudy, but easily spotted by customers.

I showed Tremain's picture in an eye doctor's place with no success. Then I entered what turned out to be a piano and sheet music store. It sat directly across from the lamp shop. A rotund man with uplifted chin padded toward me with a patronizing smile.

"Good morning, my dear. You have the look of a young lady out Christmas shopping."

"Well, yes." I glanced over my shoulder with what I hoped was a sympathetic frown. "The man who owns that lamp shop, Mr. Benning, he didn't die, did he? I came past on Tuesday and there was a CLOSED sign. Now it says it's for rent. A man next door told me Mr. Benning had taken ill."

"Oh, he's not dead. The rascal landed on his feet. I guess he did have one of his spells, but wouldn't you know it? A relative out West had just recently left him a bit of a windfall. He said since he had the wherewithal, he was going to take his doctor's advice, off he went.

"Now, what can I show you? I can make you a wonderful deal on that little maple upright in the corner."

"Oh, it's beautiful, but all I need is sheet music. It's not for Christmas, really, just a little thank-you."

"Of course. Did you have anything particular in mind?"

"Umm..."

I'd entered knowing I might need to make a small purchase to keep him chatting. It happened I knew a man who was taking piano lessons. From all indications his past work had included being a trigger man for people on the other side of the law, though I was moderately certain his current job didn't make use of those skills.

Mr. Music led the way toward three wire racks displaying music.

"These are the new ones that are all the craze here. This rack's the old standards. And of course I have stacks of other things behind the counter."

I didn't know much about Pearlie, but I knew his musical tastes.

"He likes Jellyroll Morton. Things like that."

The store owner's nostrils narrowed but he soldiered on.

"What level?"

"Intermediate."

That part could be wrong, but the thought of Pearlie walking in to exchange it gave me enjoyment. There was nothing the least unattractive about Pearlie's looks, but something in his manner made most people nervous.

I settled on something from the new arrivals rack. The owner was ringing my small purchase up when a slender woman who was still a good deal short of middle aged came down a stairway next to the counter. Everything about her was quiet except for an emerald green hat with an extravagant brim.

"Stepping out to get milk for her tea," she said briefly.

The store owner nodded without interest.

"Bring me back a couple of Butterfingers, will ya, honey?"

"Yes, Mr. Miller."

"Hope you made sure she has everything she's likely to need. I can't be running up and leaving customers if she starts thumping."

"Yes, Mr. Miller."

He slid my sheet music into a paper bag.

"There you go."

"Thanks. Say, any chance you've seen this man around? He used to be my sister's beau, but they had a silly spat. A friend of mine swore she'd seen him going into a store down here."

He started to look at the small picture of Tremain I'd produced. A murmur at the door interrupted him.

"Mrs. Arnold. Lovely to see you." His smile, which had faded considerably, returned full force. He thrust the photograph back at me. "Never saw him." He hurried to the new arrival. "I just got in the most marvelous metronomes. Absolute works of art! Let me show you."

I left without delay, hoping I might catch sight of the woman in the green hat. She, like Gil Tremain, had disappeared.

FIFTEEN

"Hey!"

The man who called to me from the opposite side of the street had sandy hair and an athletic build. As soon as there was a break in the traffic he trotted across. Up close he was about my own age or a little older with dazzling blue eyes. Mick Connelly had nice eyes the color of blue steel. This guy's were bright blue. Autumn sky blue.

"Are you passing out flyers, selling, or collecting for something?" he asked as he reached me.

"I beg your pardon?"

He grinned.

"You've been going into places up and down the street all morning. I feel left out."

"Oh really? Do you work around here?"

I'd already stopped in every place along the street. Touching my elbow, he turned me and pointed.

"Up there."

A set of stairs led up to a door with a polished brass plate and a mail slot. It faced the lamp shop across a wide brick walkway that had been a street in horse and buggy days. While its entry wasn't on Fifth, its only window was.

"You must not work very hard, if you've been keeping track of me."

"I'm puzzling over why a client's ledger doesn't tally. When I can't see an obvious way through a tangle, it helps me to go to the window and stand while I think."

Since the same held true for me, I couldn't exactly fault him. I opened my purse.

"I'm trying to find out if anybody's seen this man. He used to be my sister's boyfriend. I'm trying to patch things up between them." I was getting awfully sick of my little ditty.

He studied the photograph of Tremain with what seemed genuine seriousness. Some moments elapsed before he handed it back.

"Sorry, no." He raised an eyebrow expectantly.

"Yes? Was there something else?"

"The fellows in the insurance place said you were asking questions about the lamp shop."

At my expression he burst out laughing.

"Sorry. I was curious. I hope I don't offend you, but you looked like you'd be fun to meet."

"Wow. That's some line."

"Have a heart. Accountants don't get much chance to meet women except for middle-aged secretaries."

"And that's what you are, I take it? An accountant?" It fit the small office.

"Steve Lapinski." With a sigh that was almost comic he gave me a card.

"Maggie Quinn." I didn't give him one of mine.

"Look, I'm in for a very long day with this project I'm on. I came down thinking I'd break it up with a beer and a sandwich. Join me, won't you?" Sensing I was about to say No, he spoke quickly. "I can tell you something you may not know about the fellow who had the lamp shop."

It was nice bait.

And he did have very blue eyes.

***

"Are you sure you won't have a sandwich with that?" Lapinski asked.

"Thanks, but I had a muffin awhile ago and it filled me up. The beer hits the spot, though."

It wasn't as robust as Guinness, but good nonetheless. The small pub we were in was impeccably neat and the food smelled good. I gave my prettiest frown.

"What about the lamp shop? The thing is, some other girls and I chipped in to buy a lamp there for a present. I was in last week and put some money down, and there wasn't a sign or anything anywhere saying they were going out of business. Today I came down thinking I'd kill two birds at once, pay off the lamp and ask about Sis's beau, and boom, there's a sign up saying the place is for rent. Who can I contact to get our money back?"

It was his turn to frown.

"I'm afraid I can't help you there. But I don't think the man who ran it left town for his health. At least not in the usual sense." He waited while the waitress set down his ham sandwich. "I think he took off because he was scared."

He had my full attention now.

"Of what?"

"Don't know." He took a neat, small bite of sandwich and chewed before continuing. "About four weeks ago, though, I was locking up and saw three slicked up fellows pay him a visit. Two went in the front and one went around to the alley as if he might be planning to watch the back. They had that look about them."

"What look?"

"You know. Like men who might come around and not be polite if you owed money."

"You mean *gangsters*?"

"I'm not sure that's the word I'd use, but like that."

Amazing how easily the very questions I needed to ask could sound like flirtation.

"And how do you know what men like that look like?"

"I'm from up north."

"Detroit?"

He laughed. "No. I just meant across the river. North Dayton. When I was a kid there used to be more than a few like them that hung out up there. Bootleg bosses and men who worked for them. Fancy dressers, hard eyes. The law put most of them out of business, but there's still a numbers racket, I hear, and loan sharks and such."

I wondered whether Steve Lapinski provided accounting for any of them.

"Hey, thanks for the beer," I said standing. "And for letting me know we might as well say good-by to our down payment on that lamp."

"Hey, can I call you? What's your number?" he called to my back.

I pretended not to hear.

SIXTEEN

What I'd learned from Lapinski sat like a lump in my stomach. If what he had told me was true — and I had no cause to think otherwise — I didn't like its implications for Gil Tremain. Had Tremain gotten mixed up with Walter Benning, who had somehow run afoul of racketeers and was now missing too? It might explain the ransacking of Tremain's apartment. But the snake? The phone calls Collingswood had received? Those had to be connected.

Being short on answers and long on time before Lucille returned from her concert, I decided to pop in on Lieutenant Freeze. He didn't seem thrilled. Then again, my sunny presence never cheered him.

His desk was in the corner of the detective division allotted to homicide. They were the only specialized unit amid otherwise all-purpose detectives. Eyes narrowed against the cloud of smoke from his endless Old Golds, Freeze watched me approach as if wary I might haul my .38 out and start firing. Admittedly I had occasionally entertained thoughts of doing him in, but those involved kicking him to a pulp.

"What?" he said.

"Why, yes, my head came through the knock it took fine and dandy. Thanks for asking."

"If you'd stick to reading pulp novels instead of trying to do things women weren't meant to, you wouldn't get slugged."

I sat down in the chair in front of his desk without being asked. I knew it rubbed him the wrong way. Whoever wrote that ditty about girls being sugar and spice probably thought bland was a spice. I'd used up my supply of sugar and spice talking to the insurance guys and music store owner.

"What did you learn about Gil Tremain's bank account? Had he cleaned it out?"

Freeze caught at his cigarette as it slipped.

"Why the — why would I tell you that?"

"Because I pay my taxes? Because I'm bright as a button? Because every now and again — more often than that, actually — I bring you something useful? As a matter of fact, I have something for you right now."

"What?"

"You have a pretty limited range of questions for a homicide dick."

"I don't have time for your lip, Sullivan."

The next desk over, Boike bent his blunt, blonde head over paperwork, hoping not to get drawn in. Not many other detectives were currently in the room, but one of them snickered.

"A woman who knows Tremain from work says she saw him over on Fifth Monday morning. As nearly as I can determine, that's the last anybody set eyes on him. Last night when she finished up, two goons were waiting to grab her. When I drove up they shot out my headlight."

I'd shown my hand. He might not reciprocate. But Freeze, in his own way, was fair. He sat back. He ground out the stub of his cigarette and shook out a new one.

"Get a look at them?"

"They were by the side door where there's no light, so no. They'd left their car with the motor running. Took off fast. I started to follow, but Daisy came running out to see what was happening. I didn't want to leave her alone."

He nodded. "Daisy. That's the woman?"

"Yes."

"What was she doing there at night? How come she didn't mention seeing this genius Tremain when we were there asking questions?"

"To answer both, she's their cleaning lady. Works eight 'til midnight. She didn't even know the police had been there until I told her."

Had ace receptionist Myrtle Hawes been too rattled to mention Daisy? Or was she so protective of the company where she worked that she didn't like to share information about it with outsiders, even the police?

Freeze took his sweet time getting a match and scratching his finger across it to light his cigarette. He took a long drag.

"As near as we can tell, there's no connection between the guy you're looking for and the woman who got killed downstairs where he lived."

In other words, he wasn't that interested in what I'd just told him.

"Anything else?" he said.

"One thing. Probably not related. You know Clem Stark?"

"The gumshoe? Yeah. He's a bigger pain in the backside than you are."

I'd come up in the world.

"What's he got to do with anything?"

"Probably nothing, only the timing smells fishy. He turned up outside my building yesterday offering me a job."

One desk over, Boike made a strangled sound.

"You say something, Boike?"

"No, sir. Just made a mistake I've got to erase."

"You happen to know what kind of car he drives?" I asked.

"Stark? No. Why?"

"A brown sedan followed me twice yesterday. Beaten up, no hood ornament but it might have been a Ford. The license plate ended in twenty-six."

Freeze scraped ash off against the side of his ashtray.

"No ransom demand yet for your boy Tremain?"

"No. After going on five days there's not likely to be."

Just when I was kicking myself for not netting even one inadvertent crumb of information, he turned decent.

"Tremain's bank account's got plenty in it. He made an unusually large withdrawal Saturday morning. Nothing since."

"Do I get to know how large?"

"Large."

Tremain might have known Walter Benning. Benning might have owed money. Men who might have been collectors might have paid Benning a visit.

Or the whole tale might have been the product of a slightly bored accountant's imagination.

***

The sooner I talked to Lucille, the more productive the rest of my day was likely to be. I went across the street to the Arcade and got thin slices of tongue on rye from one of the stalls. As soon as I finished it, I drove to the Collingswood place. The housekeeper led me to the room where Lucille had been immersed in her playing on my previous visit.

Today the scene couldn't have been more different. Her violin wasn't in sight. Instead, she held a cigarette. She was pacing, arms crossed at the elbows. She scarcely seemed aware of me as I entered.

"How was your concert?" I asked.

"Concert. Oh. Fine, I guess." The fingers with the cigarette gestured me to a chair. "Have you news?"

"Yes and No. Are you all right? You seem upset."

"My father," she said shortly. "This is taking a toll on him. We're not close — nothing matters to him but his business. Still, one has a certain filial affection. I'm feeling rather... stretched with that in addition to Gil.

"Sorry, I haven't offered you anything."

She sat down, all traces of tension gone as if she'd thrown a switch. "Coffee? Whiskey? One of these?" She indicated the cigarette she was rubbing out in a pink china ashtray.

"I'm fine."

"I take it you have more questions. What did you mean, Yes and No? What did Daisy tell you?"

I told her the gist of my talk with Daisy, though not quite all of it, and about the thugs who'd been lying in wait for the cleaning woman. She listened with a calm which I found faintly disturbing.

"The place Daisy saw him is close to a lamp shop," I said. "Did Gil mention needing a lamp, or maybe a shade or some sort of part?"

"A lamp? No."

"I'm trying to find someone who might have seen him. Is there anything about him they might remember?"

"He's rather ordinary, I'm afraid. Nice looking, at least I think so, but nothing exceptional." A small smile made its way through her composure. "He does have a funny little walk. Like he's leaning into the wind. He leans off to the side on one elbow when he's scribbling away at his desk — which of course is most of the time. I suspect that's the cause. But apart from that..."

"Miss Collingswood, if something happened to your father who would benefit?"

She looked at me sharply.

"Died, you mean?"

"Or had a heart attack that left him unable to play his part at the company."

"I need a brandy." Rising abruptly she went to a small table to one side of the fire. She filled a glass from a cut glass decanter, glancing an invitation which I declined. When she returned to her seat, her eyes were as dispassionate as flint. They narrowed as she ticked off possibilities.

"Very well. If my father died, I would inherit. I would either sell or have someone I trusted a great deal manage my share of the business."

Tremain and Frank Scott both might qualify.

"If he were incapacitated but could speak and think coherently..." She swirled the brandy and took a healthy swallow. "I suppose I'd become his glorified secretary. Or perhaps he'd have the one he has at work come here. At any rate, he'd try and keep his hand in. Frank would come here to confer with him."

"And you'd be sole heir to your father's share of the business?"

The question startled her.

"Of course. Who else?"

"Maybe some to his partner? Or an employee he considered especially loyal?"

"No. When he learned the problems with his heart were serious, he talked to me. Made sure I knew how everything stood."

The rigid set of her shoulders softened and she leaned on her elbows. Resting her chin on her clasped hands, she looked into the fire. Several minutes passed before she spoke. Her voice had softened.

"I keep thinking of Eve. Both of us facing ugly possibilities we can't control. But she's so young. She simply couldn't bear it if she lost her father."

An inflection of Lucille's voice, however, suggested she might.

SEVENTEEN

Once again, no one answered when I telephoned Tremain's ex-wife. Once again, nobody answered when I drove there and rang the doorbell. I had assumed someone from C&S had contacted them as soon as the company became concerned about him. If not, I didn't welcome the thought of breaking the news, but it couldn't be helped. They, more than anyone, would know his habits and acquaintances. I knocked with no better results than I'd had from the doorbell.

Not finding anyone home at their place for two days in a row bothered me, though I couldn't say why. I stood on the porch of their pleasant brick-and-stucco bungalow, frowning in thought. Did Mrs. Tremain have a job, and Eve go somewhere after school? Or were they gone? Gone at the same time Gil Tremain himself was gone. Perhaps even with him.

Time to start talking to neighbors.

"Hi, I'm Maggie," I said when the one next door opened her door. "Is Mrs. Tremain away?"

"No, just at work."

I saw her curiosity. Neighbors are always curious when you show up asking questions.

"Mr. Tremain's office needs to update some information. Nobody answers the phone either, so they asked me to check. When does she get home?"

"Five fifteen or half past. Could I take a message?"

"Thanks, but I'll just write a note and put it in her door."

I went back to the DeSoto and contemplated writing said note. What I needed to tell her, and ask, wasn't information to come home to. As much time as I spent away from the office, there was also the problem of reaching me. Sooner rather than later I needed to find money for an answering service.

While I tried to decide my best move, a car drove slowly past. I didn't think anything about it until it came past again. This time I noticed it slowing as it passed the same house that interested me. As soon as it was out of sight, I pulled into a driveway. The car came by again. Not brown. Possibly the one that had waited at C&S Signals last night, and possibly not. In my rearview mirror I watched it slow, then continue. When it turned the corner I pulled out to follow, but by the time I reached the intersection, it was nowhere in sight.

Returning to my original spot across from the Tremain house, I scribbled a note to Nan Tremain saying C&S couldn't reach Gil and asking her to contact me or Myrtle Hawes. The receptionist was a pain in the neck, but from what I'd seen she was also a paragon of reliability. I slipped it into the mailbox and since I was on the porch anyway and bothered by the car I'd seen circling, I rang the bell again. As I was turning away I heard something inside.

It sounded like someone trying to yell with a gag in their mouth. A faint thump followed. I rang the doorbell again, then dropped to a crouch. Ducking under the window next to the door, I slid off the side of the porch into a rosebush.

For several seconds I struggled to free my legs from the thorns that had snagged in my stockings. I managed to reach a side window with a Venetian blind and peek up as a shape moved past. A man's shape. When it passed again, heading for the back of the house, I went the same way.

The back yard was small, bare at this time of year. A picket fence with rounded off tops enclosed three sides. A stoop not much wider than a sofa, and too low to merit steps, led to the back door. The door stood ajar an inch or two. From my position hunched against the corner of the house I couldn't see in, but I heard voices.

"Just some salesman. Or maybe a neighbor."

"You sure? What if somebody saw us come in?"

"They didn't. Now grab the kid and let's clear out."

I heard the sound again, definitely a muffled squeal, followed by a smack.

"You try that again and I'll pinch your nose so you swallow that rag, missy."

My jaw tightened. It must be Eve Tremain they were talking to. A girl of eleven. They were getting ready to snatch her. If I went in and the men had guns, bullets could ricochet. If they came out they could dodge in opposite directions, one making off with the girl while the other plugged me.

There was no time to plan. The Smith & Wesson came to my hand as though magnetized. Hiding the gun in the folds of my flared skirt, I breezed through the door.

"Eve honey, did you know— Oh, my! What on earth...?"

Two men goggled at me. One, with a hawk's beak, gripped a brown-haired girl by the back of her collar as she sat in a kitchen chair. Her hands were tied in front of her and a rag was stuffed so far into her mouth it was a wonder she didn't choke. The other toughie, arm's reach away from me, had a space between his front teeth. He caught my arm.

I went with it like a good little girl, then drove my knee into the back of his. His leg buckled. He went down, nearly taking me with him. As I broke free and struggled for balance, Hawk Nose brought a hand up and I caught the glint of steel.

The kid was no slouch at thinking. She somersaulted forward, escaping his grip on her collar to scramble under the heavy wooden kitchen table. I heard a shot, shattering dishes, crashing wood, all at almost the same instant I felt the breath of a bullet whiz past. I fired blindly toward its source and heard a yelp. My eyes caught bits of images: The overturned table creating a barrier between the girl and the hawk-nosed thug attempting to grab her. The one who was nearest me, the one who'd fired, clutching his arm. Hawk Nose taking a shot at me as I rolled to the side.

"Run!" yelled the one by the door. "Forget the kid!"

There was too much danger my bullet could ricochet and hit the kid if I returned Hawk Nose's fire. Unless he shot at me again.

A chunk of plaster exploded out of the wall above the table sheltering the girl as a bullet from the man by the door warned what would happen if I fired again.

"Stay down!" I screamed to Eve Tremain.

But the one with the bleeding arm already was gone. Hawk Nose lost no time following. His gun remained pointed back at the girl.

As I started after them, a bullet crashed through the open door. Sticking my nose out invited another that could hit Eve. If I went down myself, the men could come back for her.

From a window over the kitchen sink I watched the two men vault over the back fence, the injured one clumsily. By the time I reached it and looked over, they were running, making for the end of the gravel alley.

***

Eve Tremain was no longer under the table.

"Eve?"

As I moved to one side where I had a clear view of both doors in case the men returned, I caught movement between the far side of the overturned table and the kitchen cupboard. When I got close enough to peer around, she scooted back. Fear bathed her young face.

"Eve honey, I'm not going to hurt you." I held my left hand palm forward in a gesture of peace, though the .38 I still held in the other one probably didn't do much to reassure her. "Were there just the two of them?"

After several seconds she nodded. Her eyes never left me.

I tucked the .38 into its holster at the small of my back and crouched down.

"I'm a friend of Miss Collingswood. Lucille. Your father knows her. Do you?"

She nodded more vigorously.

"Would you like me to untie your hands and take that rag out of your mouth?"

For the first time I took a close look at it. A dishrag. A crocheted dishrag that had probably scoured a thousand greasy skillets. It was all I could do to keep from making a face. I took it out. She coughed and spit, then spit again and threw up.

"I can get your hands undone faster if I use a knife," I said when I'd helped her up from the floor and wiped her chin with a tea towel I found on a peg.

She hesitated.

"There." She spit the sour taste from her mouth and bobbed her head toward a drawer.

I got the smallest paring knife I could find. It would take longer, but the reassurance was worth the extra time.

"That was smart, upsetting the table," I said. "My name's Maggie. I'm a detective. Your father's boss Mr. Collingswood hired me."

While I talked, I sawed at the heavy twine binding her wrists. It wasn't as strong as rope, but the men who'd tied her had compensated by using plenty of it. From the way she was watching me, she was almost as afraid of me as she'd been of them. Even with no experience around kids, I knew asking what happened wouldn't be smart right now.

As soon as the last of the rope gave way, she jerked back several steps. One wrong blink on my part and she'd bolt.

"Is there a neighbor you're supposed to go to if you need help?" I asked softly. "Why don't you go there and ask whoever it is to call your mother. I'm going to sit on your front steps until she gets here, if that's okay."

She turned and ran while I was still speaking. I heard her unlock the front door. By the time I stepped through it into a waning day that was colder than crisp, the door of the neighbor I'd talked to was closing.

I sat down and turned my collar up. Then I took inventory. About now I could use an inch of gin. Or the whiskey I'd turned down earlier. The strength that surges to block out feeling in a fight had drained away. I didn't have enough energy left to straighten the combs in my hair.

What mattered was that Eve Tremain was unharmed. In addition, this attempt to abduct her gave me fresh hope her father might still be alive. It was no coincidence, coming on the heels of his disappearance. Someone wanted the girl to smoke him out, or to use as some kind of leverage against him.

While I was thinking about it, the woman came out next door. Her brown hair was heavily threaded with gray. She stood a moment, looking at me. Then, squaring her shoulders, she started forward.

"I called the police." The waver in her voice undermined her show of bravery.

"Good. I was hoping you would, but the girl was so scared I didn't know if I should tell her to ask."

"She said you claimed you were a detective. Well, those men who broke in told her they were from the F.B.I."

For half a second I wondered whether they might have been, given the nature of Gil Tremain's work and the fact his employer had acknowledged it could have military applications. But no, they'd been thugs.

The door behind the woman opened and Eve edged halfway out.

"Go back inside, dear," the neighbor said over her shoulder. "Your mother will be here shortly."

"I'm going to wait there where I was," I said. "I need to talk to Eve's mother. My name's Maggie Sullivan, by the way."

I'd barely gotten settled on the steps again when the first cruiser arrived. Two uniforms went up the walk next door double time. One glanced in my direction as the neighbor let them in.

Another minute passed before a taxi tore up and a woman with shiny brown hair jumped out. She ran up the walk to the neighbor's house with her hat in her hand and let herself in, calling something I couldn't hear. No sooner had the taxi left the curb than a second cruiser pulled up.

These would be cops experienced in handling robberies and burglaries. One of the beat cops who'd arrived first opened the door, they exchanged a few words, and all three looked in my direction.

A tallish cop with hair like straw moseyed my way.

"Aren't you freezing out here, Miss Sullivan?"

"Yeah, but I want to talk to Mrs. Tremain when you've asked her all you need to. That's what brought me here in the first place. You're Thompson, right?"

"That's right."

We'd met a few times at get-togethers where cops congregated.

"Boss said it was okay if we went inside. He and another man will be over directly. He's getting the girl's story now. He doesn't want to push her too hard, after what she's been through."

What Thompson wanted was to get my version of things. We were just about finished when the other two other cops arrived to sift through the kitchen. They had questions too. As soon as the boys in blue were gone, Nan Tremain and her daughter appeared from the house next door.

At sight of me on the porch, they halted their approach. Eve spoke to her mother with feverish urgency. Nan's arm circled her in a protective barricade. She stepped in front of the girl. With a look that warned she wouldn't put up with much, she strode toward me.

EIGHTEEN

"You're the one who stopped those men from taking Eve? Thank you."

Nan Tremain put out her hand. Women didn't usually initiate the ritual. It told me she had more self-assurance than most, despite the softness of her heart-shaped face and the lacy trim of the blouse collar peeking out of her coat. The firmness of her handshake confirmed it.

"I'm glad I stuck my nose in. I realize you've had an awful scare, and probably want to be left alone right now, but I need to talk to you."

"I can't. Not now. Eve's been brave as anything, but after what she's been through, and the police asking questions—"

"It's important." I hesitated. "It's about Eve's father."

I didn't like to say it in front of the girl, but it was the only card I had to play right now.

"About Gil? What—?" Nan's gaze sharpened. "You're not suggesting he had something to do with this!"

Pulling away from her mother's embrace, Eve looked from one of us to the other. Her expression had grown anxious.

"Mom... police come to see you when something's happened to someone!"

"I'm not the police," I soothed. "Mr. Collingswood hired me."

Her mother moistened her lips.

"I guess you'd better come inside."

Their front room was a pretty place. The sofa was done in sturdy, cotton-like fabric with big blue flowers that stood up like chenille. Lighter blue throw pillows snuggled into its corners. Tremain's former wife didn't stop there, however. She continued through toward the kitchen.

"Oh, my!" She came to an abrupt halt at the threshold. The police had been thoughtful enough to return the table and chairs to upright positions. It didn't hide the shattered remains of gaily colored dishes or white trails where contents of the broken sugar bowl had been spread by struggling feet or rusty stains that hadn't come from rust on the linoleum by the back door.

"I-I broke the creamer and sugar, Mom." Eve fought a sob. "I turned the table over to get away and—"

"Shhh. Shhh. It's all right." Nan cradled her daughter against her and looked at me over her head. Her eyes flicked toward the stains.

"Is that... did you...?"

"Yes. Why don't we sit in the front room? Could I make you some tea?" That and gin-and-tonic exhausted my recipe file, but it seemed right to offer.

"Thank you, no. Mona next door poured so much tea down us I don't think I could face another drop."

We settled ourselves in the room with the cheery blue sofa. Mother and daughter sat on it side by side, both with right knee crossed over the left, both with hands clasped around their crossed legs. I took a seat facing them. Between us was a braided rug with splashes of blue and yellow.

"I think it might be best if I talked to you alone, Mrs. Tremain."

"No!" The word tore not just from Eve's throat but from her heart. "If something's happened to Dad, I want to hear!"

Unclasping her hands, Nan slid an arm around her daughter's shoulders.

"We're a team, the two of us. We've had to be." Her voice shook slightly. "Eve's sensible. She's very close to her father. She needs to know."

"All right, then. You're right, Eve. Something has happened. Your dad hasn't shown up for work, and I'm trying to find him. But before I tell you what I know, you need to tell me every scrap and word you remember about those men breaking into your house. It could help me — and him."

Once she started thinking about it, she might fall apart. This was my guarantee she'd not only tell me, but would make her best effort. As the girl had proved when she rolled from her chair and upset the table to elude her captor, she was no dummy. She frowned in thought and sat up straighter.

"Mom works in the afternoon, so we lock the doors when we leave and I let myself in after school and lock up again. I'm not supposed to answer the phone or go to the door, so I don't."

Her mother smiled at her faintly and smoothed the girl's hair.

"Today... well, first the phone rang. Then a little while after that, the doorbell rang. When I didn't answer, they knocked really loud, like to make sure I could hear. I didn't know what to make of that. The knocking. Usually it's a salesman, or a store delivering something. They just ring the bell and wait a minute, then go on.

"I was in the kitchen getting a glass of milk when it happened. I waited a minute to make sure whoever it was had gone. Then I put the milk bottle back in the fridge and was going to go to my room. Only before I got out of the kitchen, there was this sound. Not big, but... and then all at once I felt a draft and knew the door had opened, and turned, and - and there they were!

"The one in front, the one with the space between his teeth—" She tapped in illustration. "—he said, 'Hello, sweetheart. Don't be afraid. Your dad sent us.'"

"You're sure he called you 'sweetheart'? He didn't use your name?"

"No." She frowned. "No. But when you came in, you did. I remember wondering about it, because I'd never met you."

The fact they hadn't used her name didn't tell me nearly as much as the fact they hadn't asked where her mother was. It told me they knew her schedule, maybe even had been watching the house.

"Anyway, they said that part about Dad sending them. They told me he had an important meeting with President Roosevelt and wanted to say good-by before he left — in case he wasn't back by Christmas.

"My dad's awfully smart, and I knew he was working on something important, but somehow it smelled fishy. I said I didn't remember seeing them at C&S Signals — that probably wasn't smart, but I was scared, with them right there in the house. The one with the gap in his teeth laughed and told me it was because they were from the F.B.I.

"I said, oh, okay, but I had to call my mom first so she wouldn't worry if she called to check on me and I didn't answer. That's when the other one grabbed me. I started to scream, but he smacked me so hard not much got out. I kicked and tried to bite him, but he held me and they tied up my hands. Every time I tried to scream, they hit me again.

"Then one of them pushed me back on the table and said fine, if I wanted it rough, he'd show me rough. He grabbed my blouse and — and—"

Her voice broke. Her eyes welled with tears.

"Oh, Evie. Baby doll!" Her mother's face had gone ashen. She held her now weeping child against her shoulder. "You didn't tell the policemen that part. Did-did the man do something else to you?"

"Of *course* he did something, Mom!" Eve pushed free and glared, making the parent who loved her an innocent target of rage and pain. "He shoved — He shoved—" Eve gagged.

My stomach sank. Nan Tremain's must be even lower.

"He shoved the smelly old dishrag into my mouth!"

A humpback clock ticked on the mantle. Her mother slumped with relief. I leaned back wondering whether the poor woman felt the same impulse toward hysterical laughter that I was fighting.

"You're pretty brave. Lots of girls would have fallen apart," I said to give Nan a chance to recover. "Can you tell me what happened next?"

Eve took a crumpled hanky from the pocket of her jumper and blew her nose.

"Then you came in, I guess. Only I didn't know who you were, or if you were with them." She turned to her mother, all misdirected anger gone. "One of them shot at her, Mom! I saw his gun. She had one too. Then there was lots of shooting. That's when I upset the table. And I think I just squeezed my eyes shut, and when I opened them, everybody was gone. So I hid."

She gulped in breath and faced me with as stern a look as an eleven year old could muster.

"Now it's your turn."

NINETEEN

There's no escaping the inevitable. I met the kid's gaze.

"Okay. Here's what I know. Your dad's been missing all week. Mr. Collingswood hired me to find him."

Eve and Nan caught each other's hands.

"Missing? What do you mean?" Nan asked.

Briefly, I related when he'd last come to work, Daisy's tale, and how thugs had been waiting for her at the end of her shift.

"The woman who makes the cinnamon rolls? Is that who you mean?" Eve's voice squeezed out, higher pitched than before.

"Daisy. Yes." Her question startled me. "You know her?"

"I met her once when Dad stopped at his office after a movie to get one of his engineering journals. She was nice. She was always leaving him treats, sometimes brownies but usually cinnamon rolls. If I was coming over, he'd save them to share."

Tremain's former wife sat with one hand pressed to her throat. She was staring at me.

"Are you saying Gil was... abducted? Like they tried to do Eve?"

"I think that's the likeliest explanation."

"But why?"

"I don't know. Did he have any enemies?"

"No! At least none I'm aware of. He's not the sort to make them. He doesn't argue, he doesn't spend time in bars—"

I held up my hand to halt her flow of words.

"Is there any chance he'd go off on his own and not tell anyone? Maybe if he was upset?"

"No!"

"Was he having any kind of financial problems?"

"Goodness no. He gave me a generous support check every month, spoiled Eve terribly. Two weeks ago he even gave me fifty dollars extra for Christmas. He said..." A hint of pink found its way through the strained whiteness of her cheeks. "He said I was to spend it mostly on myself, because I didn't have anyone buying me presents."

Two weeks ago. That meant the money hadn't come from what he'd withdrawn Saturday.

"That was the last time you saw him then? Two weeks ago?"

"Oh no. He and Eve had an outing Saturday. He sees her one day a weekend."

Gil Tremain had seen his daughter on Saturday. He'd gone out with Lucille Collingswood the following evening. Then he'd disappeared off the face of the earth.

Nan leaned toward me earnestly.

"Even if Gil did get in some kind of trouble, he'd never involve Eve. He'd never send strangers to scare her and hurt her like that."

I nodded, piecing thoughts together. If someone wanted to incapacitate Collingswood, or put him in an early grave, abducting Eve made no sense at all.

"I think someone's holding Gil prisoner. They planned to use Eve as a weapon." I sorted it out for myself at the same time I told them. "They knew if they had her and threatened to hurt her, they could force him to tell them something or do something he didn't want to. Data from an important project he'd been working on disappeared the same time he did."

Eve whimpered. Her eyes had grown huge.

"Miss Sullivan's going to help Dad, honey." Nan's voice was calm but her eyes as they met mine were hollow with fear.

"I doubt those men would come back, but it might be smart to get out of town for a few days. Just until this is sorted out."

"But surely the police..."

"They'll do what they can. I expect a patrol car will swing past every now and then, but they're stretched pretty thin."

Police resources had to be carefully allocated. The department needed more men, but the city fathers kept their purse strings tight.

"My sister lives outside Chicago," Nan said faintly. "We were going there for Christmas but—"

"Whoever has Gil knows plenty about him, including where you live and that Eve's alone after school, it appears. What about someone even Gil himself wouldn't know about?"

"Oh!" She bit her lip. "There is a woman whose daughter was in Eve's class. She was single like me, and we became friends. They moved to Terre Haute and they've asked us to visit..."

"Sophie's mom? Oh, yes! Can we?"

We unfolded the paper and found the railroad timetable. A train that went through Terre Haute departed in a couple of hours.

"If you jot down anything on your telephone pad, take the top few sheets and stick them in your purse. Write the number and time of some other train on the pad, maybe one leaving about the time yours does, and leave that. Take your address book with you," I added.

Such precautions might be unnecessary, but one woman already was dead and armed men had attempted to make off with the girl across from me. Nan's eyes told me she grasped the gravity of the situation. She nodded once before disappearing into the hall.

"Tell me about your friend." I didn't want Eve to put two and two together the way her mother had. She'd had enough scares for one day.

She did, shyly at first, then with eagerness growing. Out in the hall I heard Nan get her connection to Terre Haute.

"Miss Collingswood says you're smart, like your dad." I smiled at the girl now fidgeting on the couch.

She shrugged.

"I get good grades in school. I wish I had a talent like she does, though. She plays violin, up on a stage with other people. It's beautiful! She played for me at her house, just showing me how it's done. She let me try notes on a littler violin she used when she was my age, but all I managed to make was squawks — well, more like scratches." Eve wrinkled her nose.

"I want to play flute." She pantomimed. "Once when we went to hear Miss Collingswood's ensemble play, they had a man playing flute with them. Dad said if I was still interested after Christmas, he'd get me one and I could take lessons."

No doubt about it, the girl was a fan of Lucille Collingswood. By the sound of it, things between her father and Lucille were pretty serious.

I hurried to get in a question while we were alone.

"Those men who broke in today, did they hunt for anything? Ask you where anything was?"

She shook her head vigorously.

"Did your dad say anything about needing a lamp? Or getting one fixed?"

"A lamp? No. Why?"

Before I could ask my other question, Nan returned.

"It's all set," she said with false cheer. "Now run get your suitcase out and pack as best you can, Evie. I have to call work and do a dozen other things besides mine."

"Before you go," I said as Eve jumped up. "I'm talking to people who might have seen your dad. Can either of you think of anything about him people might notice?"

They looked at each other a moment, then giggled and spoke as one. "His walk."

Eve mimicked it, leaning one shoulder forward as she left the room. Getting up, I watched from the doorway until she disappeared into her room.

"I hope what you said earlier, about not keeping anything from her, was mostly for her sake. I need to ask about some trouble her father got in a long time ago."

Nan's whole manner went from soft to hard. She sank onto a chair.

"You mean the fact that he was a dope fiend?" The words were flat. "He went to a sanitarium. They helped him quit. He's been rock solid ever since."

"What's the chance pressure from this project he's been on, or something else, could make him—?"

"None."

Of all the nightmares she'd been exposed to today, she seemed to find this the most heinous.

"It was different when he - when he had his problems," she said angrily. "Two months after he got his first engineering job, the stock market crashed. The place he worked closed. He took the only work he could find and it bored him to death. He started... He hated himself. He tried to quit. It was awful."

"But he succeeded."

"Not until Eve was born. He was terrified he might accidentally hurt her. He tried to kill himself so we'd get his insurance. My father tied him up and locked him in a closet while he found a clinic and made arrangements. He went with him on the train to Colorado and Gil check himself in."

Her hands were balled into fists. She leaned toward me.

"He would *never* take a step back toward that kind of nightmare. Never! He'd die before he'd make Eve ashamed of him. Or Loren Collingswood, who gave him a chance. Or me, I think."

She stood up.

"I appreciate all you've done. Helping me about leaving. Especially saving Eve. But I have things to do."

TWENTY

Eve's room had a white bedstead with airy spindles. The chenille spread and polished cotton curtains were pink. Instead of a dressing table, she had a desk, with a tablet and books all stacked on it neatly like the things on her father's desk. Overseen by a pair of Raggedy Ann and Raggedy Andy dolls, a small suitcase lay open on her bed.

"Have fun with your friend," I said as I stuck my head in. Nan's okay to say good-by to the girl was contingent on not staying long, so I knew time was limited.

"If your Dad was going to buy some sort of present for Miss Collingswood that had to do with music, say a metronome, where would he go?"

"Well... she got things at a place up near Rike's, so I guess he'd go there. But for Christmas he's going to get her a music box. We were going to look for them next time he picked me up."

I'd struck out on finding a reason he might go to Fifth Street.

"I thought of something else those men said when they were here. It's probably not important though."

Eve sat down on the edge of the bed, which I interpreted as an invitation, so I went in.

"Most of my job is looking at things that may not be important. What did they say?"

"When the mean one hit me, the other one yelled at him not to hit my face. He told the mean one, 'He doesn't want bruises,' or something like that."

My theory that Gil Tremain was alive and hostage somewhere, and that whoever had him intended to use his daughter's safety as leverage to force his cooperation, grew a size.

"That actually tells me lots," I said.

"Does it?" She practically glowed.

"That's the same picture your dad keeps on his desk, isn't it?" I said reaching for the framed photograph that lay atop a folded sweater next to the suitcase.

Eve snatched it away before I could touch it.

"It's... special," she apologized holding it to her chest. "I want to take it with me."

"I understand." While part of her hoped, another part was starting to tell her she might never see her father again. She needed to have the comfort of his photograph.

"It looks like you were having fun," I said to get her past the awkwardness.

"We were, at Lakeside. Miss Collingswood took it."

"Miss Collingswood?" It surprised me to think of the staid violinist traipsing around an amusement park.

Eve grinned.

"Dad let her take half a dozen, but this was the only one that came out. She doesn't understand depth of field. Can you believe it?" She wrinkled her nose.

"I'd better get going," I said.

"You're going to find my dad, aren't you?" The plaintiveness of her question pierced me. "You're going to get him back from those men who have him?"

I've always been cozier than I should be with lying. I couldn't manage this time.

"I'm going to do my best."

I started to open the door. Words burst from the girl behind me.

"He thought somebody might be planning to steal their project. The one he'd been working on. He told me."

***

I drove to C&S Signals dizzy with what I'd learned. Eve didn't know who her father suspected or why. She didn't know anything more at all.

"He just sort of let it slip when I teased him about not listening to what I was telling him," she told me. "He made me cross my heart not to say anything."

I told her she'd done the right thing letting me know, and that she ought to tell her mother too once they got settled on the train. Then I went directly to C&S.

For the moment, it didn't seem smart to say anything about Tremain's suspicions. I had other reasons for going there. First, the man who had hired me had a right to know what had almost happened to Tremain's daughter. Second, I still suspected he was holding something back from me about those phone calls he'd received. If I was right, my news about the attempt on Eve might nudge him.

It was ten past five when I pulled in. Only one car remained in the parking lot. Three of the typists were just filing out. As I walked past they ducked furtive glances in my direction and whispered together. Interesting.

"I'm sorry, we're—" Myrtle Hawes looked up. She was watering the plant on her desk. "Oh. It's you."

"Is Mr. Collingswood still here?"

"Yes, but he's had enough aggravation for one day. He and Mr. Scott had to let someone go. He's very upset."

"Who got fired?"

"One of the typists."

"Why?"

She ignored me.

"Can't you call him at home tomorrow?"

"It's all right, Myrtle." The man I'd come to see emerged from the central area where typewriters now were silent and no voices murmured. "Go on before you miss your trolley. I'll lock up."

With a sniff the receptionist retrieved a purse from under her desk and went to a coatrack. Settling her hat on her head and shrugging into a tweed coat with cranberry slubs, she sailed out. Neither one of us spoke until the door closed behind her.

"She's excessively protective at times, I'm afraid." Collingswood smiled wearily. He had a new topcoat over his arm. "Her husband was the senior of our two employees when we started the company. He died just a few years later and, well, she needed providing for and we were nearing the point to need a receptionist.

"What brings you here?"

I offered to walk with him as he did the locking up part, but he said only the front door remained. By the time I finished telling him about Eve Tremain, we had reached his car.

"Oh dear," he said leaning back against it and closing his eyes. "This has to stop. It has to."

"It might stop faster if you leveled with me."

His eyes flew open. He looked at me sharply. "What do you mean?"

"I need you to tell me the truth about those phone calls. Everything."

His angry expression dissolved into one of despair.

"It can't have anything to do with Gil."

I waited.

"Even if it's not a wrong number, even if it's someone playing some sort of-of ugly trick..."

Dusk had thickened even since we came out. In the parking lot our two cars hunkered, solitary, buffeted by a wind that was stirring to life. Escaped handbills hawking something at a gospel mission paraded around my ankles. In spite of the chill, Collingswood made no move to don the new topcoat he carried. He swallowed and spoke.

"There was one other call. The night before I called you. They said... they said, 'Don't trust your daughter.'"

TWENTY-ONE

Another ten minutes with Collingswood left me more frustrated than informed. Like any good father, he'd insisted his daughter couldn't possibly be involved in anything unsavory. Not in anything which would harm his company, or him personally. Not in gambling or anything shameful which would make her a blackmail target.

Admittedly it seemed like a stretch, having met her and seen how involved she was in her music. Still, I couldn't forget her wry comments about hearing enough engineering talk to last her a lifetime, or her saying today that her father cared about nothing but his business.

It had been a long day and I needed the solitude of my office to think. The radiator had settled back to tepid. Home sweet home. I kicked off my shoes off and put my feet on my desk. One of my stockings had a runner an inch wide, an occupational hazard whose costs were adding up on this case. I'd replace it from the spares in my drawer before heading for Finn's.

Meanwhile, I studied the other nugget of information I'd gotten from Collingswood there in the parking lot. Pauline, the young typist with dimples was the one who'd been fired that afternoon. A two-dollar bill Mrs. Hawes kept at her desk for petty cash had gone missing. A search ensued. It hadn't turned up the money, but behind other items in Pauline's desk, jammed or stuck to the back of the drawer, was a paper with engineering symbols.

The page was from documentation on the Crescendo project. It wasn't the missing calculations, but was damning, nonetheless. Collingswood, on seeing the evidence, had fired the girl on the spot.

The incident seemed to confirm that Tremain and the project he'd worked on were the central target in everything happening. Collingswood's afflictions, the snake and the phone calls, were merely peripheral. But how? And why? Were they simply attempts to confuse the issue?

As much as I liked that idea, I didn't yet see anything to support it. I turned my thoughts to what I now knew instead.

That Gil Tremain was still alive, probably.

That he was being held against his will and hadn't given his captors something they wanted. Otherwise, why turn his apartment inside out? Why try to snatch his daughter?

The fact Eve's would-be abductors had shoved a gag into her mouth to keep her quiet just might tell me something as well. Why hadn't they used chloroform? It lasted longer and was more effective. Their choice suggested they hadn't intended to take her far, or they didn't want her throwing up when the chloroform wore off.

I was just getting to my next conclusion — that Collingswood was an innocent casualty of the situation — when two jaunty taps sounded on my door. Before I could speak, it opened and Clem Stark swaggered in.

"So this is your place, huh?" The miserable excuse for a private eye took it in. "You don't mind my saying so, you could use some better decorating." His gaze had settled on the dead plant in the corner, but only after observing my legs thoroughly enough to give evidence on them.

Slowly, so as not to give him any idea I suffered from girlish modesty, I returned them to earth and sat up.

"I don't recall anyone inviting you in. Get out."

"Come on, Maggie, don't get sore. I may have gotten ahead of you once or twice in the past—"

"You stole a case I was working on."

"Hey, let's let bygones be bygones. Aren't you going to ask me to sit down? Hear about how you'd have your own office working for me? Girl out front to take calls when you weren't around? Do your typing?"

My hand had gone under the seat of my chair, not because I felt threatened by him, but because I was furious. Sliding my Smith & Wesson out of the pocket I'd put it in a short time earlier, I leveled it at him.

"What I'm going to do is put a slug in your arm — or maybe your shoulder — unless your start telling me everything you know about the case I'm working on now and why you're interested."

Some of the color left his face.

"What? What are you talking about?"

"Your boy in the brown car is a lousy tail. If he's the best you can hire, no wonder you want to hire somebody smart."

"Hey. The men I got working for me are plenty smart. None of 'em drives a brown car, Smartypants."

He wasn't scared, I'd give him that, but he was nervous. He looked just indignant enough to make me think he was telling the truth.

"You're not going to plug me. You'd lose your license."

"Barging in after the other offices up here have closed for the day. Making a pass at me. What's a girl to do? The boys at Market House like you a whole lot less than they do me, Stark. You want to see who they believe?"

He knew I meant the detective division. He chuckled nervously.

"You got spunk, kid. I like that."

"Take off your coat."

"What?"

I bobbed the .38 in repetition.

"Okay, okay. It's off. Now what?"

Minus his suit jacket I could see he wasn't armed.

"Now you sit. And you tell me the truth."

Rounding my desk, I leaned on the corner. I put the Smith & Wesson behind me where he couldn't reach it but I could. I picked up the stapler next to my typewriter and opened it for a thick job.

"Otherwise, while I may not shoot you, I guarantee I'll use this to staple your lying mouth shut."

Stark flinched a smidgen.

"Hey, simmer down! It doesn't matter what you do to me, I don't know anything about someone tailing you. That's the God's honest truth. Or what you're working on, either."

"So out of the sky blue you've taken it into your head to offer me a job."

"I, uh, got a man who's going to be leaving. I can't afford to be short staffed, so I'm trying to line up good talent. You oughta be flattered."

The first part sounded believable. What didn't make sense was why he would come to me.

Then it hit me. Shifting the stapler thoughtfully from hand to hand, I sat staring down at him.

"What you've got is a man with a low draft number."

"Yeah, okay. You know you got a ladder in your stocking?"

I ignored the comment.

"And if we go to war, every able-bodied man in the city will be taking off, the ones who work for you included."

"Opportunity for you, kid. You'd get out of this dump, no more rent to pay. I'd get the only detective left in the city who's not gimped or blind. We'd be washing each other's backs. And while I sure wouldn't mind washing yours the other way too, I ain't the kind who gets fresh with my help."

"Help?"

"Employees."

"Yesterday it was 'colleagues'."

He grinned, not sure how to respond but unconcerned. I hopped off the desk.

"Get out, Stark. If you come back here, or waylay me again, or ever try to meddle in a case of mine, I guarantee I'll lose my temper."

I raised the stapler to give him incentive.

He left.

TWENTY-TWO

Wee Willie Ryan, my childhood friend who usually gave me a hard time as soon as I walked in the door at Finn's pub, had finished his pint and gone by the time I arrived. Seamus Hanlon, a gaunt, white haired cop who'd spent many an evening at our kitchen table from the time I could toddle until I was forced to sell the house to pay my father's medical bills, sat at the bar sipping Guinness.

"Where's Billy?" I asked as one of the regulars slid over a space to let me sit by Seamus.

He chuckled. His long-time partner Billy Leary had completed the trio whose conversation had floated around me, warming me, in the kitchen while my mother filled the front room with her constant chill.

"Kate wanted him home early so they could go to some card party." He got a kick out of how the ever-grumbling Billy fell in line when his wife put her foot down. So did I.

A look around didn't show any bowls in evidence. On Fridays, those in the know who arrived early enough could get a bowl of Irish stew that Finn's wife Rose made in their upstairs apartment then brought down to a hotplate. Apparently I'd missed out, thanks to Clem Stark's visit. It was one more thing to hold against him.

"Stew must have gone fast tonight," I observed.

"It didn't go at all." Rose set a pint topped with perfect foam in front of me. "My stove played out. I went upstairs to check and it was stone cold. No point wasting it, so I sent it home with Willie Ryan. Maire can cook it up for those little rascals of theirs."

She flitted down the bar to serve someone else. We sipped our stout in comfortable silence. Seamus was good for sitting with, each of us traversing our own thoughts. He wasn't given to idle chatter, but his quiet presence calmed and reassured like a warm hearth.

"Clem Stark's been around trying to hire me," I said at length.

Amusement navigated Seamus' craggy features.

"Bet you handed him his hat."

"I threatened to staple his mouth shut."

He gave a sly grin.

"Somebody tell him you were tired of working for yourself, did they?"

"No, he's figuring if we go to war, the men who work for him now — I think there may be three — will leave for the army."

Seamus grunted and signaled Finn for another pint. I was still working on mine.

"Are we going to war, Seamus? Lots of people seem certain."

He shook his head. "You'd need a crystal ball to answer. No telling what those men in Washington will get up to."

We shared more silence. The day had been so full I hadn't had much time for thinking. Now that I did, my thoughts kept wandering back to the abruptly closed lamp shop. There must be some way I could contact the man who'd run it, or at least find an employee or the rental agency.

"You're thinking awfully hard there," Seamus observed.

"Yeah, and I'm tired of it. Want to get a sandwich?"

His lips pursed.

"I'd need to change out of my uniform first."

"Happens you know a girl with a car."

"Did you have someplace in mind for the sandwich?"

I did, and it was in somewhat the same direction as the gaudy building whose image seemed stuck in my head.

***

"Cheese on top of tuna salad?" Seamus shook his head skeptically as I drove.

"They toast it all, and the cheese melts. It's good."

"I might skip the cheese. The toasting part sounds nice, though."

Possibly he was thinking that doing without the cheese would save him a nickel. Seamus wasn't hard up, but he was thrifty. I'd waited at the place where he roomed while he changed into a brown tweed jacket and gabardine trousers. Now we were heading south on Main.

"You mind if we take a little detour first? Drive down a stretch of Fifth a time or two?"

"I like riding in a car. Don't get to do it much now."

It had never occurred to me he might miss his daily stint in a cruiser now that his bad knee confined him mostly to desk duty. Reaching over, I squeezed his hand. I made a mental note to invite him on an occasional excursion.

It felt good having the heater on in the DeSoto. People getting on and off trolleys wore coats buttoned up. The home-bound crowd had dwindled to nothing. Now people were headed back to the heart of the city for dinner or picture shows or on dates. I waited for a trolley to pass and then turned onto Fifth. The café where I'd talked to the waitress that morning was pulling the CLOSED sign down as we passed. The music store already had called it a day. I slowed as we came abreast of the gaily painted building with the bay windows. Could Tremain have wound up there because he was following whoever he suspected was plotting to steal information about the Crescendo project?

"Working on something down here, are you?" asked Seamus.

"Yeah. A man I'm looking for supposedly was somewhere around here the last time anyone saw him, but so far I haven't been able to find hide nor hair."

Continuing for several blocks, I came around again.

There was a sauciness about the building that had housed the lamp shop. Its ornate facade flirted with passers-by as shamelessly as a woman sliding her skirt up her thigh. The windows were dark though, and the pale shape of the FOR RENT sign showed in the window. This time I didn't slow.

Seamus chuckled.

"You thinking of something funny?" I asked absently. For Seamus, taciturn as he was, a chuckle was the equivalent of hooting with laughter.

"The woman who used to own that place. The one with the little bitty towers hanging over the street. She has money enough to fill a couple of banks, and sits on a couple of highfaluting boards now, but my, twenty years ago she was a corker!" He chuckled again.

I nearly stood on my brakes. Never before had I heard Seamus say so much unprompted. Hearing him mention a woman save Kate or a few other cop wives was even more unusual. Hearing her mentioned in connection with the very place I was interested in left me wobbly as an all-night drunk.

"Tabby Warren." Oblivious to the effect he'd produce, he said the name more to himself than to me. "I had a feeling she was giving me the eye a couple of times," he confided shyly. "It didn't seem to bother her a bit that I'd arrested her."

Certain I would cause a wreck if I did otherwise, I brought the DeSoto to rest at the curb. I turned and stared at him.

"That place back there was a bawdy house?"

"Naw, and you'd never mistake Miss Warren for that kind, either. It was a speakeasy. Got raided a good dozen times, at least. I worked on some of them. Your dad too. 'Course Tab– Miss Warren wasn't there every time. I put her in the paddy wagon twice, though. Spotted her a couple of other times when we burst in, but she slipped away somehow. Some of those places had secret exits, but we never found the one there."

Seamus was smiling at memories. I leaned back and listened to this incredible flood of information about his past.

A secret way out. My thoughts were skittering. What better place to hold someone prisoner if you could somehow arrange to have the building all to yourself.... No, that was wishful thinking. There were businesses on either side. Calls for help would be heard. Still, it was the last place Gil Tremain had been seen.

***

To my surprise, Seamus decided to let them add cheese to his sandwich. Maybe memories of his younger days were making him frisky. Or maybe it was just remembering the notorious Tabby Warren.

Over supper his talkative streak continued enough to tell me about a couple of raids on the building in question. He couldn't quite hide his enjoyment as he described merry chaos when the police burst in: Screams. Whistles blowing. Socialites swinging at cops and sometimes at dates they were too drunk to recognize. Sons and daughters of high society trampling each other to get out without being slapped into handcuffs.

"Not that breaking the law is something to laugh at," he added, noting my merriment. "And however harmless the people going there and people running the place might have been, the men who kept them supplied with liquor were gangsters and killers."

I wiped my eyes.

"And you never asked Tabby Warren out? In spite of her dropping clues she was interested"

"Well, I don't know for sure she was. Anyway, I was a cop, still walking a beat, and she had all this money. Besides, she was young enough to be my daughter."

He sighed.

"My, she did make an impression though. Hard to scare. Sassed and gave lip. Back at the station the men booking her would stutter and stumble, she flustered them so." He gave me a sideways look. "Come to think of it, she was a lot like you."

TWENTY-THREE

Seamus subscribed to the early-to-bed-early-to-rise philosophy. After we'd driven around for awhile and I took him home, several hours still remained of the evening. Knowing I wouldn't be able to settle into a book if I went back to Mrs. Z's, I stopped at my office to catch up on case notes. When I finished and looked over my latest jottings, one thing niggled at me: the girl who'd been fired today.

She was young. Very young. Lots of women got manipulated by men, but girls her age were particularly vulnerable. I'd dismissed the draftsman's claim that she hung around with Tremain as spite because the dimpled typist had rejected his overtures. Now I wondered if his claim had more substance.

Could someone have used the girl, Pauline, to wangle information from Tremain? Or could she and Tremain have gotten involved romantically? In either case she knew more than she was letting on. In the first instance, she might even be willing to hide him.

At the start of my investigation, I'd managed to pry a list of C&S employees out of Mrs. Hawes. I looked at it now and copied down Pauline's address. The street name wasn't one I recognized. I went to the city map I'd had framed to hang on the wall. It was too late to pay a social call, but that wasn't what I had in mind anyway.

I swung past Mrs. Z's and picked up the key, just in case I came in after she locked up.

***

Sometimes you learn things just by taking a good look at a neighborhood. Or a house. Pauline's neighborhood was on the edge of the city. It was the sort of place where earlier in the century, modest homes had started to fill in around older farmhouses. Some of the places still kept chicken coops in their back yards. Blocks were long. Street lights were sparse. Driving around revealed a neighborhood grocery, a laundry and dry cleaning place, a beer joint — and lots of quiet.

Pauline's address looked like it might have been one of the original farmhouses. It was two-stories tall plus an attic, built like a box, and looked to be white. I couldn't make out much more than that. The windows were dark.

After sitting for fifteen minutes without so much as a car coming past, I decided to risk a look in back of the house. Now and again a shed yields something interesting. Missing items. A new coil of rope. A shotgun hidden behind a frail old lady's flowerpots. Even the yard itself can tell you things if something's discarded in haste, or more cars are in evidence than you'd expect at such a place.

I got out with a flashlight in my left hand and my Smith & Wesson in my right coat pocket. A long path with faded wheel marks suggesting it hadn't been used in a while for other than foot traffic led to the back yard. The main risk in a stunt like the one I was pulling was dogs. They could come bounding out and take a chunk out, or raise such a fuss that every light in the house went on.

I didn't encounter a dog. The back yard, from what I could see without switching the light on, looked tidy. At the back of the lot I made out the shape of a bin for burning trash, and beyond that a shed whose size suggested it might once have housed a horse and a carriage. That looked like a place to start.

If the shed had ever been painted, it had been a long time ago. Its weathered sides had seen a lot of years. As I got close, I stopped several times to listen, but there were no voices or sounds indicating it might house animals. When I reached the back of it, hidden from the house, I switched on my flashlight.

The shed opened into a dirt path with a thin coat of gravel that would disappear into mud by the end of winter. I turned and played my flashlight beam over the shed. The door on it heightened my belief it had once housed a carriage. The door was taller than it was wide, and swung outward. A heavy board that lifted out of an iron latch held it closed.

Checking to make sure no lights had gone on in houses along the lane, and listening again for noises, I lifted the board. Now came the moment of truth, easing it open, which might cause the hinges to squeak. I held my breath.

One inch, three inches, six inches. The only sound was a faint metallic grunt. The hinges had been oiled. That meant the shed was used, and probably more than occasionally.

As soon as I stepped inside, I saw an automobile. I stopped dead.

It was brown.

With quickening pulse I moved along the side. As soon as I reached the front, I saw the crumpled fender. Moving swiftly around it, I glanced at the open shed door with new caution. Then I lowered the flashlight beam so it hit the license plate.

Its last two digits were twenty-six.

TWENTY-FOUR

"Cat got you, huh?" Jolene said eyeing my legs as I came into the kitchen on Saturday morning.

"Yeah." Instead of my usual stockings, I was wearing opaque gray cotton ones. They felt dowdy, but they looked okay with my tweed suit. Mostly they hid the gauze pad covering tooth marks left by our landlady's tomcat who had ambushed me as I came in the previous evening.

"We ought to keep track of how many times each of us gets bitten," I said. "Award a prize at the end of the year."

"Maybe a new pair of stockings."

I laughed.

Escaping Mrs. Z's apartment to sink his teeth into passing ankles was the cat's favorite pastime. It was also his only exercise if girth was any indication.

Jolene closed the newspaper section she'd been reading and traded it for another.

"You must be working today, wearing a suit. You won't get so busy you forget to buy an ornament for the tree, will you?"

"Nope. Scout's honor."

Every year Mrs. Z let us put a Christmas tree up in the downstairs alcove where male visitors could wait. Now and then somebody bought an actual glass ornament to supplement the paper chains and snowflakes we constructed for its trimmings. This year I'd promised I would. We would put up the tree tomorrow when people got back from church.

Saturday morning was the only time of the week when we got to use the kitchen. I cut some bread and lowered the side of the toaster to put it in, enjoying the homey feeling that simple act produced. It was early yet. There were only the two of us. Jolene was up because she was a farm girl and had grown up milking cows or some such. I was up because I had a list of things to do. I thought about the topmost item on that list: Tabby Warren.

If I could find a listing for her in the telephone book, I'd try to get her to talk to me for two minutes. My previous dealings with socialites didn't make me optimistic. She probably wouldn't give me the time of day, or more likely her butler or whoever ran her household wouldn't. Still, it was worth a try.

It was also smart to have a fallback plan.

"Jolene," I said as mine took shape, "has anyone who works at your club ever worked anywhere around Fifth Street? The west side, I mean?"

Jolene was a cigarette girl. Her bubbly nature probably made her a natural. She'd worked at supper clubs as well as places that featured only dancing and drinks. All had been respectable, and each was nicer than the last.

She wrinkled her nose.

"I don't think there are any clubs on that end. It's too near the train station. Well, there's Lance's, of course, but I don't know anyone who's worked there. Somebody may have mentioned working in a pub down there as a bouncer, but I can't remember who. There might be places over by Wayne that call themselves clubs, but you know what that part's like."

Wayne was a cesspool ranging from bad to worse. Pickpockets. Hookers. Dope and drunks. A storefront mission or two struggled against overwhelming odds.

"You want me to ask around?" Jolene offered.

"I'd appreciate it. I need to find someplace I can show a picture and find out if anyone recognizes it."

Chances they would were probably slim. Which brought me back to Tabby Warren.

I told myself I wouldn't resort to using Seamus' name to wangle a chat with her. I hoped I wasn't fibbing.

***

Somewhat to my surprise, Tabitha Warren was listed under her own name in the telephone book. Did that mean she hadn't married? Whatever the answer, she'd be more receptive to talking to me if I waited until ten o'clock. Half past would be even smarter.

I dropped my laundry off since I'd neglected to do it on Thursday. I drove to the hat shop where I'd eluded my pursuer in the brown car. The same car I'd found last night in Pauline's garage.

What did the dimpled secretary have to do with Tremain's disappearance? If anything. According to Collingswood, she had insisted she didn't know how the sheet of engineering jargon came to be in her desk. Maybe she hadn't believed there was really a risk she'd get caught. Maybe she'd trusted someone she shouldn't have. Whatever the explanation, there was no doubt the brown car behind her house was the one that had followed me.

I went to Rike's and picked out a fancy glass Santa Claus for our tree. Even though the clerk wrapped it in layers of tissue and put it on wads of the same stuff inside a box, I decided it might be smart to drop it off at Mrs. Z's rather than have it rattle around in my car, so I did.

There was a phone message for me. It was from Nan's friend in Terre Haute saying her guests had arrived. One worry less. I'd said not to use names and she hadn't.

Since the place where Daisy Brown lived didn't have a phone, I went over there to make sure she'd made it home safely from her previous night's work. The muted sound of her singing met me as I knocked on the door.

"Who is it?"

Good. She was taking precautions.

"Maggie Sullivan."

The door opened. Daisy wore a floral patterned apron with a bib. A smudge of flour decorated one eyebrow.

"I'll bet you stopped to see if I was dead," she said cheerfully. "Well, I'm not, and I just finished frosting some orange rolls I turned out, so come on back."

My stomach gave an unseemly gurgle. I followed half a dozen steps to her kitchen. It was big enough for a two-burner stove and a sink and small Frigidaire. A drop-leaf table too small to accommodate anything but a single chair was shoved into one corner. The leaf was up and the tabletop held two batches of rolls that looked as if they were bound for customers.

"Here. Try one." She passed me a plate of extras. "Go on, sit in that chair. Just move my grocery list. Would you like some tea?"

I declined the tea and praised the roll. The frosting with flecks of orange peel was enough to make me swoon.

"Did anyone come around while you were working last night?" I asked.

"Nope. Not ones that work there or ones that didn't belong either. I made good and sure before I came out. But then that business you saw night before last, that was unusual. Now and again some of those girls who type have to come in at night, if the bosses are in a hurry on something. Nobody walks them to the trolley stop, and I've never heard a peep about one of them getting bothered."

Daisy hustled pans into the sink as she talked. My ears went up. The C&S owners had given me the impression no one came in after hours except the two of them and Gil Tremain. And of course Daisy. Now I was more than a little curious.

"Have any of the typists been in lately? I understand Mr. Tremain and some others were working on something special when he disappeared."

"Oh, yes." She nodded as she turned the water on and sifted in washing soda. "Two came in last week the same night. I think they came in separate but they left together. Another night one of the others was in. That poor girl nearly jumped out of her skin when she saw me. I guess maybe nobody told her I was around at night." She chuckled.

"Which girls?"

"I don't know names, and the first two all I saw was their backs. The one I scared, I kind of think she may be new." She attacked a muffin tin with her Brillo pad. "Has big, sweet dimples."

TWENTY-FIVE

I'd gone from killing time before I could call Tabby Warren to deciding another visit took priority. Pauline's nocturnal visit to C&S had come shortly before Gil Tremain and the final version of what he'd been working on both went missing. A page from that work had turned up in her desk. A car that had followed me sat in a shed behind Pauline's house. At last a few things were beginning to hook together.

Most places look better by daylight. The Meadows house was no exception. I could see now that it was better maintained than the shed in back. The white paint was still in good shape. Shutters on the second story gleamed dark green as did the rail surrounding the wide front porch. Rose bushes had been pruned to prevent winter kill. I rang the bell.

After a minute the door opened and I was face to face with Pauline. Her eyes were so swollen from crying they could only flinch a little at seeing me.

"Go away!"

Her voice was shrill. She tried to close the door. I had considerable experience at blocking such attempts. My shoulder was ready. It pushed the door wider, Pauline gave way and I stepped inside.

"We need to talk, Pauline."

"No! I don't want to talk to you. Go away!"

"My guess is that somebody else is at least partly to blame for the pickle you're in. Tell me who, and I'll do what I can to help you."

"No! I don't know what you're talking about."

"Pauline, what is it?" A woman appeared from another room, wiping her hands.

"She's some kind of detective! Mr. Collingswood hired her."

"I think you better leave." A man had come in behind the two women. "Our daughter doesn't have a dishonest bone in her body. You go back and tell those men who fired her that."

His neatly mended tan shirt and filled-out shoulders suggested a laborer with a good job, maybe at Frigidaire or as a plumber. He was pushing a sleeve up in a probably unconscious signal that nobody messed with his family. His wife had slipped an arm around Pauline. I held one palm out in an effort to diffuse their ire.

"Look, she seems like a nice girl. I think she may have gotten dragged into something she didn't realize was serious. Somebody she trusted may have used her."

"What are you talking about?"

"There's a good chance Pauline could end up in worse trouble than she's in right now. I may be able to stop that from happening — but only if I get some answers. Starting with that car with the bunged up fender out back."

"What does Bud's car have to do with anything?"

Pauline spoke for the first time since her parents had joined us. She looked completely confused. Maybe my theory wasn't as sound as I thought, but something was going on here. I waited for someone to say something that would nudge me in a better direction. They didn't.

"Who's Bud?" I asked.

"Our son," said Pauline's father. "Her older brother."

Was I going to end up helping one of their children only to harm another?

"I need to talk to him too."

"You can't."

"Why not?" I hoped they wouldn't tell me he was dead. In jail or an excuse with holes enough for me to take a picture through would be better.

"He's in Canada. Was, anyway. We got a letter yesterday saying they were shipping out to England."

"He's on an air crew." Pauline's pride overcame her anger at my presence.

"Maybe... maybe we should sit down," her mother suggested. "Is that alright, honey? It doesn't sound like this woman's come to hound you. Maybe there's been some sort of misunderstanding."

Pauline resisted briefly, then nodded and took the nearest seat she could find, the end of the couch. Her mother sat next to her on the arm. She nodded with strained politeness toward a chair across from them.

"You too, Miss."

"Maggie," I said. "Maggie Sullivan."

Pauline's father stood protectively behind the two women. His arms were crossed.

"When did your son leave home?"

"Two months ago. He got tired of sitting and waiting for Washington to declare war, so he went up north and enlisted."

"Who else drives the car?"

"Nobody. None of the rest of us knows how. At first we were lending it to his cousin — just until Bud came back — but the idiot didn't have it a week before he smashed the front fender. That did it. Nobody touches that car until Bud gets back."

"When did your nephew bring it back?"

His tongue traced the inside of his cheek in thought.

"Been a month at least. Maybe more. Why?"

"Daddy, I - I drove it once. After."

"What?"

Pauline flinched at his thunderous tone. Even her mother's face gave a small tic. Her arm crept around the girl's shoulder.

"Bud had been teaching me how. To drive, I mean. He'd let me take the wheel a bunch of times. Not downtown or anything; we were being real careful. He was teaching me the rules, too, so I could get my license, only — only then he went off to Canada..."

"Pauline Veronica Meadows, what have you *done*?"

Her swollen eyes began to leak tears.

"Nothing bad, honest! But one day last week I was so awfully busy at work. They had two of us typing away on a report about some big project a group of them have been racing around like ants over since I started there. I'd hurried so on the last two pages, afraid I'd miss my bus, that on the way home I started worrying I might have missed a line or a word."

She swallowed.

"I'd done that once before, left a word out. The men — they add things up above sometimes, or in the margin with an arrow. And another time I messed up a footnote. Mr. Collingswood's so strict about that. I was worried I might lose my job if I made another mistake. So that night, after you'd gone to bed, I-I slipped out to the shed and took Bud's car, and drove to work to check.

"I went really slow, Daddy, and there's not much traffic at night. I know I should have told you, but I was afraid you wouldn't let me. I'm sorry."

He exhaled, accompanied by a sound in his throat. It was one I'd heard my own father make. It meant they wanted to shake you over your foolishness, but wouldn't.

"So that's where they got that fool idea about her taking something," he said in relief. "Somebody, the watchman, I guess, saw her sneaking in at night—"

"I didn't sneak!"

"It's not unusual for the secretaries there to go in at night to work," I soothed. "But I'm starting to think somebody may have used that fact to make Pauline a scapegoat."

That was a long way from saying the girl was completely innocent. The fact her brother's car had followed me had yet to be explained. I was, however, prepared to believe she honestly might not know how the page of calculations had come to be in her desk.

"Was anyone else at the building that night?" I asked.

Pauline dabbed at her eyes with a fresh hanky. I wondered how many she'd already gone through that morning.

"Mother, could I have some tea? With lots of sugar?"

The expression she wore as she turned to her mother was a plea for more than tea.

"Of course, honey. Miss Sullivan? No? You come too, Dad. You can get back to fixing that piece of linoleum."

When the two of us were alone, I looked pointedly at Pauline, awaiting her answer.

"There's a woman who comes in to clean. I didn't know about her. She scared me to death.

"Then when I got into my car — Bud's car — to leave and I turned on the headlights, I saw Mr. Scott in the parking lot. He was talking to somebody."

TWENTY-SIX

Pauline pressed her hanky tightly between her palms. "Is this going to help me?"

"Yes, I think so," I said slowly.

Would Frank Scott try to implicate a typist in the disappearance of valuable documents unless he was behind it himself? But why would he be, when he himself stood to make a pretty penny from the very deal that disappearance was thwarting?

"What about the mistake you thought you might have made?" I asked as Mrs. Meadows appeared with tea for her daughter. Did you get it corrected?"

She broke into a smile.

"I hadn't made one after all. Everything was exactly right. Thanks, Mother. I know I look a mess, but I'm not feeling nearly so weepy."

Her mother patted her shoulder, gave me a nod, and left.

Unfortunately, Pauline's after-hours trip to the building, on top of the page from her desk compounded her appearance of guilt. Her swollen eyes and the smile of pride that had flashed over the correctness of her work suggested a different story.

"Tell me about the person Mr. Scott was taking to. Was it a man or a woman?"

"I couldn't see. They were in a car. The other person, I mean. I'd come in and out the front, which is what the girls all say you should do because there's a light there. This car was parked at the side door. I'd... forgotten to turn my lights on until I'd backed up — it's different driving at night than it is in the daytime, isn't it? So when I did — turn the lights on — all at once the other car was there. Not close, though, which was lucky. Mr. Scott turned around and I saw it was him, but I don't know who it was he was with."

I remembered how dark it was at the side door. Handy for running in to retrieve something from your desk, I supposed. But likewise a good choice if you didn't want to be seen.

"Was it someone dropping Mr. Scott off, do you think?"

Her forehead wrinkled in thought.

"I don't think so. I'm pretty sure I saw another car farther back. I didn't really notice, though. It all happened in a second or two, it seemed. Turning my lights on, and Mr. Scott straightening up and looking around."

"He was leaning into the car?"

"Like when you talk to someone. The driver. That's the side he was standing on."

It wasn't the smartest spot for a clandestine meeting, right in your own back yard.

"Then what?"

"Then I came home. I was already headed back to the street by then, and really concentrating and I honestly can't even remember driving home. I was just so glad when I got here."

I had to smile at her woebegone sound.

"Driving gets easier. Don't give up on it."

I sat forward, resting my arms on my knees.

"Look, I don't care a bit how you answer this next thing. I won't tell. How did you get into the building? I know they lock up at night."

She was drinking some tea. A hum of pleased importance escaped her. She glanced around and lowered her voice.

"The girls who work there have two keys they pass around. Promise you won't tell. I don't want to get them in trouble. Mrs. Hawes has a key that we're supposed to sign for if we know we'll need to come in, but she makes you go through a whole rigamarole, especially if the girl needing it happened to get on her bad side that day. Sometimes she makes a girl come back two or three times because she claims she's busy and can't be interrupted. Then you have to sign for it, and sign it in again the next morning.

"I guess maybe it's a good idea, but it's mostly to show she's more important than we are, and we'd better stay in her good graces. Anyway, before I started there, one of the girls got the idea she could use the key she'd checked out to get one made. So she did, and then somebody else did the same thing. Whoever used it last gives it to somebody else to take care of. It just happened it was my turn to have it."

Her animation faded. She gave a great sigh.

"And I thought, 'Boy am I lucky!'"

***

If someone wasn't setting Pauline up, I'd eat my best hat. The handsome technician she'd spurned came to mind, but there were other possibilities. Anyone who'd seen her driving it, either that night at C&S or when her brother was teaching her, would have found it an easy matter to 'borrow' the car from the shed in back.

Someone other than Pauline had used it to follow me. A man had been driving when it almost rear-ended me. Same when it had parked across from my office. Had the car been insurance in case I spotted whoever had tailed me, or a deliberate attempt to throw me off track? Either way, the page which had turned up in her desk now seemed too convenient. It also suggested I was getting closer than someone liked.

Setting the brown car aside for the moment, I now had two leads to follow. There was Scott's possibly shady meeting in the parking lot, and then there was the newly closed lamp shop. I weighed both options as I drove. The meeting might have nothing to do with the problems at C&S Signals. Maybe Scott was stepping out with a married woman. The lamp shop, on the other hand, was in the area where Tremain had vanished.

After I'd hung up my hat at the office I ran upstairs to powder my nose. When I came back I stuck my unsharpened pencil in the telephone dial and spun the number for Tabby Warren. The rich men I'd had dealings with got up and out early, making more deals and more money. Rich women, I'd discovered, were far more likely to simply enjoy their creature comforts. Catching them in the interval when they'd been awake long enough to take calls but before they headed out to lunch was an art form.

A cheerful male voice answered at Tabby Warren's place on the first ring.

"This is Maggie Sullivan. I wonder if I might speak to Miss Warren for a few minutes. It's about a building she owns, or used to own, on West Fifth."

"Just a moment," the voice said, still cheerful.

When was the last time I'd heard a butler sound merry? Did Tabby Warren have a husband, or maybe a boyfriend? The address for her in the phone book was upper-crust enough to match what Seamus had told me about her fortune. It was hard to imagine its occupants not having household staff.

"This is Tabby Warren." A new voice interrupted my speculations, this one a light but firm contralto. "I understand you're interested in my Fifth Street gaud. I'm afraid it's not for sale."

"I'm not interested in buying it, lovely as it is. I need to reach the man who used to operate the lamp shop there."

"Used to? Good heavens. I bought several lamps there. It's the only place in town to get something that's not stultifyingly virtuous."

"Do you happen to know how to reach him?"

"Mr. Benning? I'm afraid not. A real estate firm takes care of the property." She paused. "May I ask what this is about?"

I took a breath.

"I'm a private detective."

Some people hung up at this point. Others started to blather that they didn't know anything.

"How delicious," said Tabby Warren. "I presume the real estate firm is being discreet and won't give you information?"

"I don't know how to reach the real estate firm. The sign that says the place is for rent doesn't have a name or a phone number."

For about four seconds she was silent.

"That's hardly the way to run a business, I'd say." On the surface she was as pleasant as ever. Only the direction of her questions showed new caution. "How, if I may ask, did you know I owned the building? I haven't had anything to do with it directly for years."

"A policeman friend who raided it when it was a speakeasy remembered you owned it."

Delighted laughter bubbled over the line.

"Someone remembered that? Do tell me who."

"I'd rather not."

"If you want information from me, I think you'd better. No, wait. It wasn't that lovely Constable Hanlon, was it?"

I hesitated, reasoning that since she'd guessed, there was no harm in it.

"It's Sergeant Hanlon now, but yes."

"Very well, then. I don't know who looks after the building, but I'll give my business manager a call. I should have the particulars by the time you get here. Shall we say half an hour?"

She hung up.

TWENTY-SEVEN

Tabby Warren's domicile was too small to qualify as a mansion and several steps too fine to be a house. It appeared to be the offspring of hanky-panky between a Tudor and a Swiss chalet. It was three stories high with a curve of wide brick sidewalk. Across part of the front, beams formed two arms of an asymmetrical triangle that showcased sets of narrow, leaded windows. One arm of the triangle continued down to merge with the covered part of a porch at the entryway.

I was pretty sure the result was tasteful as well as attractive. It was hard to decide with part of my brain still recovering from the full-steam speed of my first conversation with the house's owner.

"Miss Sullivan?" beamed the man with the cheerful phone voice as he opened the door.

I'd never seen a butler smile before. This one wore a tuxedo outfit rather than tails. It went well with his fringe of black hair.

"Miss Warren's in the library," he said, relieving me of my coat and leading the way across a small entryway.

I had just time enough to take in carpeting that resembled leopard skin on stairs leading up on the right. We did a U-turn in the other direction to the open doorway of a room that overlooked the front lawn.

"Miss Sullivan is here."

A woman was already unwinding herself from one of two couches facing each other in a room lined with books. She came toward me with hand outstretched.

"It's so nice to meet you. I believe I've read about you in the papers. Do call me Tabby."

Her silky bronze trouser ensemble was more or less what I'd expected. The long rope of misshapen pearls knotted at her breast came as no surprise. But where I had expected reserved sophistication, I felt myself engulfed instead by a full-tilt zest for life, not to mention a very firm handshake. She moved with the litheness of a girl and the confidence of a woman her actual age, which was somewhere in the first half of her forties.

"I was terribly naughty last night, so I'm just breakfasting. Won't you join me for toast? Coffee?" She indicated a tray on the table between the couches. "Mr. Goode will be glad to bring tea."

"Just coffee, please. Black."

"That's all, then, Mr. Goode."

She swept an invitation to sit as she filled another cup with coffee and handed it to me. The walls around us were painted buff, which made the room seem airy and sun filled. Leopard print fabric reminiscent of the carpeting I'd seen on the stairs covered the couches. The morning paper and a pair of reading glasses lay discarded next to the breakfast tray.

"Hiya, Toots," rasped a new voice.

"Jasper, be quiet," scolded my hostess.

Looking around I saw a green parrot on a perch in the corner.

"I had no idea the wretched creatures lived so long when I got him," said Tabby Warren.

Resuming her seat, she tucked her feet under her.

"I'm sure you're keen to have the real estate agent's name and number." She waved a square of notepaper which she set aside. "First though, you absolutely must tell me about Sgt. Hanlon. Please don't say he's lost all his marvelous hair and is bald as an egg."

I laughed.

"His hair's all intact, although it's silvery white now."

Her own was auburn with threads of white here and there. It curled with an exuberance no perm could achieve. The fullness made a good frame for her triangular face.

"No doubt it makes him more attractive than ever." A white cat slid from the top of the couch behind her and placed a paw on her hand. She broke off a morsel of toast and let the cat lick it. "I was quite taken with him when we knew each other. I don't believe it was reciprocated."

The cat, having licked the toast, ate it out of her fingers and leaned against her, purring hopefully. I tackled terrain I wasn't equipped to traverse.

"He might have recognized the difference in your situations, you with money, him a patrolman walking a beat. He was also much older than you."

"Ah, the missed opportunities." Behind her lightness, she'd been assessing me as closely as I was her. "I suppose he's married? Grandchildren?"

"Neither. And for what it's worth, he didn't know that I would contact you, or even that I was interested in your building. I drove past because I was thinking about it. I was thunderstruck when he started reminiscing."

"Well. Tell him hello." Retrieving the folded notepaper, she slid it to me. "It occurred to me this real estate man you want to talk to might see you more promptly if I were to call him. Men have a nasty way of trying to put women off, don't you think?"

She was right on both counts.

"I'd appreciate it."

"Did you have a time in mind?"

"Two o'clock? Whenever he can manage, but the sooner the better."

"Should I tell him you're a detective? Or shall I simply say you're interested in seeing the building?"

"Just that I'm interested in seeing the building, if you don't mind. I may tell him the truth once I've gotten a feel for him."

Her forethought surprised me. As if reading it, she gave a pleased smile.

"I used to do a bit of detecting myself when I was your age. I don't believe Sgt. Hanlon knew that about me." She rose. "Help yourself to more coffee, and see Mo doesn't lick the butter off my toast. She's not entirely trustworthy."

The cat seemed disinclined to bother the toast, but as soon as Tabby Warren vanished into the hall to use the phone, it came across and hopped up for a closer look at me. I stroked behind its ears, which we both enjoyed. Meanwhile, I studied the mantle over the fireplace, or more accurately, I studied the photographs on it. No children. A woman in glasses. Two men appeared in various shots with Tabby Warren, though never together. In one of them, she and one of the men were doing some dance from the 20s and laughing.

"That was in the building you're going to see," she said returning. "It's called The Pompeii, by the way."

"The building or the speakeasy?"

She smiled. Her Cupid's bow mouth redeemed a somewhat narrow chin.

"Both, actually. I suppose at the time we thought it smart to be nihilistic.

"Two o'clock. Mr. Thompson says it's already rented, so I can't fault him for dragging his toes, despite the deficiencies of the sign you saw. I suggested to him it might be smart to have someone in the wings in case the new renter's check didn't clear, or they backed out. He agreed."

This time she didn't tuck her feet up when she returned to the couch. Instead, she clasped her hands around her crossed knees, one foot swinging. Her manner had grown more thoughtful.

"Has my building been used for some sort of criminal activity?"

"Not to my knowledge. I've been hired to find a man who went missing. He was last seen in its vicinity. It occurred about the same time the lamp shop hung its

CLOSED sign out, which happened abruptly. That's probably just a coincidence, but I'd like to talk to the man who ran the place, or some of his employees, anyway."

She was looking into the distance. A cuff-like gold bracelet at least three inches wide circled one of her wrists. I suspected it hadn't come from McCrory's.

"I'm rather fond of that little building. I care about it a great deal, in fact. It holds... memories. I should hate to have its reputation blackened."

It was hard not to grin in view of the building's past. Something else from the past had kept flirting with me. Now I gave in.

"Speakeasies had a secret way in, didn't they?"

She laughed.

"Out was more useful. Long gone in this case, I'm afraid. Bricked over. I think they use the second floor, where the speakeasy was, for repairs now; the lamp shop, that is."

"And the third floor?"

"Storage, I would guess. Do let me know if you sense anything amiss," she said as I rose. "Keep me posted in any case, won't you? My life these days is dreadfully boring. And tell Sgt. Hanlon I'd adore it if he'd stop by. I promise not to break even the teensiest law."

TWENTY-EIGHT

All the way downtown I entertained the small suspicion I might have been bamboozled. Was Tabby Warren simply a charmer unlike any I'd ever met? Or was she up to something and hiding it beneath her eagerness to help and her chatter about Seamus? She was clearly used to calling the shots, yet I somehow wasn't ready yet to call her spoiled.

A parrot.

Unbelievable.

Maybe I was nursing a grudge because Seamus had waxed on about her so. His comment that she was a lot like me rankled more than ever now that I'd met her. I had nothing in common with Tabby Warren, except maybe a firm handshake. Still, she was making it possible for me to take a step forward. Or she'd appeared to.

I went to Culp's Cafeteria and had a bowl of soup and some pie to placate my belly. At five til two I presented myself at the real estate office.

Judging by the number of file cabinets and the folders stacked in wire baskets on several desks, the place was on the up-and-up. A secretary typed placidly at one of the desks while a man paced back and forth beside her, tugging his tie. When I introduced myself another man, a sturdy fellow with a fixed smile, hurried forward to greet me and tell me his name was Thompson.

"Boss parking the car, is he?" he asked cheerfully.

"Boss?"

"Well, I sort of assumed that's who you were setting up the appointment for. Guess it's your husband, huh? Either way, you gals save us men a ton of time handling things like that." He winked.

"I don't have a boss. Or a husband. It's just little ole me."

I winked. And matched his smile.

"Uh..." The smile faded. "You mean it's you who wants to see the place on Fifth? Who wants to rent it?"

"I'd have to see it before I decided that." I trilled a laugh so silly I practically gagged on it.

"Well, uh, like I told Miss Warren, who I guess you know somehow, the building's already rented—"

"And she assured me you'd be glad to let me look at it anyway. She said things sometimes go wrong at the very last minute. In fact..." I saw an opportunity to squeeze out more information. "...she thought it unlikely you'd managed to get an actual lease drawn up and signed in such a short time."

"Well, yes. The papers won't get signed until Monday or Tuesday. They've made a deposit, though, so it's a binding agreement. Frankly, honey, you'd probably just be wasting your time going over there, and we've got one or two other places that might interest you."

"Oh, I don't mind wasting time. Not a bit. And like they say, Preparation oils the hinges in case Opportunity knocks."

"Sure. Okay. Let me grab my hat."

"Oh, and information on how to get in touch with the last man who leased it. I want to ask about, ah, noise and such. And trash pickup."

He blinked.

"Trash. Uh, sure." Going to one of the desks, he opened a drawer. He took out a folder, ripped a sheet from a desk pad and wrote. "I think he already left, though. For Arizona or wherever it was he was headed. Yeah, it is Arizona. Bad lungs." He thumped his own chest. "Only address he gave there is a post office box, for sending him monies he's owed for deposits and that."

I looked at the paper he gave me and tucked it into my breast pocket. He put on a gray fedora and we set out. I sort of liked the line I'd made up about hinges and opportunity.

***

"What kind of place are you thinking of starting? Dress shop? Hair salon? Books?"

Thompson unlocked the middle front door at the former lamp shop.

"A detective agency."

I'd anticipated the question, and on the ride from his real estate office had concluded there might be advantages to telling the truth about what I did. His mouth opened and closed a couple of times. He stared at the card I extended.

"You need someplace this big, do you?"

"Another firm has approached me with a very enticing merger offer. Multiple detectives, office staff and that." Clem Stark hadn't exactly proposed a merger, and his offer was anything but enticing, but it made good fodder for my fabrication. "Of course we'd sublet the ground floor, probably to a secretarial service that wants to expand." I was starting to fall for my own make-believe.

"You sure you want to see this place? The party who's already spoken for it put down three months' rent, so chances it'll become available are just about zero."

There was the barest hint of nervousness about his reluctance. Not the level he'd be wrestling with if he had Gil Tremain locked in one of the closets, or even knew anything about him. It was the sort of nervousness that went with cutting corners. Of taking money under the table, maybe.

"We've got two other listings that would be dandy for what you're talking about," he said eagerly. "Plenty of space, but smaller, so you wouldn't have the headache of sub-leasing."

"Maybe Monday. I just have the feeling this one might work out."

"Okay. Up to you."

He launched into his real estate spiel, ticking off how old the place was and pointing out features as he squired me around the ground floor with its maze of lamps. I got an up-close gander at the frolicking nymph. Her nipples were nicely defined. I wondered whether there'd ever been lamp with a frolicking satyr. Somehow I doubted it.

"Gee, the health trouble that made the man who had this place decide to close must have been awfully bad for him to just walk out and leave all this," I said.

"I guess. I have to say, though, he didn't look nearly as bad as I'd expected when he came in to sign the paperwork that had to be signed. Maybe he was wheezing more, but then he was always wheezing. At least he wasn't making snide comments and expecting everyone to jump when he snapped his fingers the way he usually did. He was downright chipper." Thompson chuckled. "I guess coming into money must do that to a fellow."

One of the insurance men in the neighboring building had said something about a small bequest, so the stories matched.

"Maybe it was having the weight of running a business off his shoulders," I said sympathetically.

"Say, now, I never thought of that. I guess you've learned a lot about human nature in your line of work."

I smiled and looked and listened, I wasn't sure for what. The muffled sound of a man bound and gagged in a closet? A matchbook or a conveniently dropped business card from C&S Signals that would indicate Gil Tremain had been here?

The building had two staircases, a public one at the front of the building and service stairs at the back that led into the alley. It stood more or less on a corner. On one side the brick walkway separated it from buildings across the way, including the one where Steve Lapinski had his accounting office. On the other side of The Pompeii, but only half its height, squatted the box-like structure of the insurance company.

A three-foot gap between the two buildings was bridged by gates front and back. They hid trash cans, and probably weeds in season. The Pompeii's unused coal bin, which I insisted on peeking into, greeted the real estate agent's flashlight beam with a billowing curtain of cobwebs. No one had been in there since long before Gil Tremain had gone missing.

Inside again, we toured the top two floors. The middle one had been the speakeasy. One end wall was elaborately carved and fitted with shelves to hold glasses and bottles for the long bar in front of it. Now it held lamps and shades awaiting repairs. Work tables, cabinets, and a few wooden crates of merchandise coming or going filled the center of the room where patrons once had danced and knocked back illegal booze, and Seamus and my dad along with other cops had charged up the stairs to make arrests.

I chattered questions about square footage and Thompson answered. I asked about utilities and insurance. He said he could have figures for me on Monday. All the time, I was making my way carefully around the room, trying to shake off thoughts of what this place must have been like in its heyday, trying not to miss anything in the present. Finally we climbed the stairs to the top floor.

Once it had been home to three apartments. Now their bathtubs and basins sat darkened by years of disuse. One apartment was empty, the thick coat of dust on its floor marred only by my own footprints as I went in to look in closets. Another served as storage space for new lamps and empty cartons. The third apartment was saddest of all. Stacked there, sometimes three tall, were dozens of small tables, and chairs whose velvet seats had succumbed to moths and sunlight.

Unpalatable as it was to admit a trail that I had thought promising led to a dead end, maybe it was time for me to do just that. I followed Thompson back downstairs weighted down by the sense my attempt to find some connection between this place and Gil Tremain amounted to one very wild goose chase.

Then I saw it.

Caught in a piece of molding next to the stairs to the ground floor was a single strand of yarn dyed bright, unnatural blue.

TWENTY-NINE

"Now you know I can't give you the name of the party who put money down to rent the place," Thompson chided. "Our customers expect their business to stay private, just like yours do."

Riding back to the real estate office, I'd found it hard to think about anything but the strand of blue yarn. It had to be from the muffler Eve Tremain had knitted her father. He might not be tucked away in the former lamp shop as I'd half hoped, but that strand of blue was strong evidence that he'd been there. If I could worm out the identity of the person who had rented the place with such alacrity, I could start to look for a connection.

"Oh, well." I laughed. "I thought I'd give it the old college try." Maybe the problem was I'd never been to college.

"What about Monday?" pressed Thompson. We were standing outside his real estate office and he could probably tell I didn't intend to come in. "Why don't you pick a time to look at those other two places? There's one in particular I think you'd like."

"I'll have to check my schedule. Oh, hey, I almost forgot." Diving into my purse, I brought out the envelope with Gil Tremain's photograph. "The reason I noticed your building — saw the FOR RENT sign — was that I was down there hunting this guy. Any chance you've seen him around?"

He leaned in and looked at the picture long enough to make me think he was really considering.

"No, I don't think so. Uh, why are you hunting him?"

"Now you know I can't tell you," I said playfully. "But on top of everything else, we're kind of concerned he might have a communicable disease."

Thompson bent for a closer look.

"Communicable disease, huh? So... I guess if I do see anybody who looks like him, I better call you."

***

The strand of blue yarn renewed my optimism that the sudden closing of the lamp shop connected some way to the disappearance of Gil Tremain. I hadn't been able to get the name of the building's new renter, but along with an Arizona post office box, Thompson had coughed up the local address for the previous occupant.

"I'm afraid Mr. Benning moved out the end of last week," said the landlady when I inquired.

"Oh no! I finally, finally found some information he wanted about a relative! Do you know where I could write him?"

She studied me cautiously. The house where Benning had lived was in a good neighborhood, with two apartments that must be good-sized upstairs and her apparently occupying the entire downstairs.

"You say you're a friend?"

"Well, actually I just knew him from his shop. We got to talking names one day and he said he had a cousin with the craziest name you ever heard. When he said what it was I said, 'I have a girlfriend who knew somebody named that up in Cleveland!' He got all excited and said it had to be the same person, and they'd lost touch in the twenties and was there any chance my girlfriend knew how to reach him. And now that I finally have it, he's gone."

She nodded acceptance.

"You'd better step in while I get it. It's just that two men came here day before yesterday claiming to be his friends and asking about him, and I didn't like their looks. Not that they weren't dressed very nicely. I just couldn't help feeling they were up to something. One kept looking around while the other one talked to me."

She excused herself and returned with the same address I'd gotten from Thompson. No, she didn't have a phone number for him. No, she didn't know of any friends who might. She couldn't recall Mr. Benning ever mentioning friends, or having visitors except for those two men.

"He always seemed a little too refined for his own good, if you know what I mean. Like he came from money, or thought he should, and the rest of us didn't quite measure up. Until he decided to go west. *That* certainly made him unbend. The day he left, he practically skipped down those stairs with his suitcases."

My nostrils caught a tiny, tiny whiff of something worth following. I looked at the stairs.

"He carried his suitcases down himself? They told me down at his place of business that he'd been awfully ill before he left."

Her lips blew a dismissive sound.

"He had a touch of asthma, and winter before last he caught pneumonia. But aside from that, he seemed healthy as a horse."

***

Two people now had made comments which led me to wonder if Nicholas Benning's sudden illness had been one of convenience. I found a spot to park at St. Elizabeth's and hurried in to the hospital.

"Excuse me," I said brightly as the woman at the front desk looked up. "A friend of my dad's was admitted last week. Dad asked me to stop in and say hi if he was still here. His name's Benning, Nicholas Benning."

She looked dutifully through the open pages of the register in front of her.

"I don't see anyone by that name. When did you say he came in?"

"Last week. Monday, maybe? Dad was here Friday."

Flipping through several back pages, she shook her head.

"Are you sure it was last week? I've checked admissions and discharges both."

"Oh, gee. I wonder if Dad got mixed up. He does sometimes. Well, thanks. I'm sorry to bother you."

I drove to the community hospital, Miami Valley. Repeating the same routine got the same results. The hospital had a pay phone in the lobby. Frank Scott still didn't answer at his place. I thought a minute. Since I couldn't get his account of his nighttime meeting in the parking lot last week, it might be interesting to see how his partner reacted.

***

"Miss Collingswood's upstairs. I'll tell her you're here," the housekeeper said as she let me in.

I started to correct her, but decency stopped me long enough to realize it might be wise to talk to Lucille first. Although Nicholas Benning's attack of ill health might be fabrication, I'd seen first-hand how recent worries were whittling away at the heart condition of the man who had hired me. The information I'd come to share with him might prove disastrous.

As the housekeeper's ankles vanished at the top of the stairs, a spurt of angry voices from the sitting room down the hall reached my ears. One voice, I thought, belonged to Frank Scott. I wandered closer to the partially open door to make sure.

"What do you mean you haven't cancelled the meeting?"

"We can wait until Monday. Gil may have turned up by then."

"How? That detective you hired hasn't come up with one thing!"

"It takes time, Frank."

"We don't *have* time!"

Hearing myself mentioned seemed like permission to join them. As I slipped through the door, I saw Lucille was there too. Just the top of her head showed over the back of a wing chair. Collingswood sat with his fists on his knees. Scott was pacing. None of them noticed me.

"Stop being a fool, Loren. The last thing you need is more stress from playing this down to the wire in some crazy belief Gil's going to turn up. You've been popping those heart pills like they're peppermints. It's time to step away from this and save what's left of your health.

"I'll call California on Monday and cancel the meeting. I'll tell them — I don't know what. Something that spares the company egg on its face. Then, Loren, we need to talk about my buying you out. You need to start taking things easy. Enjoying life."

"I started that company!"

"*We* started that company."

The housekeeper's timorous knock interrupted.

"Oh, Miss Lucille! I didn't know where you'd gotten to. I didn't mean for her—"

Those present had noticed me now.

"It's... all right. We were expecting Miss Sullivan," Collingswood managed. Spots of color tinted his otherwise pale cheeks, but he didn't look shaky now. He just looked angry. Not at me though.

All three were too intent on their own set-to to ask what I wanted. Standing seemed a good option. Scott lighted a cigarette.

"Lucille's worried about you," he resumed as the housekeeper left. "She said you're already thinking of selling."

"Lucille!" The censure in Collingswood's voice was unmistakable.

"You've been talking about it, Father."

"Yes, but how dare you! How dare you presume to speak for me?"

"How dare *you* tell a man I could have been happy with that he couldn't marry me?" Lucille sprang to her feet. "Go ahead and kill yourself, then! See if I care. I'm twenty-nine years old and I've spent my whole life doing what you wanted — being your little hostess, nursing you and worrying every time you landed in the hospital. And you? All you've ever cared about or felt the least scrap of affection for is that damned business!"

"Lucille—"

"Well, no more! I've had it. First thing Monday, as soon as the station opens, I'm buying a ticket and catching the train to New York!" She burst into tears.

Her father was too stricken to speak. Scott, too, seemed caught off guard.

"I hate to intrude on this little discussion," I said, "but I've got a date. Contrary to what Mr. Scott thinks, I've managed to learn a few things. I could move faster if I found out a few more, starting with the name of the man you had the late-night chat with outside your office last week and what you were chatting about."

Surprise swept Scott's face as I looked at him, awaiting an answer. He snorted derisively.

"Ike Wiggins."

"Wiggins!" his partner exclaimed. "He came to see you again?"

"Apparently he thought me worth another pass."

"The nerve of him!"

"Who's Ike Wiggins?" I asked.

Lucille was regaining control of herself. She looked as puzzled as I was.

"He owns a rival engineering company," Scott said. "Here in town. It's about the size of ours."

"Several weeks ago, he approached us each individually. He... he offered each of us money," added Collingswood.

"Money."

"For... for letting him see a copy of our calculations."

"Giving it to him, you mean."

Collingswood nodded.

"I told Frank about it, and he said the unprincipled scoundrel had been to see him as well."

"And neither of you saw fit to mention this to me?" I dug my nails into my palms to control my temper.

"We... I..."

"Were afraid he might have made Gil Tremain the same offer?"

"Gil would have turned him down just like we did!"

"You can't know that," Scott said through his teeth.

"If you want me to keep on working for you," I said, "I strongly suggest you give me an address for Wiggins."

THIRTY

When the afternoon was young, I'd envisioned getting back to Mrs. Z's in time for a bath and leisurely primping, and relaxing with my feet up for a while before Connelly came to take me to dinner. By the time I'd started my hospital visits, I'd given up on the relaxing part. Now, heading for the address of the man Pauline had seen Frank Scott talking to in the parking lot, I worried Connelly might show up at Mrs. Z's before I did.

Before I passed a phone booth, I spotted a dumpy hotel. Pulling to the curb, I ran in and called Connelly's place to let him know I'd be delayed an hour. No one answered. I called Mrs. Z's. Esther, who'd been dating someone lately, picked the receiver up on the first ring.

"You must be going out," I said. The phone was on a little table across from the foot of the stairs.

Esther laughed. "As a matter of fact, I am. I just put my coat on."

"Do me a favor. Officer Connelly's coming to meet me, and I'm running late. If Genevieve's going to be around, ask her to tell him. If she's going out, ask Mrs. Z."

Assured I'd done all I could in that department, I hopped back into my DeSoto to drop in on Ike Wiggins, who from what I'd heard, qualified as a snake in the grass.

Wiggins lived in a nice brick house where a middle-aged woman getting her money's worth from her corset opened the door.

"Whatever you're selling, we don't want any," she snapped.

I stiff-armed the door as she started to close it.

"I'm not selling anything. I'm here to see Mr. Wiggins. I'm doing some work for C&S Signals."

Her nice wool dress and the wisp of a hat in her hand suggested she was the missus. A cat with rumpled fur looked happier than she did. The woman looked me up and down.

"You don't look like a floozie, and if you are you're welcome to him. With that cast on he smells like a billy goat, and has just about the same disposition. He's in there." She gestured.

"Oh, dear. How long has he been in a cast?"

"Too long," she said darkly. Standing in front of a hall mirror nearly as tall as she was, she jammed her hat on her head. "Doreen!"

A woman in a starched white apron appeared from somewhere at the rear of the house.

"I'm going to my sister's so I can have some pleasant conversation with my dinner. If Mr. Wiggins doesn't want to sit at the table, take him a tray in his study. If you and Jules are ready to leave before he wants to go up to bed, put a pillow and quilt on the sofa and he can sleep there."

"Ellen!" bellowed a voice from a room on the right. "Get back in here and tune this radio properly. I'm getting more static than program!"

As if she hadn't heard, his wife went out and closed the door.

"Miss? May I help?" the woman in the apron asked timidly.

"I'm on my way to see Mr. Wiggins, thanks. Mrs. Wiggins and I were just having a chat. How long has the poor man been in a cast?"

"Two weeks tomorrow. If you want anything, he's got a bell to ring, though he may have thrown it at something."

I thanked her and a few seconds later stepped through the doorway indicated by Wiggins' departing wife. A man with sloping shoulders sat in a wheelchair that held one of his legs out before him. It was encased, thigh to toe, in a plaster cast. If he'd had it on two weeks, he wasn't the one who had met Frank Scott the night Pauline saw them. At any rate, he hadn't driven there.

His back was toward me. He was struggling to reach the dials of a large console radio next to a lounge chair. He couldn't manage because the cast sticking out in front of him and the wheels of his chair kept hitting the cabinet. Loathe to startle him since he was leaning halfway out of his seat, I cleared my throat.

"You took your own sweet time about coming."

"It's not your wife, Mr. Wiggins."

Collapsing back, he spun the chair around.

"Who are you? What do you want?"

"My name's Maggie Sullivan." I sat down, the better to be eye-to-eye with him. "And I want to know what you discussed with Frank Scott at your moonlight rendezvous in his office parking lot last week."

Wiggins' top lip bunched and he stared.

"What are you talking about? I haven't been out of the house since I broke my leg tripping over that worthless, yappy mutt of my wife's."

As he spoke, he reached for a cushion behind him — to adjust it, I thought. Instead, he heaved it toward the door I'd just come through. I looked around in time to see a pint-sized pooch with bulging eyes take off down the hall.

"Now give me that." Wiggins stabbed a finger toward the cushion.

I picked it up and handed it to him.

"I haven't seen Scott since a month ago."

"When you tried to bribe him."

He cocked his head, looking wary now, but not particularly worried.

"I wouldn't call it a bribe. I offered him a road to profit. What business is it of yours, anyway?"

"I'm a detective." He didn't need to know what kind. "Who else at C&S did you offer a road to profit?"

"Hey, what's this about? I haven't done anything wrong."

"You also tried to bribe Loren Collingswood."

"I already told you, it wasn't— Okay, he might have misinterpreted. The man acts like he's got a poker hanging out of his backside. Gave a spiel about loyalty and integrity."

"And Scott?"

"Scott laughed in my face. Said he stood to make a lot more than whatever I could offer. In the way of, uh, profits, that is. From better marketing. That's all I was trying to interest them in. They're both owners, they got a right to sell whatever they want, don't they?"

"Who did you try to make headway with at C&S who wasn't an owner?"

His upper lip bunched again. A mannerism of his that said I'd lost him.

"What? Nobody."

"What about Gil Tremain?"

Wiggins shook his head slowly.

"Sounds kind of familiar. What's this about, anyway? If C&S are claiming I did something wrong, they better think twice. My word's as good as theirs."

"It's about an employee of theirs. The engineer who made the breakthrough on the project you tried to get your hands on." I decided to gamble. "A project of considerable interest to the War Department."

He snorted.

"No, it ain't. That project of theirs wouldn't do a thing to keep planes in the air, but to some outfit wanting to mix pictures with sound, or make sound better than it is on that piece of junk radio there, it's worth a bundle."

The cushion sailed past me again. I heard a snarl and bark, but the dog already had vanished. Getting up, I retrieved the cushion and tossed it to Wiggins. He wasn't exactly overcome with gratitude.

"I don't know what your game is, girlie, but you can tell Collingswood it's not going to work. I'm like this with my councilman." He held up two crossed fingers. "If he or Scott tries spreading tales about me, I'll sue them for slander. Now fix my radio on your way out."

I walked to the console, smiled at Wiggins, and yanked the plug from the wall.

THIRTY-ONE

As if I weren't already late enough, my gas gauge was dancing with Empty. I pulled into a station. Handing the attendant a buck, I told him to skip the oil check and window wash, just put in five gallons.

While I drummed my fingers on the steering wheel, I thought about the two men who'd turned up to see Benning's landlady. Her description of them fit what Lapinski, the blue-eyed accountant, had told me about the pair who sometime earlier had called on Benning at his place of business. I was more inclined to believe that now. There were probably several kingpins in town who ran illegal gambling operations and wouldn't take kindly to those who didn't pay debts. I only knew of one, a man named Nico. I didn't know his last name, I'd only met him once, and I had no desire to repeat that experience.

The attendant closed up my gas tank. I waved thanks and drove on. When I got to Mrs. Z's, I dashed up the steps still entertaining a small hope I might have gotten there ahead of Connelly.

It evaporated the minute I came through the door. He stood at the foot of the stairs chatting with Mrs. Z. I stared, slack-jawed with disbelief. At shoulder level Connelly's upturned palm provided a perch for Mrs. Z's cat, who lay there docilely, legs dangling. The vicious, sneaky wad of fur was even purring.

"Ah, here she is now." Connelly turned with a smile. A lock of brick brown hair curled onto his forehead.

The cat looked at me and hissed.

"There, there, puss. Maggie looks meaner than she actually is."

Swinging the cat down, he gave its ears a parting rub as he passed it to Mrs. Z. Eyes twinkling, he watched me try not to glower at the cat in front of my landlady.

"Butterball was a naughty boy," she said fondly. "When I opened the door, he shot right past my feet. Officer Connelly was kind enough to scoop him up for me. I do believe Butterball's taken a shine to you, Officer Connelly."

"I have a way with cats." Connelly's eyes met mine. His lips twitched.

Mrs. Z disappeared back into her apartment.

"Sure you haven't been telling fibs about that pussy cat?" he grinned when the door had closed. "It seemed friendly as all get-out to me."

"Yeah? Well, maybe I should show you where it sunk its teeth into my ankle last night. Or maybe you should talk to Jolene and some of the others."

I unbuttoned my coat. My intended apology for being late had evaporated.

"I won't be long. Just let me freshen up and pour more peroxide over the bite marks."

Connelly looked as if he might choke as I started upstairs. Gripping the newel post, he leaned around to call after me.

"Jaysus, Maggie! Tell me that's not how you really care for a wound!"

I ignored him.

***

I skipped the hydrogen peroxide part, but after I'd washed my face and combed my hair, I did slap a fresh bandage over the teeth marks. They weren't as bad as some the cat had given me. I shed my suit in favor of the new red dress I'd splurged on for the holidays and put on fresh lipstick. My brain was overloaded from trying to figure out where Gil Tremain was and why. I wasn't going to think about it tonight. Although I wasn't about to puff up Connelly's fine opinion of himself by acknowledging it, I was looking forward to the evening.

"Don't you look a treat," he said when I came back down. Popping remnants of something white into his mouth, he brushed the crumbs from his lips with a fingertip. "Lovely divinity, Mrs. Z. I don't know when I've tasted better."

Mrs. Z beamed. While I was upstairs, she'd come into the hall again, bearing a plate. This time the cat was nowhere in sight.

"Never have cared much for divinity," Connelly confided as we crossed the porch and stepped into an evening whose damp air hovered just above freezing. "Nor any sort of candy other than fudge, come to that. Why women feel some need to churn it out at Christmastime like it's part of setting up the crèche is beyond me. But talking of that, what should St. Nick bring you?"

"Somebody's in a good mood," I said.

There was always a spring in his step, but tonight it was even more pronounced.

"Someone better be, the mood you looked to be in when you stomped upstairs. But yeah. Had a letter from Ma and the kids. That's better than finding an extra ten in my pay."

"And don't think I haven't noticed that you never answered my question."

I tossed him my car keys.

"You driving or not?"

Connelly didn't own a car, but at least half the time when we set off somewhere, he drove. He claimed to like sitting behind the wheel of something that wasn't a cop car. For me it was a treat to be a passenger.

We decided on a place that served fried chicken, which we both liked. It was something of an indulgence, but Christmas was a time for indulgence as well as for charity. Over whiskey for him and a martini for me, he told me about the letter he'd had from Ireland. Though he always referred to "Ma and the kids", the youngest, his baby brother, was twenty-five now, the same age I'd been when I met Connelly. I knew he missed them, probably even more at this time of year, so I asked him about the little things they did to celebrate, the cooking and get-togethers and that. Talking about it allowed him to be there, at least in his mind.

When our dinners came, we ate in silence for a minute.

"Thanks, Maggie. For listening."

I nodded, embarrassed. To prevent the moment's becoming overly serious, I made a big show of looking around as if about to divulge the deepest of secrets.

"Has Seamus ever mentioned the law-breaking rich woman he was smitten with? It appears she reciprocated."

Connelly halted his efficient demolition of a drumstick.

"Are you talking about the Seamus I know? White-haired gent? Bad knee? Doesn't say half a dozen words unless you pry them out with a crowbar?"

"That's the one."

A grin crawled over his face and he sat back.

"Even you couldn't make up a whopper like that. And no, I've never even heard him mention a woman, except for you, of course, or when he does something with Billy and Kate. I always supposed maybe he'd had a sweetheart when he was young back in Ireland, and that she'd died or married someone else after he came over. It happens often enough."

"Did it with you?"

The instant the question was out, I regretted it. Connelly shrugged, his gaze holding mine too intently for me to break free.

"There was a girl I thought mattered. A few months after I left, I realized she hadn't." He bit off some chicken. "You going to tell me how you came by this gem about Seamus, or are you sworn to secrecy?"

I laughed.

"Not formally, but it might be wise not to mention it. He was so caught up in the past, I doubt he realized he was chattering like a magpie. Shy as he is, I'd hate to see him razzed — which I know you wouldn't."

Connelly was as fond of Seamus as I was, though he'd known him but a fraction of the time.

"Spill all, then."

His eyes weren't as blue as Steve Lapinski's, but when they twinkled the way they did now, they took my breath away. And so, as we ate our chicken and mashed potatoes and carrots, I told him all about Seamus and Tabby Warren. Connelly's baritone chuckle rumbled under my narrative like an accompaniment.

Yet all the time we laughed and enjoyed ourselves, rustling at the edge of my mind like an intruder whose identity and intentions need to be determined, was the thought that I was missing something. Some stone I hadn't turned over. Some two-plus-two I hadn't added. Something that could mean the difference in finding Gil Tremain alive and finding him dead.

THIRTY-TWO

When the waitress brought our coffee, what had started as a pleasant evening began to deteriorate.

"Maggie, as delicate as your skin is, you're daft to be using peroxide on a cut," Connelly commenced.

"It's better than water. It foams a cut clean."

"And who told you that? Your Da, I suppose. Well, he might have been wrong about one or two things. It's way too strong. I'll bet your skin turns red as anything where you pour it."

I squirmed.

"It irritates, Maggie, and that's just begging for infection."

"You can be pretty irritating yourself, so quit harping. I'm not going to try dandelion fluff gathered during a waning moon and mixed with spit from a black cat." I had a hunch that when he could, Connelly used some of the old home remedies he'd grown up with.

"Who said anything about dandelions? Use water and mild soap. Then dab on salve or Unguentine. A puncture wound from an animal bite especially wants tender handling."

"Did I ask for advice? You're sounding like somebody's granny."

"You'd be better off having a granny. She might be able to talk some sense through your thick skull." Reaching across the table, he walked two fingertips up the back of my hand. "She might even be able to teach you how to get along with cats."

My mouth had gone dry. The magnetic tug where our bodies connected held me motionless. Reclaiming my hand, I reached for my coffee cup.

"I get along fine with cats that are normal. So drop it. That goes for the flirting too."

"My, my," he said mildly. "Apart from me, what's ruffling your feathers? Was it tangling with Freeze? Or is it because some private dick's trying to hire you? I understand bets have been made over whether you slug him or not."

My mouth dropped open. Too furious to speak, I snatched my napkin from my lap and threw it onto the table.

"Do you coppers sit around all day swapping gossip about me? Or does somebody pin a daily announcement about Maggie Sullivan on the bulletin board for everyone to snicker at going off shift?"

I started to rise. Connelly caught the same hand he'd teased a moment earlier, this time urging me down and restraining me. At a nearby table a young fellow with sideburns halfway to his chin was watching us with interest. Rather than entertain the entire restaurant, I sat.

"Maggie, calm down. The fellows like you. They get a kick out of how you hold your own with people. You say things to Freeze and the other brass that none of us would dare. And the talk's not entirely focused on you, for your information. There's a rumor Freeze may be looking at having to work with you if we go to war. Some think it would be fine entertainment watching him squirm. Me, I might feel sorrier for him than for you."

If I'd been speechless before, I was doubly so now.

"What are you talking about?" I managed at last.

"There's talk the department would be losing men to the draft. Detectives too. A door was ajar that shouldn't have been a week or two back. Someone heard your name mentioned in a meeting the chief was having with Freeze and somebody else, probably the division commander."

I shook my head.

"First I've heard about it."

"And why should you unless and until something's decided?"

I struggled to process what I'd just heard. The Selective Service sign-ups that had gone into effect a year ago didn't include women. But surely if Freeze was forced to have a woman under his wing, it would be one who was already a cop. One working under Lulu Sollers in the Women's Department.

"Any idea whether it's Freeze or Chief Wurstner behind this?"

"No idea. And it could all be rumor. It's pretty clear there's some kind of planning going on, though. These last six months, maybe more, there's been meeting after meeting among the command staff. So, yeah, there's been a bit of joshing about whether you'd be more likely to say okay to Freeze or this private fellow, who appears to be about as popular as a carbuncle."

If he was right about the scuttlebutt, it showed the same sort of looking ahead that Clem Stark was doing. Somehow that thought was odious.

A waitress had stopped and was offering to warm our coffee.

"If it cheers you any, Freeze thinks he comes away with the short straw as often as you do when you two butt heads," Connelly said when we were alone again. "Boike says Freeze thinks you're holding back something that could help with that woman who got shot to death a few days ago. I gather that's connected with a case of yours?"

"Boike, huh? I didn't realize the two of you were friends."

"We get on. He's not the one told me about the meetings and that, by the way."

I sighed. "Freeze gives me too much credit for knowing things. Never to my face, I might add. As to my supposed wealth of knowledge..."

I ticked it off on my fingers.

"Either or both of the men who own the company that hired me could be responsible for the disappearance of the man they hired me to find. Thus possibly behind the shooting in question.

"One of them might likewise be the target of efforts to give him a heart attack — possibly fatal — as part of the mix. Then there's his daughter, who nurses more than a couple of grievances and stands to inherit if anything happens to him. Nor can I overlook a young secretary who asked the missing man about equations and terms in papers she typed. A page from a missing project turned up in her desk yesterday and she got fired. I don't believe she's involved, but a car that followed me a couple of times is parked in back of her house."

"All of which Freeze knows about?"

"If he's at all competent, which to give the devil his due, Freeze is."

It occurred to me he might not know about Pauline's firing. The image of him spewing smoke while he browbeat the already miserable girl made me less than eager to remedy that.

"Look, Freeze turned his nose up at half a dozen leads I offered. Given what you've told me about all the meetings, and knowing the department's understaffed as it is, I guess I should cut him some slack on that. But what in the name of sense does the man think I'm holding back?"

"That I can't answer." Connelly searched his memory for a minute. "Apparently accusations were traded between him and the men investigating an abduction attempt yesterday. That's probably making him sore. And apparently he's peeved at not finding even a hint what your man who vanished meant to do with the thousand dollars he took from his bank account right beforehand."

By sheer force of will, I kept my breathing even.

"Well, I assure you I know absolutely nothing about that thousand dollars."

Including the fact the 'large withdrawal' Freeze had mentioned amounted to that much.

I frowned at my coffee cup with the intensity of a gypsy attempting to expand her reading skills beyond tea leaves. I didn't want Connelly to see the information had startled me. Freeze had told me Gil Tremain had made a "good-sized" withdrawal last Saturday, but it had never crossed my mind he was talking about that much money. He'd also said Tremain's bank account still contained a healthy balance. At the time, all I'd been interested in was whether Tremain had cleaned it out like someone about to skip town, or it showed a trail of regular payments that might suggest blackmail.

"There is something new I've come across, though," I said slowly. "Just this afternoon, in fact. Whether it's worth mentioning to Freeze, I don't know."

While Connelly listened intently, I outlined how Walt Benning had abruptly closed his long-time business and left town after two men known to encourage people to cough up money they owed came calling. I told about the same two men turning up later at the place he'd been living.

"And you think Tremain might have taken money out for something to do with this fellow? Because the building was the last place he was seen, and the bit of yarn proving he'd been there?"

"I don't know. He'd also talked about buying his daughter a flute."

"Not for that kind of money, unless it was gold plated."

"He'd proposed to his girlfriend, or was close to it. Maybe it was for a ring."

Connelly whistled skepticism at such a large outlay.

"The two men, though. They're likely candidates for the same ones who tried to snatch Tremain's daughter."

I shook my head.

"The ones who tied up Eve were street thugs. Not bottom of the barrel, but not fancy, either. The witness who told me about the ones who came to see Walt Benning intimated they work for a man somewhere near the top of the local crime ladder. I'm wondering if it's a man named Nico."

Connelly leaned back, staring.

"Jaysus, Maggie. Do you mean Nico Caras?" He picked up the check and rose in a single motion. "Let's talk outside."

THIRTY-THREE

That made two things I'd learned in the last five minutes. Gil Tremain had withdrawn a thousand bucks — more than I made in two years — from his bank account two days before he vanished, yet according to Freeze, the account had still enjoyed robust health. I'd also learned the full name of a man who, even before Connelly's reaction, I had known was a crime kingpin who, as nearly as I could tell, managed mostly to stay in the shadows. Not bad for an evening when I'd resolved to put work out of my mind. Maybe I should go on dates more often.

"Mind walking?" Connelly asked as we reached the sidewalk.

At heart he'd always be an Irish country lad. He missed walking. I shook my head.

"Matter of fact, I was hoping we'd look at the lights."

"We'll do that, then."

The temperature still hovered just above freezing. Damp from the river beaded moisture on parked cars and gave the air a rawness independent of the thermometer. It wasn't quite cold enough for our breath to make clouds, but little curtains of fog hovered in front of us when we spoke.

Drawing my hand through the crook of his arm Connelly held it in place. The closeness made conversation easier.

"Now then." His eyes pierced me with his don't-give-me-malarkey warning. "How do you come to even know the name Nico Caras?"

"I met him once."

"Where?"

"In a vacant lot north of the river. Not recently. It was several years back. I needed information."

I heard him swear under his breath.

"From what I've heard, *I* wouldn't want to meet the man! Not without half a dozen other cops backing me up."

"It probably wasn't the smartest thing I've ever done."

He spun to face me. A couple leaving a restaurant a block past the one we'd been in stepped around us.

"Smartest? You've taken more than your share of daft risks since I've known you, but that takes the prize for stupidest."

"Yeah, I know. He had two bodyguard in his car, and two goons in a car following." I skipped the part where one of the goons had patted me down, and had a swell time doing it. "After we'd had our chat and I'd driven far enough to hope I wasn't going to get a bullet in my head, I pulled over and thought I'd never stop shaking."

Connelly resettled my hand in the crook of his arm and we walked on. His mouth was grim.

"So what have you heard about Caras?" I asked after a time. 'What kind of rackets does he control? Numbers? Gambling?"

"Both."

"So the lamp shop owner who up and left town for his health could have left because he owed Nico money."

"In which case he might need to go pretty far to stay healthy," Connelly said drily.

"Arizona, according to the forwarding address he left."

"Which if he's half smart is phony."

Could Gil Tremain have owed the lamp shop owner money, I wondered? Could he have taken that thousand dollars to pay off a debt? Or help a man to whom he somehow had a connection?

"What about your man Tremain?" Connelly asked, his thoughts apparently traveling the same route. "He a gambler? Could he be the one Caras is hunting?"

"Not from everything I've learned so far. All he did was work and spend time with his daughter or his girlfriend."

I couldn't see a gangster like Caras dabbling in engineering developments and the prospect of making money on them. Since Connelly was the one who'd opened this door, I saw no harm in trying a few more questions.

"What about drugs? Caras mixed up in that?"

"Could be. Bear in mind, I'm only a beat cop. I get scraps, not a full plate like the detectives."

"Heroin?"

Connelly fell silent. He was starting to realize I had more than passing interest.

"Not much heroin here. Mostly snow. It's not like some cities."

For two years before coming here, he'd worked a beat in Boston. I figured he was comparing. His arm flexed, pinning my hand to his ribs.

"If you think either man we've been talking about could be mixed up in that, leave it be, *mavourneen*. That's an ugly world."

We were in the center of downtown now. On our left was the courthouse. Up ahead, Rike's department store blazed with lights. The marquee of the Victory Theater advertised its current bill. Hotels beckoned customers to dance and dine. Movie palaces, gin mills and dance halls offered enticements for Saturday evening.

And Gil Tremain was out there somewhere. Alive or dead. My job was to find him. His daughter trusted me.

"The thing is, Connelly, Freeze told me Tremain's bank account still had a hefty balance, even with that chunk out at the end. If Tremain was a gambler who didn't know when to stop, or if he was a dope fiend, it would be emptier, wouldn't it?"

He rubbed a hand across his chin. "You'd think."

"Should I pass it on to Freeze about muscle working for Caras sniffing around?"

"Yeah, I would. And I wouldn't let grass grow before I did. It's not likely to help with his homicide, but he'll know the right person to tell. Someone at Market House is bound to be interested. And who knows, if it makes him look good, he might view you more favorably next time you want something."

"I won't hold my breath."

He chuckled.

"Now then. The night is young. We've wasted enough breath on work. We're supposed to be having a good time. What shall we do? Movie? Dance? Have a drink somewhere?"

Crossing Second had brought us to the first window of Rike's department store. Mannequins depicted Mom and Dad beaming at son and daughter under the Christmas tree on Christmas morning. The kids were rapturous over a wee train running around its track, a little toy cookstove, and other delights. Grandma and Grandpa looked on in the background. Everyone was in robes and pajamas (for sale inside). They were cozy and happy.

It wasn't the kind of family I'd grown up in, or Lucille Collingwood, or Eve Tremain, but maybe all of us needed to believe in families like that. I paused, along with several couples and a family with sleepy children in tow, to take in the scene. The crisp peal of a Salvation Army handbell above a collection kettle silvered the air.

"Maybe a drink later, but right now, if it's all the same, what I'd rather do is just walk and look at things."

"Window shopping?"

I smiled at the teasing in his voice as we moved on.

True, the windows also displayed items for Christmas giving — jackets and new toasters; humidors and jewelry. But somewhere ahead or around the corner would be scenes with Santa, and one with a snowman. The windows showed a world free of thugs and blood-soaked rugs and shattered families. I loved the once-a-year familiarity. The hope. The peacefulness.

"Mostly I just want to look at decorations and smell the air and pretend I'm a normal person," I said.

Connelly spun to face me, gripping my shoulders.

"A normal person doesn't meet gangsters in vacant lots," he said fiercely. "A normal person doesn't get herself beaten up or duck bullets." The hardness of his face dissolved. "You wouldn't be half the woman you are if you were one, Maggie *mavourneen*."

His head bent so close to mine I could feel his breath on my face. Several moments crept by. Finally he turned my collar up and gave it a little tug and we set off again.

His hand rested gently at the base of my neck. It wasn't a courting claim like holding hands. It was intimate. There were people in the streets, coming out of picture shows, going into clubs, gazing in windows the same way we were. Yet there in the midst of it, the two of us were alone in the world.

THIRTY-FOUR

"Oh, Maggie, the Santa ornament's perfect!" Jolene said, admiring it in its box. "With the glass ball and the fancy wax ones and the paper chain, it's going to look like a real Christmas tree!"

It was Sunday afternoon. Jolene and I and three of the other girls were in the little downstairs guest parlor that was currently almost filled by the evergreen tree we'd just set up. The space wasn't much more than an alcove. By the time the other girls finished changing their clothes after church or Sunday dinner and came down to join us, we'd be bumping elbows every time we moved and laughing.

One of the girls who'd rushed up to change had the room at the top of the stairs. She also owned a radio. The faint sound of Sammy Kaye's Orchestra trickled down to add to the festive atmosphere. The plate of divinity Mrs. Z had made for us sat on a tea table just outside the arch that formed the entry to the parlor. Jolene already had pronounced it first-rate.

"Hey, I was almost right." She moved closer to me and lowered her voice. "It was one of the assistant managers, not a bartender, who used to work in that area you were asking about. Rich is his name. Anyway, he tended bar at a place called... Let me think. Fun? No. Revels! That was it, Revels. He said it's still there, or was six months ago, last time he stopped in."

Jolene could say a whole paragraph, maybe a whole page, without taking a breath.

"It's clean, and fairly respectable and Rich said any woman with one or two brains in her head would be okay going there by herself, except maybe late on Saturdays. I told him you had plenty in the brains department. The owner's named Barney and most of the time he tends bar.

Rich said if you tell him you're a friend of his — Rich's, I mean — he'd be as friendly as they came.

"The place is around the corner where Sixth would be if it went through there, Rich said. On some brick walkway that used to be a street but isn't now. One of the waitresses heard us talking and said that's called a 'close', but Rich didn't think so."

While Jolene chattered on, I ruminated over the thin sliver of help. By light of day, the things I'd learned from Connelly last night were causing my hopes of finding Gil Tremain alive to dwindle again. Two days ago, the attempt to make off with his daughter had fed logic telling me he was alive. Clearly they'd intended to use her as a lever to force him into giving them the information they wanted. A kid her age couldn't carry around a string of complicated calculations in her head.

That logic held up through the moment her would-be abductors fled without her. For all I knew, at that point, whoever was holding Tremain would have given up. For all I knew, Tremain had been dead since Friday. At what point did people willing to kill potential witnesses and snatch terrified kids cut their losses? At what point did a prisoner who refused to talk despite beatings and who-knew-what other pressures become a liability?

I'd found a strand of blue wool at The Pompeii. I knew it had come from Tremain's scarf. I knew he had been there. But I'd been over every inch of that building, and I hadn't seen him.

He *had* been there.

He wasn't there now.

He could have been removed, struggling, the very night I'd managed to thwart the attempt on his daughter. Or taken out unconscious and limp. Or taken out dead.

What was his connection to the man who had owned the lamp shop? To Nico Caras? Should I—

A scream from upstairs splintered the afternoon, a sound with fear and grief and anger all rolled into one. We rushed into the hall as the girl with the radio burst from her room. She seized the post at the top of the stairs and clung to it as if to keep herself upright.

"Come quick!" she screamed. "The announcer — the Japanese have bombed some place of ours! Some navy base in the Pacific!"

Time shattered and reassembled in kaleidoscope bits. Someone thought to fetch Mrs. Z. We were all crowded into one room, a dozen young women and our landlady, pressing together. My hand was on Mrs. Z's shoulder. She was gripping it to keep it from moving.

In New York, or maybe Washington, some newscaster relayed what the President had said, along with periodic bulletins. Planes attacking. American battleships sinking. Lives lost. Until the papers came out, the station we were listening to, part of NBC Red, was our only available source of news. In between bulletins the network went back to its regular programs while our nerves stretched with the waiting. We'd expected to slug it out with the Germans eventually, but attack had come from a totally different direction, without any declaration of war, and even as the Japanese envoy pretended to negotiate.

"Why hasn't FDR come on?" Esther's voice cracked. "Something's happened to him!"

"No. He's just busy." My words came out short because I, too, longed to hear him.

Our President's voice had coaxed us back up from the very pit of the Depression. It hadn't solved every problem, but banks had stabilized and factories had reopened. That voice had explained new programs and encouraged us in countless Fireside Chats. It was familiar. More than that, it reassured us.

For more than half an hour we stood or sat on the floor or on the bed and listened to the shards of information that cut in. One said Manilla had also been bombed, which wasn't true then but was later. Someone scooted the room's single chair around for Mrs. Z. Someone was sobbing. I heard the recitation of a rosary.

"I need to call home," Jolene said suddenly. "My brother..." She headed downstairs.

Her brother was a year older. He'd most likely put on a uniform. Her family lived on a farm less than twenty miles from here, but right now, to her, they probably seemed farther away than the distant speck of land whose fate had turned life as we knew it upside down.

Was my brother still alive? Fed up with lack of normal interaction and the corrosive silence that passed as our home life, Ger had run away when he was fourteen and we'd never heard from him. If he was alive, would he go off to war now? Did he have a family himself?

All at once I was gripped by the need to be with the people I was closest to. I slipped from the room, hungry for the faces and sounds of Finn's.

***

As I drove I could almost pick out which people knew and which didn't in those I passed. Some came out waving cheery good-byes from Sunday dinner at a relative's house. Others hurried along with elbows tucked, eager to find refuge.

In Finn's, voices were muted. Rose set a glass in front of a customer, then dabbed at her eyes when she'd turned away. Finn, passing her, gave her waist a squeeze in place of his usual guff. Seamus left his spot at the bar and came to meet me.

"You doing okay, girl?"

His hand rubbed up and down my shoulder. He hadn't reassured like that since I was a kid. I nodded.

"You?"

His snowy head bobbed.

"Guess I won't be putting in for my pension as soon as I'd planned. The younger ones will be wanted to fight, but the city'll still need coppers. I can manage a couple more years."

It was the first time all afternoon that I'd teared up. I drew a knuckle through the wetness.

"Let's get a table, shall we?" he said. "Billy and Kate are like to show up."

"Or Kate's already volunteering for something down at the parish hall and dragged Billy with her." My attempt at humor was shaky, but enough to make him smile.

Connelly stood talking to two of the regulars. His set of uilleann pipes, minus the chanter, still hung around his waist. He must have been practicing in the back room when news about the attack filtered in. Sliding his arm from the bellows strap and unbuckling the rest of the apparatus, he laid the instrument in a battered valise and came to join us.

"So it's finally come." He gave my hand a squeeze.

Rose, who knew our habits as well as she knew her own, appeared at the table. She set a fresh Guinness down before Connelly and one before me.

"We'll be okay," she said firmly. "We've got smart people in Washington. The ones that have argued for keeping our noses out will sing a different tune now."

She whizzed off as Seamus, having fetched his half-finished pint from the spot he'd vacated, rejoined us. Connelly looked older than he had last night. Strain tightened his features.

"You're worried your ma and the others will be wondering if you're safe, I guess."

He attempted a smile.

"It'll take a bit for them to get the word on this business. RTE signal doesn't reach out where they are." Meaning no radio. "I thought about sending a telegram, let them know I'm okay, but Ma might get scared and imagine the worst before she even opened it."

"He tried calling a cousin in town to ask him to go out to the farm, but the cable across the Atlantic was busy," Seamus put in.

Other people were drifting in after me. Wee Willie and his brood came through the door. Willie and his oldest, who was all of nine, were lugging their radio. Finn cleared a place behind the bar for them to plug it in. Maire, with kids trailing, made a beeline to sit beside me.

"Oh, Maggie! What if Willie has to go?" She caught my hand and held on so hard it hurt.

"With every nun that ever knew him saying he'd take first place for being a troublemaker? The devil wouldn't have him, let alone the army."

We both knew it was a lie, but it made her smile. She kept holding my hand, though. Their daughter, who was youngest, climbed into her lap. Willie joined us, and Maire let go of my hand to take his. We made stabs at conversation. Now and then news trickled in on the radio. We'd shot down some Japanese planes. There were fires. NBC said a report they'd been getting from a station in Hawaii had been cut off by a telephone operator who said the line was needed for emergency use.

I felt wrapped in layers and layers of gauze. Everything seemed distant. People. Voices. Even my own. Yet as I sat and listened and looked, something started to wear a pinhole through the cocoon encasing me. A man. At the bar.

"Maggie?" Connelly was frowning at me.

"That man at the bar, the one just right of the taps. Has he been in before?" I didn't ordinarily come to Finn's on a Sunday. Maybe there was a different crowd.

"Can't say I've ever seen him," Connelly said.

Maybe it was someone new in town, or passing through, someone in need of other people around this afternoon like the rest of us. Except...

Except I'd seen him somewhere.

He wasn't one of the thugs who'd tried to snatch Eve. Maybe I was only imagining a familiarity. Maybe I'd noticed him only because his tweed casual jacket didn't show signs of wear like others in Finn's. It was belted, and fit him so perfectly it had to be tailored. I'd bet a couple of nickels his cap was also top of the line. And his hair...

He had sideburns. That was it. Sideburns. Like the man in the restaurant last night.

I rose.

"Be right back," I murmured in response to Connelly's puzzled expression.

Behind the bar, running its length, a mirror taller than Finn's head gave anyone sitting there a view of the room. As I started forward, the man I was watching slid from his stool. He sauntered toward the door. I picked up my pace. So did he. As I drew within six feet of him, a man burst in from the street.

"If there's any cops in here, you better phone the station!" he shouted, wild eyed. "Them Gamewell call boxes are flashing like crazy!"

THIRTY-FIVE

When I heard Connelly swear under his breath, I realized he'd followed me. He rounded the bar with swiftness that bordered on running and snatched up the phone. By the time I looked back at the door to the street, the man in the dandified clothes had vanished.

I pushed outside and looked and saw a man's figure ducking into an alley. Torn between choices, I went back inside.

Connelly was already dropping the receiver into its cradle. He stuck two fingers in his mouth and gave a piercing whistle. His voice rang with sudden authority as everyone turned.

"Any cops in here — you're to suit up and get to the station immediately. Nothing's happened, but we're to patrol to make sure it doesn't. Cop or not, if you've got a car and can take lads home to change so they get there quicker, wait by the door."

This is how he sounded in Ireland, I thought. Giving directions that might make the difference between life and death.

"I'll take you and Seamus and a couple of others," I said.

Wee Willie had jumped up to drive. Seamus was heading toward us, his long stride marred on one side by the hitching of his bad knee. Connelly was shaking his head.

"No, you take Seamus and whoever else you can fit in. I'd best wait in case there are questions, or anyone looks to be dragging toes. I'll catch a ride with whoever's last out. And when you come back, take my chanter apart and put the reed up, eh?"

Seizing my shoulders, he planted a kiss on my forehead.

"We'll be all right, Maggie." He ducked his head to look into my eyes. "We'll be all right."

I wasn't sure if he was talking about the war, or safety here at home. In that still dazed moment, he might even have been talking about the two of us.

***

By the time I returned to Finn's, only a handful of customers remained. Wee Willie had collected family and radio. I went to the set of blackwood and ivory pipes Connelly had abandoned. Once they had belonged to my father. Smoothing my hand along the leather bag and the silken wood made me feel less alone.

In the back room, I set the valise containing the pipes on a table. I drew a breath to steady my hands. Carefully, carefully I drew off the cylinder covering the long, fragile reed at the top of the chanter. I eased the reed from its base and laid it in a nest of tissue paper in a box secured by a rubber band.

I seldom performed the delicate task. The concentration required for it had left me no room for thoughts. Now they engulfed me. The fellow with the sideburns, the snappy dresser, had been in the restaurant last night. He had turned up here. He was following me.

Where and when had I acquired him? Had he been waiting today when I came out of Mrs. Z's? Did he know where I lived? Had I put a houseful of innocent women at risk?

I couldn't answer. The fact he was following me, and that he wasn't either of the men I'd surprised in Eve Tremain's kitchen, was all my mind had strength left to grapple with.

"Closing's in half an hour," Rose murmured when I emerged from packing the pipes. "Stay and come up for a bite. It's a night for company."

I demurred, but Rose insisted until I gave in. When she and Finn had locked up, I followed them and two other regulars upstairs to their apartment. Rose cooked up potatoes with onions and bits of leftover bacon, but no one around the table ate very much. No one showed much appetite for the whiskey Finn poured for us, either. We talked more than we had downstairs. The men said the war would be over fast, now that the U.S. was in.

"Guess I'd better get that radio you've been wanting, though" Finn said reaching to pat his wife's hand. "We'll want to keep up with what's happening."

Eventually, I took my leave. I needed to walk. I needed to see my city and be reassured it was safe.

***

At first I walked without direction. The river still hugged the city the same as it had when the first settlers arrived. Lights blazed in The Engineer's Club. The fancy white confection that was Market House was also alight. Chief Wurstner and the city's entire police command would likely be working there all night.

I turned down Fourth toward the *Daily News.* A squad car pulled abreast of me.

"Miss Sullivan? That you?"

I couldn't see the cop inside, but I stepped over.

"Chief Wurstner's asking people to stay off the streets so we can keep an eye on things better."

"Okay. I'll get back to my car and head home."

But I didn't. Instead I turned into an alley. My .38 was in my coat pocket, wearing out the lining but handy if I needed it. I was only a block or so from The Pompeii where I'd found the strand of blue wool. Did I want to get my crochet out and pick the lock? Maybe there was something in the desk or files that Walt Benning had abandoned when he left town that would give me a clue to how he and Gil Tremain or someone else at C&S Signals tied together.

Stepping out on Temple, I spotted another cruiser approaching. Dayton police cars came in two patterns. The one that had stopped me was white on black. This one was black on white. They must be making rounds almost constantly, keeping an eye on the train station three blocks away. I ducked back quickly.

When I did, my ears caught a small clank of tin in the alley behind me. A garbage can. A stray cat jumping off a garbage can.

Or maybe not.

Cogs in my brain that the day's events had disrupted started to turn again. When I left Finn's, had I checked to make sure the stranger with sideburns who'd scooted the minute I noticed him hadn't followed me? I couldn't be certain. While I walked I'd had bursts of alertness during which I remembered to listen for footsteps behind me. But only bursts. Habits of self-preservation that had served me for years had been abandoned. Now I drew a breath and set about correcting my own sloppiness.

If some ordinary citizen had turned into the alley after me and stubbed his toe on a garbage can, his footsteps would continue. The alley was silent. If the sound had come from a foraging animal, in which case I had no need to worry, I'd find out soon enough.

I stepped to the mouth of the alley and made a big pretense of peeking out to see if the coast was clear. If I ran into a foot patrol, my plan would be spoiled, but I didn't. I headed east, and as soon as I came to a shop front spaced far enough from a streetlight to give the right reflection, I ducked into the doorway. A minute later, a man's shape emerged from the end of the alley.

He looked left and right, clearly wondering what had become of me. Wandering back out, I bent as if for a final look at merchandise in the shop window. Careful not to notice the man behind me, I moved on. My pace was unhurried. Just before reaching the corner, I limped once and took off my shoe. I didn't hear footsteps. If anyone was following me, they were making a better job of it now. I didn't look back.

With shoe in place again, I crossed the street. Only one car had passed me, an old bug-eyed thing whose engine wheezed. Up ahead was the alley for this block. I turned in, and immediately flattened myself against the wall.

Now there were footsteps all right, accelerating. My Smith & Wesson was out. The second I caught sight of someone turning in, I extended my foot and sent him sprawling.

It didn't last long. He was fast as a cat. In a single motion he pivoted back on his feet. But I was mad. My forearm slammed his windpipe, rendering him unable to breathe and driving the back of his head into a brick wall with force enough to daze him.

"Move and I'll keep shooting you until I run out of bullets," I said. "Spread your arms."

He shook his head to clear it and spit in my face. Somewhere he probably carried a weapon, but all I could tell was that it wasn't in his hand. My eyes were still adjusting. I kicked his legs apart.

"Well, well. If it isn't 'Burns." I could make out the caterpillars of hair crawling down his cheeks now. "Funny, you don't look much like a poet. Or maybe you do, with that Napoleon Bonaparte hairdo."

"What? What are you talking about? You crazy or something?"

Always a good impression to give. My free hand grabbed his belt and jerked it open. The move, on top of the blow to his head, was enough to confuse him long enough for me to shift my grip to the waist of his pants and spin him face-first to the wall.

"Keep those hands out, pal. Palms on the brick."

I relieved him of a nice semi-automatic.

"I don't like being followed. Who sent you?"

He sneered. "You'll find out, and you're going to be sorry you laid a finger on me."

An iceberg floated into my stomach. The words, the cockiness, the way he dressed gave me a good idea who had sent him.

I gave the back of his skull a tap to make sure he slept for a couple of hours.

THIRTY-SIX

I slid onto a stool at McCrory's wondering whether it might be the last time. The slicked up guy I'd tangled with in the alley last night, worked, I suspected, for Nico Caras. He might even be a relative, given how clumsy he was at trailing someone.

"You doing okay?" I asked Izzy as she set my tea down. Her eyes were red and she wasn't whizzing quite as fast as usual.

"What if they drop bombs on us while my boy's in school and I'm here?" she whispered. She moved on before I could answer.

"Planes can't fly that far. There won't be bombs," I said when she returned with my oatmeal.

She paused and blinked at the thought. Then she was gone, refilling coffee cups along the counter and taking an order. I didn't know whether what I'd told her was true. If it made her feel better, that was what mattered.

I unfolded the paper whose 72-point headline taught us the words PEARL HARBOR if we hadn't heard them before. I read until I couldn't bear to read any more. Wire photos showed the destruction. A map inside showed where the Hawaiian Islands were, and where the naval base was.

It was a relief to turn my thoughts to Nico Caras. If I was right about pretty boy Sideburns working for him, his interest in me had to be connected somehow to Gil Tremain. I wouldn't call Caras a gangster exactly. He probably hadn't dirtied his hands in years. He had the trappings and the manners of a gentleman. Gangsters worked for him. He was a crime boss.

Most of Caras' boys were considerably more competent — and dangerous — than the one who spit in my face last night. They would know where I lived. They would know where I ate. If they wanted to have a chat with me, they would turn up.

That strongly suggested the smartest thing I could do for Gil Tremain, as well as my own health, was find him and sort things out before they found me.

***

"Where is everyone?" I asked Mrs. Hawes, who sat solidly as ever behind her receptionist's desk. C&S Signals had never been noisy, but today the place was almost silent. No murmur of voices came from the work area. Only the pecking of a single typewriter filtered out.

"Mr. Collingswood and Mr. Scott decided people didn't need to come in today, that they could stay home with their families if they wanted. Lydia and I called everyone first thing this morning to tell them."

I looked in the direction of the pecking typewriter.

"A few did come in," she said, noticing. "Some of the young men, mostly. Better than sitting around doing nothing."

"I need to see Mr. Collingswood just for a minute. I promise not to stay long."

"He didn't come in. Mr. Scott's minding things. Would you like to see him?"

Even better, I thought. Nico Caras was only one of the things I had to discuss with Scott.

The receptionist picked up her phone. A moment later Scott met me at the door to his office. He had a stubble of beard which made him more attractive.

"There's coffee in the back room. Would you care for some?" He waved me toward a chair.

"No thanks."

"Rotten business losing those ships, all those lives."

He sank heavily into the chair behind his desk. His eyes drifted toward the sailboat picture on his wall.

"The shock of it didn't make Mr. Collingswood's health worse, I hope."

Scott gave a half laugh.

"If anything, it's put him back on his feet. It made him go sentimental, though — as it has a lot of people. Worried about their families. He wanted to stay with Lucille. She didn't take off for New York, in case you were wondering. Not that I supposed for a minute she would. But he thought our employees needed a day to recover, listen to news if they wanted, adjust to the idea we're now at war, or will be once Congress meets and makes it official."

"Why not just close for the day?"

"We both agreed someone should be here. We have valuable equipment, and data from research going on besides the project you know about. According to the grapevine — engineering grapevine, that is — the police were called out to patrol around factories and some of the research places last night. Protecting against sabotage.

"I volunteered to keep an eye on things. My health's fine, and if Gil comes strolling in, I want to be here to knock his teeth down his throat."

I was stunned.

"You still think Tremain disappeared voluntarily?"

"I wouldn't put it past him. As I told you in the beginning, he has a flair for the dramatic. Walk in at the eleventh hour, announce he's made some improvement on the project in time for the meeting, et cetera. Won't he be surprised to hear it's off until all the dust from Hawaii settles?"

He slammed a partly open desk drawer closed. Time to change course.

"I paid a visit to Ike Wiggins."

A flare of irritation faded as he gave a whoop.

"I'd hate to bet which of you ground your teeth more!"

"His leg's in a cast. He's worn it for more than two weeks. He's using a wheelchair."

Several seconds passed before he saw where I was headed.

"Ah. Your question Saturday about who I was talking to in the parking lot." He rubbed at his forehead. "What day was that again?"

I smiled without answering. He shrugged.

"Maybe I got the time frame wrong. These last six weeks I've been in and out quite a few nights seeing that blasted project to its completion. Maybe I got the week wrong."

Picking up the dice I'd noticed when I searched his office, he rocked them in his hand.

"There was a man who pulled in one night just as I was leaving. He wanted directions."

A fast fabrication to cover his lie? If so, he'd seen Pauline's car and taken steps to make her look untrustworthy.

Or it could be the truth. It was feasible.

He let the dice spill onto his desk and picked them up again. "He said he was from out of town and how did he get back to the highway? I pointed the way and explained it three times, but he still got part of it wrong when he repeated it back." Scott grimaced. "Other than that, Wiggins is the only one I recall talking with outside."

To Pauline, already nervous about driving home, pointing to give directions could have looked like an argument. I watched Scott thumb one of the dice over the top of a finger back into his palm.

"Are you a craps shooter, Mr. Scott?"

He laughed.

"You mean do I play against other people? No. I just enjoy the feel of the dice. How they fall is too random for my taste. I play poker every week or two. There's thought there. Analysis."

"What about Tremain? Did he ever go to one of those games?"

"Gil?" Scott snorted. "We couldn't even interest him in a friendly game at lunchtime."

"How about Walter Benning?"

The dice clicking back and forth in his hand missed a beat.

"Not a name I recognize. What's this about?"

"Tremain was seen going into a business he owned the day he vanished."

"You mean that tale that Daisy told... wait. Walter?"

"Yes."

He put the dice down, stacking one on the other, and blew through his fingertips.

"There's a man named Walt who plays most of the time. He shouldn't. I never caught his last name, though."

"Why did you say he shouldn't play?"

Scott leaned back.

"First off, he tries to bluff when he shouldn't. Makes risky bets sometimes when he's in the hole. A month or so back I was the last one leaving the game. Answering a call of nature. When I got to where I'd left my car, I noticed Walt across the street. We'd arrived the same time, so I knew it was his car.

"Two fellows had him by the arms and... it didn't look friendly. Walt was nodding his head. They slammed him back against his car. I wasn't sure what to do. I wasn't keen to stick my nose in to help someone I didn't know. They let him go about then, but one shoved his face close to Walt's. I wondered afterward if Walt owed money or something."

"What made you think that?"

He frowned in thought.

"I'm not sure, really. The way they moved. Swift. Smooth. The whole thing couldn't have taken a minute. And the car they left in — it was dark, and they'd parked away from the streetlight, but when it took off and light hit it, you could tell it was polished to the nth degree. A third man was driving."

It sounded like Nico's boys all right.

"Has Walt played poker since?"

"I think so... yes. Two weeks ago. I remember thinking he wasn't laying down chips as freely as usual. And he made it a point to leave with the group. I can't say whether he played last week. I didn't go, what with the uproar over Gil already starting. What on earth makes you think the two of them might have known each other?"

I stood up and smiled again.

"Just a hunch."

THIRTY-SEVEN

Loren Collingswood and his daughter were in the room where I'd last seen them arguing, only this time they had a card table set up next to the fireplace and were playing two-handed bridge.

"It's not the ideal way to play, but we enjoy it." Lucille patted her father's hand. He smiled in return.

"I'm afraid we haven't had a game in ages. Things like yesterday make you realize you ought to appreciate what you have. Frank offered to mind the shop today so I could stay home. The outfit that was flying in for the meeting called me here this morning and asked to postpone it, so that pressure's off for a bit. Have you brought news?"

"Dribs and drabs."

Shedding my coat so as not to overheat in the warm room, I leaned against the mantelpiece. They watched me expectantly.

"I'm curious. Is Mr. Tremain a bridge player?"

"We tried to interest him a few times, but he said it just didn't appeal to him."

"What about poker? Did that ever appeal to him?"

"Poker!" Collingswood seemed taken aback at the mere thought.

Lucille burst out laughing.

"He was too polite to say so to Father, but Gil thinks card games are a colossal waste of time. Poor Eve begged him to play Rook with her one day when it was raining. He didn't even last half a game."

"What about dice? Did they interest him?"

"You mean gambling with them? Trying to roll certain numbers? Good heavens no."

"These are very odd questions," frowned Collingswood. "What are you getting at?"

"I'm trying to find out how he might have known a man who owed money to loan sharks."

***

Nico Caras knew Walt Benning. Benning had played cards with Scott. Scott worked with Tremain. The problem, I reflected as I walked to my car, was the lack of a connection between Tremain and anyone else.

Tremain was at the center of things. Viewed from another angle, he was at one end of a chain. Maybe I should take a look at the other end. Maybe I should try to talk to Nico Caras.

Good sense and my knotted stomach told me that was a very bad idea. I told Good Sense to scram.

Getting in touch with Caras would be tricky, though. The only other time I'd had cause to try, I'd contacted someone who contacted someone who contacted who-knows-how-many other someones to set up a meeting. Today, with routines disrupted and people jittery, no telling how long it would take. Meanwhile, if Gil Tremain was still alive, and his disappearance had something to do with the high-stakes meeting that had now been canceled, he had now become more a liability than an asset.

That pest Good Sense tugged at my sleeve, reminding me there was one other place I hadn't checked for the link I needed to put my chain together: The bartender at the watering hole Jolene had told me about yesterday.

Keeping one eye peeled for a tag-along I drove to Fifth and found a parking space. The coffee shop I'd sat in the first day was open, but the newsy waitress wasn't there. The music store was closed. Ever alert to the possibilities of disaster, the insurance place was open. I passed The Pompeii and turned into the brick walkway. Down a bit, about where Sixth ought to be, I found Revels.

It was bigger than I'd expected, plain looking but clean. Behind the bar, a good-sized fellow with dark hair polished glasses. A single customer, who sat with his elbows propped on the bar, looked around at the sound of the door opening. It was blue-eyed Steve Lapinski. He recognized me.

"You didn't give me your phone number," he complained in wounded tones.

"You're better off."

The bartender listened with interest.

"Beer." I slid onto the neighboring stool. "The darkest you've got. Get him another of whatever he's drinking."

Lapinski debated and then nodded thanks. He knocked back the remnants of what appeared to be whiskey and soda.

"Are you Barney?"

"Except when the bill collector comes calling." The bartender flashed me a grin.

"A man who used to work here says you're okay. He thought you'd be willing to talk to me, let me know if you've seen someone I'm looking for."

I slid him one of my cards as he set down our drinks. Barney whistled.

"You tried to make time with a gumshoe, Lap? You're lucky she didn't feed you your hat."

Lapinski had read the card as it passed.

"You even lied about your name!"

"Mr. Lapinski has his charms." I figured I owed him that much.

"You must be a good detective to find any." Barney snapped his bar rag at the man beside me. "He's been coming in ever since I've been here, and I've never noticed 'em."

Men talk more freely when I get them joshing with me, and with each other. I let the two of them go on for a minute. When they began to run down, I brought out my picture of Gil Tremain and did my routine.

Barney held the photograph up in front of him and gave it thoughtful study.

"Nope. Haven't seen anyone looked like him come in. Only ones I recall other than regulars these last few weeks were a pair of fellows who came in a few times. They were older than the one you're looking for, or maybe just harder. I might not have noticed them except they always came in late, maybe half an hour before closing. That and they argued one night."

"About what?"

"Don't know. I heard one of them say they weren't getting paid enough."

The mention of two men had caught my attention. Thugs or gangsters? I'd encountered one pair; heard reports of the other.

"Suits?" I asked.

"No." The bartender made no bones about his curiosity. "Why?"

Lapinski had turned on one elbow to listen.

"Because," I said, "a pair who work for a man named Nico Caras may be hunting him too." I heard a sharply drawn breath. "Or they could be looking for Walter Benning, who ran the lamp shop around the corner. Those two wear suits, though."

I swiveled so I was looking directly at Lapinski.

"How does it happen you recognized the name Nico Caras?"

He shrugged.

"Like I told you, I also have an office north of the river. I grew up there. Nico and some other men used to hang out at a place over there, a little dump of a Greek joint on Herman just off Main. People gave them a wide margin. When I was in high school and thought I knew just about everything there was to know, my pop cautioned me to steer clear of the place – not to get within two blocks, he said."

"And did you? Steer clear?"

Lapinski chuckled and took a good swig of whiskey. By the sound of his words, he'd already had a couple before I came in.

"Yeah, mostly," he said. "Might've gone past once so I could brag I'd seen the place."

"The two who came in here." I swiveled back to face Barney. "What can you tell me about them?"

He folded his arms and leaned back against the counter under the shelves that held his bottles of liquor. Whether to aid his memory or because of his dearth of customers, he pulled himself a beer and sipped.

"Always came in late, an hour or so before closing. The first one would order two drinks. Then when the second one came–"

"They didn't come in together?"

"Nope. More like they were meeting. Anyway, the bigger one always came in first. Then his friend would turn up. Sometimes they'd talk for a while – like when they had the argument – other times it was only a couple of minutes. The one who came first would knock back his drink and then leave. The other one generally stuck around and took his time finishing."

Maybe just two pals meeting up after work, I thought. Except I couldn't think of anything close that would be running a night shift. Otterbein Press was a few blocks north, and farther still, in opposite directions, the two newspapers. This was awfully far for someone working at those places to stop for an after work drink.

"Any sort of factory or warehouse around here with people getting off work around that time?"

"None I can think of. You, Lap?"

Lapinski shook his head.

"Used to be a warehouse over toward Main, but it finally went under '38, '39. Been sitting vacant ever since."

"When was the last time they came in?"

Barney rubbed his chin.

"Saturday, must have been. This place was dead as a tomb last night. I closed early. "Say!" His fingers snapped. "One night the two of them had just started jawing when another guy joined them. He tore into both of them, and *he* had a suit on."

"Can you describe them? What did they look like?"

"Didn't really notice the one in the suit. As soon as he'd lambasted them he left, and the one who came first trotted out after him. The one in the suit was older than Lap here, I think. Can't remember him being a blond or a redhead, so his hair must have been dark."

"What about the other two?"

"One had a beak on him that looked like it might have been broken a time or two. The other one ..." The bartender made a face. "The other one was wearing the most God-awful blue muffler I've ever seen."

THIRTY-EIGHT

If Nico Caras had anyone looking for me today, they'd have an easier time spotting my car than they would me, I reasoned, so I walked. I walked with my eyes peeled for a tagalong, afoot or awheel, and for vacant buildings where a man who didn't want to be there could be stashed for a week.

Once Barney mentioned the blue scarf, I'd had no doubt the duo who'd been meeting in his pub were the same ones who'd tried to make off with Eve Tremain. Further questioning of the barman confirmed it. The one in the blue scarf had "bad teeth" he said. When I pressed him, he mentioned the gap, and the fact one eye tooth stopped halfway above its neighbors. Amazing how when you're being shot at, you miss such details.

The way I'd pieced things together, the two of them meeting but one of them leaving almost immediately indicated a shift change. One was coming and one was going and I'd bet my bottom dollar they were taking turns guarding Gil Tremain. The spot where they were rendezvousing suggested he couldn't be too far away. If not in The Pompeii, where Tremain or the thug now wearing his scarf had been, then where?

I worked my way several blocks south of where I'd left Barney and Steve Lapinski, back and forth and then along cross streets. Most places of business were open, though the ones in retail didn't look very busy. It surprised me to see how few places were vacant when only five or six years ago businesses big and small had been going under. The ones with FOR SALE or FOR RENT signs were small, save one in a building with other tenants. In all of them, a captive man who managed to yell or make some sort of noise would attract attention.

It occurred to me I should have thought to contact the real estate man and ask to see some of the other buildings he'd been so keen to show me. I passed a drugstore and noticed it had a soda counter. Maybe it would have a pay phone too. It did, but when I called the real estate office no one answered. I had a cup of coffee and mince pie to rest my feet, then set out again.

Ten minutes later I was on a stretch of Wayne where people got robbed and assaulted at night and drunks slept off their excesses during the day. The warehouse Barney had mentioned was just on the fringe. It was also farther than I could see anyone walking to meet and pass along information at Barney's place, especially anyone guarding a prisoner who shouldn't be left alone too long. For that reason I hadn't started there. Now I had no other possibilities.

I had my tweed suit on today, and serviceable shoes. Glad both could take dust and a scrape or two squeezing through tight places if they had to, I approached the front door of the two-story warehouse. It had a padlock. A sturdy one that I held little hope would yield to the coaxing of my crochet hook. In any case, I wasn't keen to stand there on a busy street in broad daylight while I tried. Looking to see if anyone apart from denizens of the area disinterested in legal niceties was taking note of me, I tootled around to the side of the building.

All the downstairs windows and most of those on the top had wood nailed over them, inside or out. Edging along the wall, I tested those that faced the weed-grown parking lot. None gave. The door to a loading bay had a bar welded across it as well as a padlock. I made my way around to the back. Pry marks on both doorframe and hinges at the door there attested to numerous attempts at entry. Some possibly had been successful, judging by the extra locks. If worse came to worse, I'd try to work my way through all of them.

On the last side, however, I spotted a boarded-up window held in place only by two loose nails at the top. Keeping flat to the wall, I got close enough to try it. The bottom edge pulled out a foot, maybe more. I wore a drab little gray beret, handy for when I didn't want to stand out. I found a piece of broken handle and eased my hat through the opening. Nobody shot at it. Going in blind was risky, but the way I saw it, I had no choice. Smith & Wesson in one hand, I hauled myself over the window ledge into the building.

The stench of the place made me gag. As I struggled for breath, a crouching shape sprang at me, lifting a club. I spun to the side with my .38 leveled.

"Don'tshootdon'tshoot!" a voice whined. The man with the club thrust his hands up, dropping it.

A second voice yelped and someone swayed up to a sitting position.

"Didn't mean you no harm," the man moaned. "Oh, please don't shoot!"

My eyes were getting used to the dim. My nose wasn't faring as well. The stink of unwashed bodies and human waste was overwhelming. I breathed through my mouth.

"It's one of those Japs! They've bombed here now," the voice from the floor wailed. A woman's voice, I was pretty sure. She clutched a blanket to her chin.

The man swayed. The woman did too. They were both drunk as skunks.

"I'm not a Jap," I said sharply. "And if you stop yelling and answer some questions, I won't tell the cops about you. Who else is in here?"

"Jis us 'n Frank, 'n Leon over there. Leon coughs blood, so best not go near him."

I made out other shapes now, one a few feet away, another in a distant corner. At least I supposed the shape in the corner was that of another wino like the two I was talking to. When I left home this morning, I hadn't anticipated breaking into a place floored in grime and curtained in cobwebs, or I might have dressed in something with room for a flashlight. The one I'd tucked into my waistband had gotten lost in my tumble over the windowsill, so for all I knew the shape in the corner could have been a gunny sack or just a shadow.

"Where are the stairs?"

The man pointed.

"Anyone up there?"

He shook his head.

How would he know?

"Did anybody come here with a man who didn't want to be here? One who was unconscious or tied up?"

Then man's jaw worked like he was repeating my words to get them up to his brain.

"No."

"You sleep here most of the time?"

He worked his chin again.

"Mostly. Me and her."

I sighed. Asking if anybody they didn't know had come here recently would be pointless. They probably wouldn't remember me five minutes after I left. I told the man to sit down, that I was just going upstairs.

Halfway up, a cobweb hit me full in the face, persuasive evidence no one had been up or down for a while. I continued anyway, only to find a great empty space not quite as wide as the downstairs. I went back down and made a circuit to make sure I hadn't missed anything. The duo I'd talked to, after a fashion, were sitting shoulder to shoulder and muttering to each other. I don't think they even noticed when I squeezed back out over the windowsill.

THIRTY-NINE

Fresh air had never smelled so good. I stood outside the warehouse and filled my lungs, then tried to bat away the cobwebs that clung to my face. For several minutes I fought them, pulling them from my hair, my skin, my collar only to have them attach themselves somewhere else. Finally I removed my beret and beat it against my skirt to shake dust out of both. When I'd given my jacket a good shaking, I used the nubby tweed to scrub my face. I'd be imagining sticky threads even after a bath.

The idea The Pompeii somehow held the key to finding Tremain came back to sting like the splinter lodged in my palm as a souvenir of my breaking and entering. I couldn't get the splinter out without tweezers, and I couldn't resist the urge to detour past The Pompeii, so I did. When I came within sight of it, my pace accelerated.

A workman bent over buckets and other equipment. He straightened and his arm went up. He was washing windows. I crossed the street.

"Getting the place spruced up for the new business going in, huh?" I said with my breeziest charm.

He halfway glanced at me.

"Yep."

"How you going to get the ones higher up? Not with that." I nodded at a small stepladder.

"Take most of a day just on these down here, with all those doors being glass too. Then there's polishing up the brass. Man who hired me said he uses an outfit with platforms who do the top ones."

"Who was that? Who hired you, I mean. Thompson, that real estate guy?"

He switched his rag for a squeegee and towel, giving me a good look over.

"You're mighty nosey. Man might give me more work. Mind your own business."

He turned his back to scrape and wipe, scrape and wipe. Impressed by my ability to cultivate small talk, I crossed the street again. Yesterday's shock had altered the way people walked. They moved resolutely, some with eyes on the sidewalk, some with shoulders thrown back. Relaxation wasn't in vogue today.

Suddenly a sensational emerald green hat caught my eye. Hoping I was right, I abandoned my intent to go a different direction and walked toward its owner. Yes. It was the woman from the music store.

"Excuse me," I said. "You work at the music store, don't you?"

She smiled politely.

"I'm afraid I only take care of the owner's mother. I'm her companion. They'll open at noon today, if that's what you're wondering."

"Actually, it's you I wanted to talk to," I said as she took a step to continue. "You stay with his mother full time? Get room and board in exchange?" That's how it usually worked for a companion.

"Yes."

"And you live upstairs? Facing the lamp shop?"

Curiosity overcame her growing frustration at the delay.

"You were in several days ago, weren't you? Asking Mr. Miller whether he'd seen someone, he said. Did someone break in at the lamp place? Was there a burglary?"

It caught me off balance.

"What makes you think that?"

Her cheeks grew pink.

"I'm sorry. It was a ridiculous question. I need to get back. Mrs. Miller gets cross if her dinner is late." She held up a small cloth shopping bag and started to move again.

"And her son will be wanting his Butterfinger."

My comment won me a wry smile.

"Look, I'm a detective. A man I'm hunting was last seen in front of the lamp shop. He's got a kid hoping he comes home for Christmas. Just spare me two minutes and tell me why you asked about a burglary."

"I just supposed..." She glanced around and indicated a pocket of space with a bench and an evergreen shrub between two buildings. If her employer happened past, he'd be less likely to see her. "I supposed you were someone who worked there—"

"You've never stopped in?"

"No. Mrs. Miller doesn't like to be alone. And her son doesn't get along—" She brushed a hand in dismissal. "Anyway. She wakes up at night and wants hot milk. By the time I've made it for her, I'm usually wide awake. Often I sit at the window until I feel drowsy. There's nothing to see. I just like... looking out."

Toward freedom, I thought. I felt sorry for her. Probably she was widowed with nothing to live on, or had taken care of parents who died, and therefore had no work experience except taking care of demanding old people.

"Really, I'm embarrassed I brought the whole thing up," she was saying. "It's just that the night before you came in, I was sitting there and I thought I saw just a pinprick of light. Bobbling around upstairs. I expect it was just a reflection of some sort, only..."

"Only?"

"Well, a few minutes later, one of the front doors opened. A man came out and jumped in a car that pulled over for him and took off. He had a sack in his hand."

It wasn't much, but it was something.

"And that was the only time you've seen anything?"

"Well, no. Last night ... who could sleep soundly? Except Mrs. Miller, whose only concern was that all the news coming in interfered with her programs. Sometimes I don't see a single car if it's one or two in the morning. Last night it seemed like police cars came past every ten minutes.

"Right after one of them, a man came walking along, looking over his shoulder as if he didn't want to be seen. He went up to the door by the corner, and someone inside let him right in. A few minutes later he came back out — or someone did. But surely it was just someone checking to make sure things were safe, don't you think? Since it's sitting there with no one around since the lamp shop closed."

***

The splinter in my hand stung like the devil. My stockings were in tatters. When I got into my car and caught a glimpse of myself in the rearview mirror, I discovered I'd had a cobweb dangling from one side of my hair the whole time I talked to the woman in the green hat. Time to retreat to my office and regroup.

When I'd washed up, I borrowed a pair of tweezers from a woman I was friendly with at the sock wholesaler down the hall.

"The President's going to speak after he meets with Congress," she said when I returned them. "Come listen with us if you like."

"Thanks. If I'm around I will."

Her mother-in-law, the other occupant of the office, looked poison at me. She would hold me personally responsible if the country went to war. She'd done her best to keep FDR from getting elected a third time.

With splinter now removed, I washed its entry site a second time. I took the gin bottle from the bottom drawer of my desk and poured half an inch in a glass. Standing over the pot in the corner that held a dead plant, I dribbled a fine stream over where the splinter had been. It wasn't peroxide. I drank the gin left in the glass so I wouldn't waste it.

Besides, I deserved a toast. Something was going on at The Pompeii. It had still been going on as late as last night.

Circling my desk a time or two, I picked up the phone, and the pencil I used for dialing.

"This is Maggie Sullivan. It's urgent that I speak to Miss Warren. There's a problem at her building."

Seconds later Tabby Warren came on.

"What's this about? I'm on my way to a Civilian Defense board meeting. Emergency session. What sort of problem?"

"When you asked me if The Pompeii was being used for illegal purposes, I said no. I think otherwise now. You told me an exit had been bricked over. Is there a space attached to it, or anywhere — *anywhere* else in the building a man could be hidden so well that I, and the real estate man who showed me around, could have walked right past him?"

Silence followed.

"Miss Warren—"

"Possibly. I don't see how."

"Where?"

"I'd have to show you."

"I can't wait. Just tell—"

"Impossible. And if you believe it's your missing man, and he's being held against his will, then trying to reach him in daytime puts his life at risk. Meet me at The Pompeii's back door at eleven tonight."

She hung up.

Mine was more of a slam.

I wasn't going to sit around all day waiting for answers. If Tabby Warren insisted on taking her sweet time about helping me, I'd have to try to force the hand of someone who might shed enough light for me to move on my own.

FORTY

Steve Lapinski's unwitting mention of where Nico Caras and his boys hung out had been just specific enough to let me find it. As I walked toward a dumpy café with red checkered curtains covering the lower half of the windows and Greek words painted above them, I found myself thinking of funerals. Mine in particular. I opened the door and was nearly flattened by the smell of garlic.

"Place isn't open."

A bruiser in a well-cut jacket with no need of shoulder padding stepped in front of me, crossing his arms. A few men sat drinking coffee and reading papers at the front of the place, and another pair halfway back.

"Looks open to me."

"Men only."

"I'm here to see Mr. Caras."

Before the name was out, the bruiser and another man seized my arms. This was the place I was hunting, all right. Caras sat with half a dozen other men at a table near the back of the restaurant.

"How about letting Pete be the one who pats me down?" I said as they jerked my arms out. "He keeps his mind on business instead of groping like a schoolboy on his first visit to a cathouse."

If the one who did the honors had entertained any such inclination, my mention of a name he recognized was enough to render him brisk and efficient. I'd had sufficient brains to leave my Smith & Wesson in the car before I came in. My hope was that I didn't lose any before I left.

My escorts all but lifted me off my feet as they marched me toward the back of the restaurant. It was four times as deep as it was wide. The man who had searched me had, as I'd intended, discovered one of my business cards. We stopped halfway back and he handed it to one of the men who sat there, who in turn hotfooted to Caras. Another man where we'd stopped had thrust his jacket back, ready to draw in an instant.

Caras waved the card away. He'd noted me from the moment I entered. I felt myself being assisted forward again. Caras sat behind an oblong table. Two men lounged on one side of him and three on the other. Except I knew they weren't really lounging. Nor was the one who stood one step behind him and to the right. He was the one who'd searched me the other time I'd met Caras, the one named Pete.

Caras was short and fleshy without being fat. Dipping a radish into a plate of tan goo, he popped it into his mouth as I was jerked to a stop before him.

"You're interrupting my breakfast."

He patted his mouth with a red checkered napkin. At this time of day, most people were starting lunch. I thought it wise not to mention that.

"I apologize. For that and for roughing your pretty boy up last night. It's a nasty habit of mine when a man I don't know follows me into and alley and won't tell me who he is or what he wants."

This time Caras tore a morsel from a loaf of bread and dipped it in the goo. He chewed in silence, staring at me without interest.

"I thought you said Curly's nephew lost her because some cop pulled up and gave her a ride," he said to someone behind me.

"That's how he told Curly it happened."

Caras grunted. His pinkie flicked, which apparently was an invitation to sit since a hand shoved me into a chair.

"Keep your hands where I can see 'em," the man who'd assisted me growled in my ear.

Obedient as a freshman who had finished her math test in Sister Matthew Elizabeth's class, I folded them on the table

"Where's Walter Benning, Miss Sullivan?" Caras selected an olive from a dish I hadn't noticed and chewed daintily.

"Your guess is as good as mine. All I've managed to get on him is a forwarding address, a post office box which is probably phony. I'm guessing you have that too. He didn't have friends unless you count an occasional chat with the owner of a music store across from his lamp shop, who bought Benning's story about coming into money from a relative and taking off for his health. I've also learned he played poker in one of your games, and lost enough that two of your boys paid him a visit not long before he took off.

"Now. How about you tell me about the other two goons I keep crossing paths with since I started hunting Benning. They're bargain basement compared with your boys. Are they after Benning too, or are they part of some beef with you? Or should I be asking what your interest is in C&S Signals, or maybe Gil Tremain?"

The man across from me had stopped chewing. Covering his mouth, he spit the olive pit into his palm and dropped it onto his plate. His eyes cut along the men to his left, then those to his right.

"Anybody know what she's talking about?"

Silence.

Pinkie lifted, Caras sipped coffee from a miniature china cup. He pushed the dish of olives toward me.

"Have one, Miss Sullivan."

A knot the size of a softball was lodged in my gut. Anything I swallowed would come right back up.

"It's a little early in the day for me, but thanks."

"These two men. Describe them."

"Muscle for hire. No suits, but not ragged either. Fully equipped with car and guns. Poor at tailing, though. They tried to snatch the kid of the man I'm hunting. That also didn't seem like your style."

I wasn't sure about that part, but when you're outnumbered a dozen to one, and you've been fool enough to put yourself in that situation voluntarily, flattery can't hurt.

"One's nondescript and currently nursing a sore arm, courtesy of my bullet. The other one's bigger, with a gap between his front teeth wide enough for another half tooth."

"Anyone?"

This time Caras didn't slice his men with his eyes. He waited with the confidence of one whose organization kept more up to date on the street than the cops did.

"The one with the gap sounds like a guy used to be around called Arnold," a voice behind me said. "Last I knew, he was doing a stretch for auto theft, though."

"Maybe he got sprung. See if anyone knows."

I listened to footsteps moving and stopping as men at the various tables were questioned. Caras broke off a morsel of bread and handed it to me.

"Dip this in and try it. You'll like it."

For the first time, I noticed Caras was the only one eating. The tan goo, whatever it was, had a tantalizing aroma. I dipped tentatively and managed to push it into my mouth. My taste buds fell in love, but my stomach warned not to send any more after it.

"Delicious," I said, and meant it.

"You never explained your interest in Benning."

"He doesn't interest me in the least. I've been hired to find a man who vanished around the same time Benning took off. He was last seen near Benning's lamp shop. I have cause to believe he'd been inside the building."

"That's why you went poking around there Saturday."

"Yes."

Comprehension hit me. That was when Sideburns had started following me. Caras had men watching the building. Benning must owe him a bundle. Either that, or Caras was sore that he'd managed to skip town.

"The man you're hunting," said Caras.

"Tremain."

"Tremain. How's he connected to Benning?"

"He's not, as far as I know. But one of the men he works for plays in a poker game your outfit runs. If you're willing to tell me whether Tremain ever sat in, or had any sort of dealings with you, it might help us both. You've probably never met him, but one of your men may have. I have a photograph. In my purse, in an envelope."

One of the men had my purse jammed up under his armpit. At a signal from Caras, he opened it as if it might have cooties on it and dug out the envelope.

Soft footsteps came up behind me.

"Arnold got out about two months ago. Place he used to live before he got sent away got torn down though. Might take a day or two to find out where he is now."

"Georgie, see it gets done."

One of the boys at the table jumped up and left. Another moved the plate to the side so Caras could spread the envelope's contents on the table before him.

"The one on the right's Tremain." I'd picked up two others before setting out.

"And the others?"

"One of the men he works for and Tremain's fiancée."

"Why are you looking for him? What's his importance?"

"He's an engineer. He was working on a project worth big money to his company. Some data from it disappeared the same time he did. I think maybe he hid it. I think someone snatched him and is trying to get it.

"Anything you could find out about dealings he might have had with your... associates, or with people who had dealings with you might help me. Added to what I've told you, it might help you find Benning."

"Tit for tat."

"Yes."

Caras' hands were crossed, one on top of the other, on the table. He rocked them in thought.

"Very well. I can tell you one thing."

He beckoned me closer. I leaned forward. His open palm struck my face with such force I would have been knocked from my chair if two of his henchmen hadn't pinned my shoulders back.

"I don't like women who don't know their place. You haven't been slapped around enough to learn yours. It's unattractive."

The hand that had hit me splayed across the photographs, dispelling any thought he might return them. His eyes held mine.

"Get out while you still can. If you ever come here again, you won't be that lucky."

FORTY-ONE

My cheek stung and one side of my lip would be the size of a Frankfurter by the time I got back downtown. I had a score to settle with Caras now, not that I ever expected to have a chance to do so, or, hopefully, be fool enough to try. All the nerve I'd expended walking into that café had gotten me absolutely nothing. It might even have made things worse if it brought any of Caras' lackeys sniffing around The Pompeii before I got in there tonight.

I gritted my teeth and mentally cursed Tabby Warren. The few words we'd exchanged on the phone confirmed there was some sort of hidey-hole in her building that I'd missed Saturday. Why couldn't the wretched woman simply have told me how to find it? Just because she'd found some socialite's missing earring or something of that magnitude twenty years ago didn't mean she was a detective, and it definitely didn't mean she belonged where she might encounter men who would knock her teeth out — or worse. I needed to get in without her. If the window washer had finished, I'd take my chances going in now, tap walls again, keep my eyes peeled for something I'd missed.

But when I approached The Pompeii, the window washer still was plying his squeegee. He also was casting sulky looks at two painters who were deftly refreshing the building's bright colors. A single look sufficed to tell me they weren't the pair I'd met in Eve Tremain's kitchen. Their movements marked them as experienced at the work they were doing. Nonetheless, I began to wonder whether all of them had been put into place to make certain no one unwanted got inside.

I was starving and, I realized, somewhat shaky. The latter might have something to do with my recent encounter with Caras, though. Making sure neither his emissaries nor anyone else was tagging along, I went to the Arcade. I got a fresh ham sandwich and an orangeade and a couple of apple fritters and sat on a bench to think.

The window washer had been in place before I talked to Tabby Warren. Maybe he and the painters all had been hired by the real estate firm to spruce the building up for new occupants.

Or maybe they'd been hired by whoever gave Walt Benning a wad of cash to skip out on his business along with debts that could get his kneecaps broken.

"I hoped I might run into you here." Matt Jenkins, my photographer pal from the *Daily News*, dropped onto the bench beside me. "Holy Hannah, how'd you get that fat lip?"

My hand rose involuntarily to the souvenir of Nico Caras.

"Being polite."

"Hah." He repositioned the camera equipment around his neck and let out a breath as though weary. "I stopped by your office a couple of times. You doing okay?"

"Yeah. How about you and Ione?"

His wife wrote stories for magazines from Cincinnati to New York and Chicago. The three of us had spent a lot of evenings together. Jenkins scrubbed his fringe of red-gold curls and fought a yawn.

"I kind of hated leaving her alone. I went in when I heard the news last night and haven't been home since. She wasn't herself when I left. Quiet and wandering around the apartment. I think she's worrying I'll have to put on a uniform, which I guess I will. I don't mind. Newsroom's crazy today, wire machines ringing almost constantly."

"Want an apple fritter?"

"Thanks."

Our very conversation sounded different. Hollow. The bombs that had fallen last night in Hawaii had reshaped everything.

"Did you know they have their own newspaper?" Jenkins asked. He sounded positively besotted.

"The wire services?"

"The Army. *Stars and Stripes*."

I glanced over. His eyes were shining.

"Got to go." He hopped up. "Thanks for the donut."

He loped off to take pictures.

I got back to detecting.

***

Killing time was a skill that eluded me. I bought a copy of the afternoon edition and sat at my desk reading items which had been updated since I read the same paper at breakfast. I called to check on Seamus and hear his familiar voice, but a stranger answered his phone.

"They have Seamus back riding patrol. He said if you called, tell you not to worry." The man I was talking to had retired a year and a half ago. He and other retirees had been called back to handle booking and office chores, and thus free every man who was able for street duty.

I typed up what I'd learned and what I suspected about the disappearance of Gil Tremain and folded the carbon copy into an envelope. When I finished, I addressed it to a post office box I kept. The short walk to mail it gave me a chance to stretch my legs. If something went wrong tonight and I wasn't around to tell them, it would give the cops someplace to start.

My adventures in the warehouse that morning had left me with a jagged nail which attention from my emery board hadn't completely solved. I was making another attempt when the door to my office flew open. Two men who worked for Caras came in, splitting left and right as one of them closed it.

"Don't try for a gun," his pal warned. He tossed something onto my desk.

I raised my brows in question. It was the envelope of photos Caras had kept.

"Nobody working for Mr. Caras knows your boy Tremain. He don't owe money."

"What about the other two?"

He stared at me from a face that was shaped like a dustpan.

"What do I look like, a broad to be beatin' my gums when I'd already learned what I was supposed to?"

"Okay. Tell Mr. Caras thanks."

He nodded and turned to leave while the other one watched to make sure I didn't turn hostile. All at once the one who spoken whirled back.

"Nobody remembers seeing the dame in the pictures. The guy who ain't Tremain's pretty regular at a poker game. Those two don't owe anything either." He leveled a finger. "Ain't no question you've got maximum moxie, toots, but there's such a thing as having too much. Don't bother Mr. Caras again, or you'll leave feet first."

***

By nine o'clock it had been dark for hours. I got up from a long nap on top of my bed and washed my face to wake myself to full alertness. Then I changed into clothes I kept for creeping through alleys at night or heading into places I wasn't supposed to be.

When I'd pulled on men's trousers, an undershirt and a sweater, I twisted my hair up as tightly as possible and hid it under a knitted hat that also held it in place. Like the short pea coat holding my Smith & Wesson and extra cartridges, the other items in my ensemble were black.

Then I had nothing to do except sit and fidget. Out in the hall, two of the girls were squabbling about who was guilty of getting something sticky on the bottom of the iron we shared. Finally it was time to set out.

A bit of zig-zagging ensured I wasn't followed. The police were out in force again tonight. They must be exhausted. I thought about letting someone know what I was about to do in case I got into a fix, but I wasn't a hundred percent sure I'd find Tremain or even a trace of him in The Pompeii. Besides, the police had enough on their hands.

Parking my car, I replayed my zig-zag game on foot. Shortly before ten I stood half a block away surveying the former speakeasy. Nico's boys were watching the front of the building. I couldn't see them, but that's how they'd known about my visit with the real estate agent. The question was, were members of their merry band also watching the back?

With no idea what to do about it if they were, I went a block south and came up the walkway where the alley dead ended. For perhaps five minutes I stood and watched and listened without catching any hint of activity. Then, with .38 in hand, I eased forward, shifting my weight from foot to foot and sticking close to the wall of the former speakeasy.

Not a sound broke the silence; no snuffle of a stray dog hunting food; no creak of wood or scrape of metal. I slid into the doorway at the back of The Pompeii. Pressing my ear to the door, I listened for sounds inside. I drew in quiet breaths to check for cigarette smoke or aftershave. Reassured, I shifted the gun to my left hand and took out my crochet hook.

Behind me I felt a stir of movement. As I started to spin someone spoke.

"You're later than I expected."

FORTY-TWO

Tabby Warren came even with me, her hands tucked into the pockets of a jacket. Her hair was completely hidden under a tightly tied black scarf that would do a pirate credit. She kept mostly in shadows. Only a wedge of her face was visible in pale light from stars and a distant street lamp.

"You're left handed." She tilted her head at the .38.

"Only with a gun, and when I need the other one for something more important."

"I thought you'd come early. I would have twenty years ago." She'd blackened her cheeks and forehead with something, but I could make out her smile. "From here on out, however, you're in charge. By the little you've told me, I gather we may encounter people inside who take exception to our presence. I know the layout of the building better than you. It's dearer to me than most of the lovers I've had. So I may make a suggestion or two, but I'll do as you say."

The fact she understood the risks of the situation didn't diffuse my anger.

"There's a very unpleasant man who has two of his enforcers watching the front of this place. He may also have some watching back here, in which case you've just guaranteed we were seen."

"Highly unlikely. The man in that house keeps hunting dogs." She indicated a yard across the way with a sturdy iron fence. "They raise holy Ned if anything stirs back here after dark. His father bought the place from me a few years after the speakeasy closed. He was kind enough to take the dogs in fifteen minutes ago. I've been watching here since."

"Swell." It was all the graciousness I could muster.

"You believe the man you're looking for is being held here against his will?"

"Yes."

"With someone guarding him?"

"Probably."

"Then depending how much he's worth, or how important he is, they also may have someone keeping an eye on the back door from the inside, don't you think?"

"Maybe. When I first came to you, you mentioned an exit that had been bricked over. I assume that's it?" I pointed toward the corner of the building near the walkway.

"Yes. The wall's rock solid now."

"Besides front and back, is there any other way in? Through the coal bin, maybe?"

"Not the coal bin, but..."

She darted down the back of the building and into the weed-infested utility space I'd noticed between it and the insurance place. Hands on hips, she stood staring up at an old iron fire ladder that ended two stories up.

"There used to be a taller building where that new one is now. It came all the way over. We'd come down the ladder, drop onto its roof and make our way to the street." Still staring, she shook her head. "Even if we managed to toss a rope around one of the rungs and climb, the window coming out probably hasn't been used in twenty years."

Layers of paint would have glued it closed. Breaking the glass risked being heard by anyone inside. Even attempting the venture would waste time.

"We'll have to go in the back way then."

We returned to the door.

"Once we're in, Jasper will sound the alarm if anyone else comes in," Tabby said optimistically.

As I tried to make sense of her words, a shape moved in the darkness next to us. I heard what I realized was the rustle of wings. We'd held our voices to whispers. Now I struggled to keep mine from rising.

"You brought your damn *parrot*?"

"He's quite a good lookout. He played the role frequently when this was a speak."

"He stays outside."

"He's useless there. He has a place he likes to perch just inside."

***

Arguing would only waste time. We planned, then moved swiftly. Tabby tossed pebbles at a window to one side of the door and watched to see if it drew anyone. After several pebbles and no response, I eased the back door open and entered, ducking down in case I got a welcome. Half a minute later, just long enough to be prudent, she came in after me.

"Do you have any sort of weapon?" I asked, my mouth to her ear.

She flashed a small revolver.

"Have you ever used it?"

"Yes. On a man who deserved it."

The calm in her voice gave me pause. I began to wonder if I'd underestimated her.

With me in the lead, and my flashlight beam trained on the floor to keep us from stumbling while encouraging the emergence of our night vision, we made our way slowly up the back stairs, checking the back half of each floor before we moved on to the next. When we reached the third floor, we moved to the front and repeated the same process going down.

So far, we'd been checking to make sure no one was guarding the spaces we'd been through. They weren't.

"Now what? Where's this secret spot they may have stashed him?"

"Second floor. Let me take the lead. Stay close."

The awareness of minutes ticking past made me tense. If Gil Tremain was here, and whoever was guarding him left to meet the man relieving him, as the rendezvous at Revels suggested, it could give us an opening to get Tremain out quickly. But chances were even better the departing guard could surprise us. It wasn't looking out for myself that concerned me. It was being responsible for Tabby Warren as well.

Reaching the second floor increased my edginess. Except for the bar, the walls surrounding what had been the speakeasy dance floor were mirrored. Although tarnished by age, they would immediately reveal our images to anyone climbing the stairs. The middle-aged woman ahead of me moved swiftly along one mirrored side. In spots her stride lengthened as if to miss a floorboard which she knew might squeak.

Her destination was the beautiful, finely carved wooden wall behind the bar. When she reached it, she motioned for me to stop and stood staring at it as if waiting for her eyes to soak up every particle of light in what appeared to be pure darkness. Finally she stepped closer and stooped to squint at something. Her nose was almost touching the wall itself.

Straightening, she slipped behind the bar with its line of lampshades awaiting repairs. She stood looking down. Placing her finger against her lips in a gesture of silence, she beckoned me. When I joined her, she pointed her toe to a spot where the wall behind the bar met the floor. A thin line of light met my eyes. Its length was no more than an inch.

I looked at her in question, but she had stooped for a closer look. Balanced on her haunches, limber as a cat, she watched the line, then rose. A gesture of her hand urged me back. As soon as we were free of the narrow space behind the bar, she took the lead again. An archway that led to the bathrooms provided a vantage point from which we could watch both stairs and bar without being seen. Her voice was a mere breath of sound.

"There's a small space behind the bar. Not an exit. It was for hiding. If our lives were in danger. One or two of the local bootleggers took exception to speakeasy owners who chose not to buy from them."

She turned to me and her light-hearted air had been replaced by cold, hard anger.

"There's a place in the carving that slides one of the panels back, and I bloody well want to know how someone knew about it. The day we closed The Pompeii, I personally jammed a nail in the mechanism to keep it from working. Only three other people knew about it, all of them dead by then!"

"Show it to me, and then, please, won't you leave?"

"You don't understand. The space is terribly narrow. Not much wider than a lane at a bowling alley. Any shot that misses its target will ricochet. And the guard, if he has any sense at all, will be watching the way he's always come in and out."

Her phrasing hinted at something.

"Are you saying there's another way in?"

"Up there." She pointed to the floor above us.

FORTY-THREE

I shone my flashlight on the back wall of one of the bedroom closets. Tabby poked and prodded.

"It's been plastered over," she said. "The bottom half used to hinge down. There are rungs on the wall that lead up from below, like a ladder. Scramble up, crawl through, out the window onto the fire escape and drop to the building next door. It was something of a lark to us."

She sighed softly. I tapped the wall.

"It doesn't sound like very thick plaster. There may be laths behind it, but we could break through if we had a hammer or mallet."

"And bring somebody running with the racket," Tabby said.

I was thinking.

"Do you have a watch?"

Tabby blinked at me. "Yes, of course."

From one of what I now could see were numerous pockets on her jacket, she produced a man's wristwatch. It had a dial that glowed in the dark.

"There's a train due in ten minutes, assuming yesterday didn't throw everything off," I said. "A long one with freight." I knew because it also passed within a block of my office, and I'd watched it a time or two. "As close to the rail yards as this is, it's bound be noisy."

"Yes! I'd forgotten. Some of those freight trains made such a racket they'd drown out the band."

"And somewhere I saw a hammer. On top of a crate, maybe down on two."

"Look for it. I'll be behind these cartons sketching a schematic of the passage so you'll have an idea what you're going into."

***

Trying not to feel like a duck in a shooting gallery amid the mirrored walls of the second floor, I made my way quickly through rows of benches and boxes. I spotted the large wooden crate. Not only was there a hammer on its partially open lid, a crowbar lay on the floor beside it. The crowbar could serve multiple uses. I took both tools.

When I got back, Tabby was sitting cross legged behind the cartons. One hand held her flashlight, the other a stub of pencil. I crouched beside her.

"Here's the back of the closet." Her finger began to trace what she'd drawn on the pasteboard. "The rungs are set close to the wall, so make sure your foot doesn't slip. They're iron, not wood, thank goodness, but some may have rusted. Test before you put your weight on."

If we were discussing breaking down a wall to get to the ladder, I knew it couldn't lead directly into the hidden space behind the bar.

"What's at the foot of the ladder?"

"A space big enough for two or three people squashed together. Facing the ladder is a sliding panel. It opens directly into the hiding place."

"The place where we saw light."

"Yes. There'll be a hand grip on the left with a latch that lifts up." She hesitated. "At least that's how I believe it works. I never actually had occasion to go in this way, only to come up."

We looked at each other.

"If it means surprising whoever's inside, it's worth a try. How much time?"

"Until the train?" She checked her watch. "Two minutes."

"So I'll be coming straight into one end of the narrow room. The entrance at the opposite end is the sliding panel?"

"Yes."

"So that entrance faces the bar."

"Yes."

"Meaning I'll come in at right angles to a guard or guards."

"If they're facing what they believe is the only entrance. At least that's what I'd do."

"Me too." I got to my feet. "How wide's the room?"

"Four feet, maybe five."

She'd meant it when she said narrow. No matter where Tremain was, he'd be in the line of fire if there was shooting. My guess was he'd be at the end where I came in. I hoped to heaven he wouldn't be right where I'd lose precious seconds getting around him.

Faint, but growing in volume, there was the sound of a train. I went into the closet and picked up the hammer. When the train noise was too loud for conversation, I swung the hammer. Bam-bam-bam-bam.

A half-dollar sized chunk of plaster fell out. I swung harder. Bam-bam-bam-BAM. Another chunk, a small hole, and maybe the feel of something giving. That was all. I needed a sledge, not an ordinary carpenter's hammer. Panic set in.

Tabby reached for the hammer. I shook my head. I motioned for her to step back and picked up the crowbar. Holding the shaft like a bat, with the solid part of the crook turned toward the wall, I swung. My batting aim hadn't been great in softball, but when I connected, I connected hard. I did now. Again and again.

Palm sized holes appeared as chunks of plaster fell. A lath was visible. My next swing splintered it. I wasn't making fast enough progress, though. Top volume from the train wouldn't last long. I jammed the crook of the crowbar under the lath and hooked it around, then slid it up so its middle was in back of the lath.

"Grab the other end," I shouted at Tabby.

She gripped the shaft. We tugged and rocked. The lath gave way. Falling plaster exposed one ten inches below it. I clobbered it a couple of times to weaken the middle. Then the two of us attacked it too and it snapped.

I battered away at a third, but had to stop for breath. Tabby picked up the hammer. Bam-bam-BAM. Bam-bam-BAM. She whaled away at one side of the crack I'd made in the wood and a piece broke off. She repeated it on the other side: Bam-bam-BAM. Bam-bam-BAM. As the noise of the train began to diminish, she was matching the sound of the rails. I made the crowbar into a bat again, nodded for her to step clear, and picked up her rhythm.

We took turns, whittling away weakened edges, widening what we'd begun. By the time further work became risky, we'd made a hole large enough for me to squeeze through. We both sat down panting.

"When you're down, flick your light off and on. Then I'll come down," Tabby said.

"No." I flexed my hands. The spot where I'd dug the splinter out that morning burned. "Once I have my footing on the ladder, I want you to leave."

"No."

"You said I could call the shots."

"Sometimes I lie."

Maybe we were alike.

"A space as small as we're talking about, you'll get in my way. If you want to help, leave, wait ten minutes, and call the police."

"And if you go down and the latch down there doesn't work? You have no idea how to trigger the one at the bar and get in that way."

I could have slugged her. Instead, I stood up and checked to make sure the .38 was secure in my pocket since I would need both hands going down.

"Fine. Wait for me behind the bar in case I need to get in that way, then. But if you hear shooting, clear out and get the police. Agreed?"

She didn't respond.

"Agreed?"

"Yes, fine."

I got on my knees by the hole in the wall and stuck one leg through. The angle was awkward, but finally my toe found a rung of the ladder. I got my other leg through and managed something that passed for a foothold. With Tabby holding my shoulders, I drew an arm through and caught onto a rung. Then, testing my weight on every step, I started down toward a door that might or might not open.

Cobwebs caught at my legs.

Lots of cobwebs.

I'd had my fill of cobwebs.

FORTY-FOUR

The handhold at the bottom of the ladder was exactly as Tabby had described. It yielded on the first try and slid noiselessly. Halfway open it stuck. I shoved. It gave a piercing shriek.

"Hands on your head," I said to the man who had turned and was reaching under his jacket. "*Now*, or I'll give you worse than a slug in your arm!"

It was one of the men who'd tried to snatch Eve Tremain, the one at the door whom I'd shot. He sat at the opposite end of the tunnel-like space. He obeyed sullenly. Keeping my gun on him, I yanked off my cap, partly to rid a few square inches of my body of cobwebs, but mostly to reassure the other man in the room, who sat gagged and tied hand and foot to a chair on my right.

"Gil. I'm going to get you out of here. Mr. Collingswood hired me to find you."

Glassy eyes stared at me without comprehension. His head lolled as if he couldn't support it. I wasn't entirely sure it was Gil Tremain, he'd been beaten so badly. I pulled his gag down, then turned my full attention back to the guard.

"Lock your fingers together and bring them down behind your neck. Then get on your knees. Give so much as a twitch I don't like and I'll shoot you. Understand?"

He muttered under his breath.

"Yeah, I've been called that before," I said as I patted him down. I relieved him of a snub-nosed .38 which I stuck in my waist.

"Who else is here besides you?"

"You tell me."

"When's your pal with the gap in his teeth supposed to relieve you?"

"What pal?"

I kicked him in the back.

"Get over there and sit with your back glued to the wall. Legs out, crossed at the ankle. Keep those hands the way I told you."

I shifted so I could see them both.

"Tremain!"

His eyes had closed.

"Did you hear what I said about Collingswood hiring me? He and Lucille have been worried sick about you. So's your daughter."

The eyes fluttered.

"Eve..."

It was little more than a croak. He was in bad shape, face purple and yellow and caked with dried blood. His lips were cracked and peeling as if he'd been denied water. He needed to get to a hospital. Had I told Tabby what to do if she *didn't* hear shots?

A vacuum bottle sat by the chair vacated by the thug who now sat glaring at me and waiting for a chance to even scores if I let down my guard. I sat and pinned the bottle between my knees, removing the top with my left hand.

A taste reassured me it was nothing but coffee. I let Tremain have a few sips. His lips reached for them desperately, but most of the liquid ran down his chin, he was so weak. He needed someone to hold his head while he drank, which I couldn't do while keeping a gun trained on the thug on the floor.

"Gil! How many others are there? Keeping you here? Besides this one?" I gave him another few sips. Those went down better.

"One... two... Tell Eve I didn't..."

"You'll be able to tell her yourself. Help's on the way."

"Tell her!" He began to cough.

I held the lid of coffee to his mouth.

"Take it easy. I understand. You wouldn't tell them where to find what they wanted from the Crescendo project.

You'd hidden it because you smelled a rat. They tried to beat it out of you. More than once, by the looks of it."

"But I didn't... that."

His head and eyes swerved toward the wall facing him. I turned slowly to follow his gaze without losing sight of the man who was spoiling to jump me. What I saw made me sick at heart.

One of the tables from the long vanished speakeasy sat against the wall. It held a syringe and spoon and an unfolded piece of wax paper displaying a white substance I guessed was heroin.

Rage boiled through me.

"They beat you, and when that didn't work, they offered you heroin."

His head bobbed agreement.

"Told me... stop pain. I didn't. I didn't."

I stormed to the entrance the guard had been watching. Too angry to see how the panel opened without taking my eyes from the guard, I pounded my palm on the wood.

"Tabby! Open up. Everything's okay."

Surely as determined as she'd been to help, she hadn't left.

The panel shot into its pocket. Tabby came through so briskly I had to fall back a step. Her eyes were ablaze.

Behind her, holding a gun to her head, was Frank Scott.

FORTY-FIVE

"Jasper's ordinarily quite reliable as a guard, so I assume these unpleasant individuals came in the front. They caught me dab in the middle of the dance floor. I'm afraid they took my revolver," Tabby said calmly.

"Put the gun down or I shoot her right now," Scott said. "Nobody named Jasper or anything else is coming to help you."

The goon with bad teeth had come in after him. Also visibly armed. And wearing Tremain's blue muffler. Two men with weapons drawn, plus the one on the floor who already was shifting to grab my ankles and bring me down if I tried anything. Behind me, Tremain was in desperate need of medical care. The gun poking into the ribs of a woman who'd helped me was the decisive factor.

"Okay, Frank. Anything you say."

Stooping carefully, my free hand raised in reassurance, I placed my .38 on the floor. The man I'd surprised when I came in snatched it gleefully. Getting to his feet, he reclaimed his own weapon from the back of my waistband.

"How the hell did she get past you?" Scott snapped.

"She didn't. There's a place back there that opens like the one we've been using."

The light from the single overhead light wasn't great, but it was enough to see Scott's face color.

"Walk away now, Frank, before you make a worse mess for yourself," I said. "That woman you're threatening is pals with the mayor and sits on more civic boards than you have fingers. Hurt her and they'll be hunting you from here to kingdom come."

All the antagonism toward me he'd been hiding showed in his smile.

"Is that the best you can do? It's all I would have expected when Loren first hired you. Now that I've seen how effective you are, I'm disappointed you'd resort to fairytales."

"Then maybe you should consider I might be telling the truth. She owns this building."

"And I would like to know how you discovered the mechanism that opens the panel and figured out how to use it," Tabby demanded.

Scott sneered without even glancing at her.

"I made pocket change delivering flowers when I was a kid. I brought some here one day and a big blond guy showed me."

Tabby looked devastated.

"Look, she only came down to let me in. I had no idea she'd stick around. She doesn't know anything, not even who you are. Let her go."

"Ah, but the two of you, nuisances though you are for making more work, will help sell the idea Gil's death is an accident — an ugly end to a promising life. Who knows when or why he started using heroin again? When he doesn't show up for work, his concerned employers hire you to find him. You do just that, but something goes wrong. He's hopped up on drugs... maybe jumped you to rob you... shoots you and your friend with your own gun. After which he collapses, having taken too big a dose."

The rage I'd felt when I saw the drug paraphernalia multiplied beyond measure. Gil Tremain had endured beatings and, by the looks of it starvation, rather than give up information to a traitor. Now his name would be disgraced in the ugliest way imaginable, his daughter left to believe the last thing he'd want her to believe about him.

"Why, Frank? Just tell me why you hate him so much." I could guess, but I needed time to clear my head. I needed time to think.

"I got tired of hearing how he walked on water. Tired of Loren never taking my advice on anything even though we were partners."

"So you decided to give him a heart attack. With the phone calls, and taking Gil and his calculations and finally the snake."

"I didn't take the calculations. He hid them. He heard me talking to someone and began to mistrust me. I could tell. The mule-headed idiot won't tell me what he changed or where he put them. It's his own fault it ends like this. He could have died quickly. Painlessly. Without disgrace."

But he would have been disgraced in his own eyes, and his daughter would have believed that he was a dope fiend.

I couldn't let that happen.

I couldn't.

My eyes searched desperately in the small space for something — anything — I could use as a weapon. Three men with guns. Against Tabby, me, Tremain. The latter tied in his chair and too weak to move if he could.

"Arnold. Take care of Miss High Society."

Scott shoved Tabby toward the gap-toothed thug. The burly, unshaven specimen hooked an arm across the front of her shoulders and pulled her against his body. It immobilized her more than Scott's way had, but Arnold's gun was pointed forward and five inches from the side of her head rather than pressed to her skull.

"If you try anything smart, your friend gets it. Understand?" Scott brushed past me.

"If you shoot either one of us here, your tale about Tremain shooting us will be hard to swallow. Traces of blood where they shouldn't be and missing where they should be. Then the cops discover you played poker with Benning, and how he conveniently disappeared the same time Tremain went missing."

"You won't take a chance on it."

"How did you get him to meet you down here?"

"Wouldn't you like to know?"

He was smug beyond fear. As if to emphasize my helplessness, he seized Tremain's chin. He put his own face close.

"Time to say good-by, Gil. I won. We may not make that fat deal, thanks to you, but sooner or later I'll see the same flaw you did in our original calculations. Meanwhile C&S will keep on making dandy profits and I'll get my share. Loren will be oh, so glad I'm there to steady the ship. Who knows? Maybe I'll even woo Lucille again. And since Miss Sullivan here worked so hard to find you, it seems only fair that she put the needle in your arm."

I stared at him in loathing.

"I won't."

He leveled his gun at me.

"You will, or Arnold twists Miss High Society's arm from the socket. He's remarkably useful. Even knows a vacant lot where we can dump bodies without being noticed, just like he knew where to buy the treat you're going to give Gil.

"Go on." He motioned me toward the little round table against the wall. "Strap first. Pick it up."

I stared at a leather strap I hadn't noticed before. I stared at the table holding it and the needle and other items. Was the table light enough I could swing it up and knock Scott's gun from his fingers? He was barely an arm's length away.

I raised my eyes in hopes I'd catch Tabby's. I never had a chance.

"Coppers! Coppers!" a voice screeched through the open door to the bar.

Jasper's voice.

In the split second Scott and his two henchmen froze in confusion, Tabby gave what resembled a bow. The man who'd been imprisoning her catapulted over her head to land on his back. My fingers closed on the empty syringe. I drove it into Frank Scott's cheek.

As he howled in pain I rammed my shoulder and the full force of my body into his side. I went down with him. One of his hands had grabbed at the source of the pain in his cheek — the needle — but the other still held a gun. I caught his arm with both hands and smashed his wrist against the floor as he began to hit ineffectually at my head. From elsewhere in the room there was a shriek, a male shriek, then a shot. I slammed Scott's wrist down again and he lost his grip on the gun.

Once my fingers were in possession of it, I rolled to my feet. Unable to see behind him, and unsure what was happening, Scott made the smart decision to go motionless. I blinked once to make sure I wasn't imagining the tableau that met my eyes.

Tabby Warren stood straddling the gap-toothed thug who had been her captor a moment earlier. She was leveling his own .22 automatic at him. She held it very nicely, one hand supporting the other.

Sprawling with his back to the wall, in almost the exact spot I'd forced him to sit, was Scott's other lackey. A throwing knife like I'd seen at carnivals lodged in his inner thigh.

"One acquires unusual skills growing up on the vaudeville circuit," the socialite said noting my expression.

Then, soundless as a cat, one of Nico Caras' men stepped through the opening behind the bar.

FORTY-SIX

He was one of the ones who'd sat at the table with Caras that morning, the one Caras had called Georgie. His topcoat was cashmere, he had the hard, cold look of a trigger man, and he hadn't come empty handed.

"Lose your pieces." He waggled the .45 he held to make his point.

"He doesn't have any quarrel with us, and we don't have any with him," I said to Tabby.

Nodding, she put her gun on the floor and used her toe to nudge it out of gap-toothed Arnold's reach. He slid back on his elbows, looking nervously at the man who'd entered.

"You followed me." I was irritated at myself for failing to spot him.

"Followed Arnold. Since he and his friend came in the front way, I figured it might be smart to come in the back."

Like most of Caras' men, he was probably half of a pair.

"Where's your pal?"

"Outside in the car. This won't take long." His eyes flicked to Tremain, who was now unconscious. "That the man you were hunting?"

"Yes. And he needs a doctor fast."

"Like you told the other dame, I've got no quarrel with you. As soon as I take care of some business here, I'll be on my way."

The trouble was, I had a feeling I might not like how he planned to take care of that business. He was ignoring the fact that instead of putting my gun down I'd merely lowered it to my side, but he'd noticed. Taking two steps into the room, he gave Scott the once-over.

"He the one who helped Benning get out of town, Arnold?"

"The-the guy who had the business downstairs?" Arnold nodded in full-blown panic.

"I didn't help him. I just paid him to close up shop and let me use this building," Scott said irritably. He got to his feet. "Who are you, anyway?"

"Where is he?"

"Benning? I have no idea."

"I'm not going to ask you again."

"He doesn't know," I said.

"Shut up. Nico was right, you need to learn manners. Last chance, pal."

"I don't—"

Georgie squeezed the trigger. Frank Scott screamed and fell to the floor clutching his knee.

"Where?"

"Idon'tknowIdon'tknow! Knew he owed somebody money. Oh, God, my knee! I needed a place. An empty building. That's all. I don't *know* where Benning went! I just paid him to-to go."

Georgie's arm raised languidly.

"Don't," I said.

"Nico wants it like this."

I wanted Frank Scott alive. I wanted him to suffer like he'd made Gil Tremain suffer. I wanted the cops to wring every last detail of what he'd done out of him in case Tremain didn't make it.

"Killing him's not going to find Benning."

"It sends a message."

An emptiness came into his eyes. I knew what it signaled. I pulled the trigger.

He fell back with an awkwardness that looked out of place with his cashmere coat and well-barbered face. After several moments Tabby reached gingerly to slide his gun from his fingers.

All around us the tunnel-like room was silent. Then the mewling sound of held-in whimpers reached my ears. Scott or the thug with the knife in his thigh. I couldn't tell and didn't care.

Tabby glanced around and changed the oversized gun in her hand for the smaller snub nose. Rubbing absently at one smudged cheek, she surveyed the scene.

"Four ruffians down and a missing man rescued. Not a bad night's work for two women, do you think?"

Nervous chatter, because we both recognized how close we'd come to never indulging in any sort of chatter again.

"Two women and a parrot," I said. "Don't forget the parrot."

FORTY-SEVEN

It felt as though the city's spirits had put on widow's weeds that Christmas. Kids' heads were still filled with thoughts of presents and candy and visits from St. Nick. For adults, though, choirs and mistletoe and bright shop windows couldn't crowd out the reality and uncertainty of a country at war.

After three days in the hospital, Gil Tremain went home with the Collingswoods to recover. When I visited a week before Christmas, Lucille was wearing a fine new diamond engagement ring.

Frank Scott had gotten the lump of coal he deserved in his stocking. He'd be spending the holiday behind bars, and based on mounting evidence against him, a good many to come.

On Christmas Eve, Seamus and I went to Mass. I hadn't been since my dad died. It didn't make me any friendlier toward God, but it soothed somehow. It was familiar. In the glow of the candles I sat looking at faces I knew. How many of them would be here next year, and the year after that?

Tabby Warren invited Seamus and me to a bash at her place on New Year's Eve, but we both chose the one at Finn's instead. Even there, the laughter rang hollow, at least to my ears. Sometime before midnight I slipped away and went to my office. Leaving the lights off, I went to the window and stood looking out at the city. I thought of all the people, good and bad, moving through it, and wondered as I sometimes did, whether what I did made a difference.

Behind me the door opened softly. I didn't turn. I sensed who it was.

"Thought I might find you here," said Connelly's voice. "Party too much for you?"

"Something like that. I didn't want to be a wet blanket."

He settled beside me. "It's been a rough few weeks all right."

"Glad you had tonight off."

"Me too, even though it means going in bright and early. Okay if I twirl a strand of your hair?"

"No."

He did it anyway, chuckling. I pressed my cheek to the teasing finger.

Outside it had started to snow. Just a few flakes.

"Everything's going to change, isn't it?" My breath made a cloud on the window. "Because of the war."

"Yeah." His arm slid around my waist and I settled into it. "Everything except there's still good people around to get us through it. And us. We won't change, Maggie *mavouneen*."

The words traveled not through the air, but from his ribs to mine. Adam and Eve. We stood in darkness, watching the snow fall.

— The End —

ABOUT THE AUTHOR

M. Ruth Myers received a Shamus Award from Private Eye Writers of America for the third book in her Maggie Sullivan mysteries series. She is the author of more than a dozen books in assorted genres, some written under the name Mary Ruth Myers. If you shine a bright light in her eyes, she'll admit to one husband, one daughter, one son-in-law, one grandson and one cat – all of whom she adores. She lives in Ohio.

Made in the USA
Las Vegas, NV
11 April 2022

47287355R00152